FILTHY

TIA LOUISE

This book is a work of fiction. Names, characters, places, and incidents are products of the author's imagination or are used fictitiously. Any resemblance to actual events or locales or persons, living or dead, is entirely coincidental.

To the Mermaids.

"You fill the empty places in my heart."
-Onur Taskiran
(variation)

He watches her like she's something he's never seen before,
like a Viking entranced by a mermaid.
—Tia Louise, Fearless

PROLOGUE

Oskar

Seven years ago

WIND WHIPS THROUGH THE CAB OF OUR MILITARY-ISSUE RANGE Rover, and we're traveling home in peace, no assignments left to complete.

My elbow is propped on the open window, and the unusually warm breeze twists loose strands of my hair around my eyes, hidden behind aviator sunglasses.

My partner Hutchence Winston, or Hutch as everyone calls him, is light. He's finished, retiring from active duty after four years in country.

I don't share his status, and my mood is not as light.

"Varna's a far cry from what you expected when you got here four years ago." Glancing at him, I consider all we've seen in our time together. I consider how it will be when he's gone, and my stomach pinches with sadness. "No black and white ice deserts or peasants standing in bread lines."

"Was I that much of a stereotype?" Hutch laughs, gripping

the steering wheel as the vehicle takes a hard bounce over the rough terrain into Bucharest.

"You were just another American."

Hutch is a typical, bold Marine. He's big, although not as tall as me. He's stubborn and a natural leader, but unlike the other Marines I've encountered, he doesn't act like he knows everything or like Langley is the center of the universe.

We're actually good friends.

"This country is beautiful… when it's not trying to freeze you to death. Which isn't often enough for my taste." He glances from the road to me. "Sure you don't want to come back with me? You are an American, after all."

An old bitterness twists in my chest at his words. "Only on paper, my friend. America is a stranger to me now."

"Only a stranger if you don't have friends, and you have them."

Lifting my chin, I look away, out the window. I have no reason to be loyal to this place. Without explanation, my father dumped me here at the age of six, to be raised by strangers who were promised a pension to keep me alive. I grew up no better than a foster child with a resentful family waiting for their monthly check.

I was hidden away from my family, my friends, until I was nothing.

Alone, I taught myself to hunt, to shoot, to use tools and build things by hand. I learned geography and where the moneyed class went for holidays. I studied and went to college, and as soon as I was old enough, I joined the military and eventually found myself working with the Americans, tracking down terrorists and flushing out spies.

"That paper is all you need." Hutch pulls me back to the present. "I could use you in the States. You're the best tracker I know, and one of the few people I'd trust with my life."

I feel the same about him, but I don't say it out loud. He

doesn't need to know my reasons for staying, about the letter burning a hole in my pocket.

"It's not so easy to drop everything and leave for a whole different country."

The letter arrived last night via special courier. It was hand-written on expensive stationery bearing a Muscovite stamp. I read it quickly, then stuffed it in my pocket as I tried to make sense of the words. None of it made sense.

It was from a man named Simon Petrovich, and it said my time had come. I had to take my place in line, pay my dues. It said I couldn't run from who I am.

Who am I?

Dipping my chin, I look out at the barren terrain. "I have unfinished business."

Hutch doesn't miss a beat, letting out a low chuckle before turning the wheel onto a narrow, country road. "Any chance that business has long hair and soft curves?"

He's joking, and I'm about to reply when my eye catches on a column of smoke off the road up ahead. Dread pits my stomach as we get closer, and I see a crowd gathered in the parking lot surrounding a one-story building.

"What's that?" The closer we get, the less I have to ask.

"Krasivoy Kafe?" Hutch downshifts, reading the sign, and we turn into the parking lot.

Hopping out fast, we join the crowd surrounding the white-planked structure. Black smoke pours out of the large, glass windows, and the heat forces us all to step back.

Firetrucks are nowhere to be seen, and the restaurant is going up like a box of tinder.

"What happened?" I shout in Russian as we locate a paunchy man with a tag indicating he's a manager. His hair is slicked with sweat and his white, button-down shirt stretches over his swollen belly.

"We got as many out as we could," he shouts in Russian, face lined.

A woman in a black trench coat with long pearl earrings runs to where Hutch and I stand, frantically pulling my arm. "My daughter is trapped inside! Please, you have to save her!"

My chest tightens, and I look to Hutch. He's waiting for me to translate.

"Kitchen fire?" I ask in Russian.

The man turns his wide eyes on me, like I asked him why grass is green. "What else?"

"Please," The woman jerks my arm again. "She went to the bathroom, and they dragged me out…"

I can't believe anyone could still be alive, but I don't see flames–only thick smoke. A small cry meets my ears, and my jaw clenches.

"Oh my God!" the woman screams. "My father has money, connections…"

"The firemen are on their way." The man's black eyes meet mine.

"It will be too late!" she screams

"God will save her little soul," the man says.

Fuck. My shirt is over my head while he's still speaking, and Hutch is right behind me. "What the fuck are you doing?"

"A little girl is trapped inside." I'm not a hero. I've never been the type of guy to run into a burning building, but that little voice will haunt me forever if I do nothing.

"Oskar, stop." Hutch is right beside me. "You're not prepared for this."

"You should know, Marine, we're never prepared for hell." I twist my long hair in a bun, tucking it under a beanie, then I dunk my shirt in a nearby bucket of water and squeeze it over my head.

"Cover your face." Hutch shoves his canvas jacket over my torso. "Bring her to me here. If you get disoriented, listen for my voice."

Diving through the window, I'm immediately disoriented.

Thick black smoke steals my breath and my vision. I drop to my knees, coughing as I crawl across the open dining area.

Fire roars from the kitchen like a freight train overhead, and I follow the path to the back where the bathrooms would be.

It's closer to the kitchen, and the heat is overwhelming. Panic constricts my lungs.

Pausing to center my mind, I close my eyes and force calm, remember my training, my instincts… and listen. A whimpering cry is to my left, and I dash in that direction, pulling up short as a flaming board slams to the ground in front of me.

With a lunge, I reach him. A little boy is huddled in a corner.

"Come here," I say in Russian, but I don't wait for his cooperation. Bending to scoop him up, pain flashes through my shin. "Shit! Don't kick me!"

He's in my arms, but at my full height, the smoke is disorienting.

"Hutch?" I yell.

Faintly, through the darkness, I hear my name and run for it. When I reach my partner, he takes the boy as I dive through the opening.

"No little girl." I drop to my knees, gulping at fresh air. "I didn't make it to the bathroom. It's too hot—I'm afraid it's too late."

"Please!" The woman's face distorts as tears streak her cheeks. "My father has so much money. He will give you all the money you want."

"What good is money if you're dead?" The manager shouts at her.

The woman's eyes go wild, and she lunges forward as if she'll run into the building. Hutch catches her around the waist, and she crumples in his arms, crying "No…"

My chest burns hotter than the fire at her display of grief.

I don't know if the cry I heard was the little boy or her daughter. I only know I have to try one more time.

Turning on my heel, I charge again into the burning darkness. It's more of the same—heat, blindness, impossible to breathe—only now I feel light-headed from smoke inhalation.

I can't pass out. I have to hold on a little longer.

The roar of burning is sliced by a loud groan overhead. The beams holding up the roof are almost burned through, and the clock is ticking. I'm on a fool's errand. A child in here this long would have certainly inhaled too much smoke or succumbed to the heat.

Giving the room one final sweep, I hear Hutch screaming for me to get out when my eyes land on hers across the dining room. Oversized dark eyes, pale, ashy hair. She's so tiny, crouched in the corner, watching me as if from another plane of existence.

She doesn't seem traumatized or overcome. She seems to be waiting for me to save her, wondering why it took me so long.

Another loud groan echoes overhead, and holding my forearm over my nose and mouth, I look up to see the rafters wavering precariously. It's going to fall on us. A load-bearing beam crumbles like a broken toothpick.

I'm out of time.

Closing the space, I scoop her up and hold her close as I pump my legs, running hard, frantic to get to safety before it's too late. Her small head tucks beneath my chin, and her little hand clings to my arm.

My heart pounds in my chest. I'm not going to make it.

I *have* to make it. I can't let her die.

Hutch's green eyes stand out in the black soot covering his face. They're twisted in horror as another loud groan turns into a long rip. The roof is coming down. I have no choice but to throw her. Tiny nails scratch my skin as I rip her from my chest.

It's a sensation I'll never forget, her cry a sound that will echo in my mind.

"Oskar!" Hutch's shout is the last word I remember.

Flashes of light, of pain, so much pain.

Crying, roaring, screaming.

Then black.

I'm on my stomach in a hospital bed with bandages over my eyes. Hutch's voice is at my side, but it's several days before I register what he said to me.

"I can't stay any longer, friend." He sounds so troubled. "I've got to get back to my family. Come find me when you're well. I'll have a place for you."

But the little girl… *What happened to the little girl?*

It's mist and shadows. The pain medication keeps me in a dreamlike state, and I count time by the nurses tending to me. One speaks in Russian, saying my first round of skin grafts was very successful. She places a device in my hand and says to press the white button if the pain becomes too great.

Her tone is light, and she says I'm a hero. She says everyone in the city is talking about me.

"The little girl–" My voice is thick from lack of use. "Is she alive?"

"Her family came to thank you, to give you money. Your American friend spoke to them. He told them you were not able to see anyone."

She's moving things around, rustling papers. She keeps talking, saying my picture is all over the Internet, on the news, in magazines. *No, fuck no,* I think before a wall of pain hits me so hard, I press the button, passing out as the meds drench my system.

The bandages are off my eyes now, and someone has placed a mirror below me tilted toward the window. I assume so I'll have a view of the sky and trees. I want to see my face, my body, but I'm unable to move in this bed. At least the pain has subsided, and I no longer hold the device with the small, white button.

"You're very lucky." A man speaks in Russian at my bedside as if conjured from nothing. "Your face and hands were spared. You're unscarred from the waist down."

A long stretch of silence follows, and I feel I should say something. "Thank you."

"I'm signing your release order. Your skin grafts are nearly healed, and you will continue to improve with time."

Release order. I'm able to leave, but where do I go? The last thing I remember is the letter, but I'm sure whatever it was about has expired or been forgotten.

"Your bill is paid in full, and your relative brought you clothes." He places a yellow sheet on a nearby chair. "When you're ready, you're free to go."

My brow furrows—what relative?

He leaves, and I realize I can get out of the bed. Placing my hands on the sides of the mattress, I'm stiff and sore, and bandages cover my torso and arms.

Stepping to the mirror over the sink, I recoil at my reflection. My beard is unkempt, and my hair is dirty and matted. My eyes are white-blue, stark against the darkness of my skin, and at the tops of the bandages I see the destruction. Melted bits of skin not quite covered with gauze. I look like I've been to hell and met the devil.

Only I was wrong, the devil is here to meet me.

My door opens, and a short man with flat blue eyes and light brown hair enters the room. He isn't smiling. His face is unlined, as if he's never smiled a day in his life.

I tower over him, and in these bandages, my crazy beard in need of a trim, and my wild hair, I imagine I look like a demon.

"Get dressed." He speaks English with a slight accent.

"You'll stay in Minsk until you're well enough to assume your post in New York."

"You're supposed to be my relative?"

Dead eyes blink up to me, and he nods briefly. "Simon Petrovich." He produces a document that looks suspiciously like a birth certificate. "Your father gave you to me long ago when he could no longer pay his debts. You're in my service now."

"Why am I meeting you for the first time today?"

"It was supposed to be six weeks ago. This pointless act is costing me time."

Pointless act. "I'm not going with you. I don't know you, and I owe you nothing."

His voice lowers to a growl. "If it weren't for me, you'd be dead along with your entire family. Now you'll get your strength back and go to my brother in New York. He needs a bodyguard, and you'll do nicely."

Hesitating, I turn the paper over and back. "My last name is Lourde, not Petrovich. You are not related to me. If you provided for me financially, I thank you, but this is not legally binding."

Another cold smile stretches Simon's lips. "You look at me and think, I am not afraid of this man. I have rights. I am a hero. I am somebody."

"I don't think I'm a hero."

"You are nobody. You are a freak and a monster, and you will follow my orders or I will have you arrested for war crimes and executed."

"War crimes?"

"You aided the Americans in the destruction of several hospitals on the border of Belarus. Innocent civilians were killed, your countrymen."

"I did no such thing–"

"Your arguments are pointless. You will take your place

in my service or you will not take another breath." Turning his wrist over, he glances at his watch. "I'll see you in the car."

He leaves me to finish pulling on the soft-knit pants and long-sleeved shirt. The fabric is clearly expensive, and the weave is loose to cover my bandages. From everything Simon has said, he's clearly very wealthy, which means he's dangerous.

I'm too weak to fight, and Russian thugs can be problematic. For now, I'll go to Minsk and get stronger, then I'll see what this bodyguard duty entails. I'm not afraid to walk away, but I want to have a fighting chance before I gamble my life.

CHAPTER 1

Hana

Present Day

HIS FACE IS MARRED BY SHADOWS, AND HE LEERS AT ME THROUGH the darkness. "You were dancing the first time I saw you." His voice is gravel scraping against concrete, tensing my spine and constricting my throat. "An ethereal, delicate ballerina."

I cross my arms over my chest as his eyes slide down my body. Rubbing my palms against my upper arms, I try to create warmth on my exposed skin.

He would sit on the front row with my parents, my mother between him and my father, watching. My heart would beat so fast, and in my pale pink leotard, I felt exposed, completely nude. An oily smile curled his lips, exposing large teeth, black eyes lit with evil.

I stopped dancing when I was thirteen, when my father died, but it didn't stop him.

Sweaty palms grip my shoulders in the darkness and my stomach knots. *Just a taste…*

I can't breathe, and tears burn my eyes. He holds me down. Claustrophobia presses against my temples. I wave my hands, twist my body.

You like this. Your body doesn't lie.

I want to scream, *I don't!* I don't like it. I want to kill him.

Rage billows and grows into a mushroom cloud in my belly, flooding my chest with hate. It leaks out of my pores and steams in my eyes. I'm a walking column of red-hot fury.

He's gone, but his destruction remains.

Make me forget.

Drugs… So many drugs.

Alcohol… Pour more alcohol on it.

It only makes the fire bigger.

A dark room, a circle of men chanting. I'm standing in the center like a statue, holding a torch as an old man approaches to kneel at my feet. *Just a taste…*

How does he know? *Hit him with the torch*–my arm doesn't listen. Burn this place to the ground, kill them all, send the demons to hell.

My brain is cloudy, but he's here. I blink away the smoke and see him lying at my feet, facing up. His black eyes are empty, glassy, and satisfaction unfurls in my stomach.

A voice at my back, *He's dead.*

Cold filters through my chest. I did it, but I'm still not free.

Kicking against the covers, I bat my arms against the nightmare, flinging blankets across the room as I jump out of my bed and scamper to the other side of my elegant, oversized suite.

Crickets…

I'm in Hamiltown, alone in my bedroom.

He's gone, and I'm fighting ghosts in the darkness.

"No." My voice is a broken whisper. "I said *No.*"

Staring into the black, my eyeballs ache, and I realize it was all a dream, a nightmare.

"Oh, God." I exhale heavily, dropping my head.

My shoulders tremble as I cry. I'm safe in this beautiful room in Uncle Hugh's posh estate. Correction, our posh *family* estate in my family's town.

Pressing the heels of my hands against my eyes, I exhale a growl. I have to move past this. I'm surrounded by people who care about me. I'm twenty-one, my trust has matured. I have all the money in the world… And I can't forget.

Sitting on my butt on the warm wood floors, I need a drink. I need a drug. My eyes are wet as I wipe them. I need *him*.

When he enters the room, his presence calms me. I'm safe.

The first day I got here, our eyes met, and the earth moved. He reached out and caught my hand to steady me, to keep me from falling. He never touched me except to protect me.

I close my eyes, and I see him there, always there, silently guarding. He's tall and ripped, with long hair and intimidating ink. His expression says *just try to fuck with me*, and his scars say he'd walk into the fire to save me. He's beaten hell, and the demons fear him.

Lying at his side was the first time I'd slept in so long. I curled up and closed my eyes, and everything slipped away. I never wanted to leave, so he did.

He walked away, but his last words were a promise.

Placing my hands on the floor, I crawl to my bed again and slide under the sheets. I curl into a ball like before and slide my fingers over my eyes. Tingles in my fingers and toes. I focus on his wolf eyes and steady gaze. He's not here, but I believe he's watching over me.

He's the only memory I want to keep.

"You're up early." My sister Blake leans on her elbow at the bar, swiping her finger across the face of an oversized iPad pro. "Do you have an appointment?"

The sun shines bright through the wall of windows in our kitchen, illuminating the white countertops and contrasting them with the rough-hewn wood floors and cabinets. It's warm and homey, and I glance out the window through the drooping wisteria towards the stables.

When Blake and I were little, our dad brought us here a few times to visit our uncle and get to know our home, but we never went into town or met the locals. We rode horses or played in the large rooms, running through the wide halls and sliding down the banisters.

It imbued this house with memories of safety, of a life before the nightmares began.

Going to the coffee press, I pour myself a mug. "Appointment for what?"

She looks up at me, her silver eyes full of concern. "A photo shoot? You usually sleep late."

I usually don't fall asleep until dawn, but I don't tell her that. I've been trying to turn over a new leaf and not leave Blake to clean up my messes or worry about where I am anymore. Not that I ever expected her to do those things.

Still, she did.

Blake has fretted over me since we were kids, even more after our father died and our mother sent her away to boarding school. She texted constantly, asking what was happening, how I was doing.

I was going through hell, so she asked her friend Debbie to help. That's when my life really blew up. Debbie's mom was one of our mother's high-end drinking buddies. They were obsessed with betting on thoroughbreds, taking ski trips to St. Moritz, and gossiping about other women's husbands. Debbie was the wild-child product of neglect.

She was a year older than Blake, which made her four years older than me, and she affectionately pulled me under her wing–into her world of wild parties, fake IDs, high fashion, alcohol, and drugs. That's when I discovered drinking made you forget, and Molly made you have fun. I wasn't stupid enough to do anything addictive like heroin, but I was too young, and I got too close to the edge too many times.

It stopped the nightmares, and I thought I could control it. I guess that's what everyone thinks starting out.

Now Debbie's dead, and I've got a lot of making up to do, a lot of debts to repay.

Wrapping my hands around my mug, I can't help a shiver, but I do my best to distract my mind. I can only take my past one day at a time. "What are you looking at? Wedding dresses?"

Her furrowed brow relaxes with a smile, and she returns to the screen. "No, I've already found my dress. I was looking for a place to hold the ceremony. I'm not sure how many people will attend, and I don't know. Uncle Hugh says he loves having us here, but he's been doing things on his own so long. It feels like an imposition–"

"If you don't have your ceremony in the carriage house, Uncle Hugh will shit a brick." Walking around the bar to where she's standing, I lean in for a closer look. "I can also stage early photos, since you're making me be in the ceremony."

"You're my sister. You have to be in the ceremony." She tugs a blonde spiral curl hanging by my cheek. "You're my maid of honor."

"I'm your sister, which means I'm better at capturing your emotions. No one would love this job as much as me."

Not to mention, I'd rather be behind the lens instead of onstage for everyone to stare at and whisper. Still, she's right, I guess. If I weren't in the ceremony, people would think I don't like Hutch or had some problem with their marriage, which is absolutely not true–even if her future husband only recently decided to give me a chance.

I can't be angry with him for being hesitant, and I do like Hutch Winston, even if I was surprised when Blake said she was falling for him.

For years, she blamed him for her being sent to the nuns,

but I think Mama really wanted her out of the house. Blake didn't approve of Uncle Victor–and said so, *loudly*. Hutch just gave our mother the perfect excuse to get rid of her.

Then, when we came here, and Hutch appeared, looking like a mashup of an *Esquire* cover model and a *Playgirl* centerfold, saying our uncle hired him to keep us safe… I guess I can't blame a girl for letting all that anger bubble over into crazy-hot sex.

She would still fight with him, but they sorted it out in the bedroom. Now they're getting married.

"I still can't get over you in love." I wrinkle my nose at her. "It's a big change. I like it."

She tries to act coy. "I don't know what you mean. I'm the same as I've always been."

"No, you're not. Before you were always so controlled and formal. Now look at you with your hair in pigtails and your cheeks all pink. You're wearing jeans and a tank."

"I've always worn jeans."

"Not ripped jeans, and definitely not with a tank top. You said tank tops showed too much skin." Blake always worried her curvy body attracted the wrong kind of attention.

Those nuns really fucked her up, but Hutch seems to have undone the damage.

She starts to wave me away, but pauses, touching my chin lightly. "Why are your eyes so tired? Are you sick?"

Pressing my lips together, I wish I'd minded my own business. Things always go sideways when I start talking too much.

"I'm fine." I try to pull away, but she holds my forearm.

"Talk to me, Hana. What's going on?"

She probably thinks I'm using drugs again, and I don't have the right to be angry with her for assuming it. My only choice is to be honest.

"I haven't been sleeping so great is all." I lift my arm to drink more coffee, and her hand falls away. "I'm probably still adjusting to being here. It'll pass."

"We've been here almost a year. Why aren't you sleeping?"

Anxiety knots my stomach. I don't want to tell her about my nightmares–they're not her fault. Victor Petrov was *not* our uncle. He was a vile, wicked man who stole from our family and abused me. The people who should have protected us failed, and now we're doing our best to pick up the pieces.

It's what my therapist would say, and I'm trying so hard to grow and get stronger. I'm trying to stand on my own and not use crutches.

Lowering my mug, I push off the bar. "I do need to work today. The light is perfect, and I should get Pepper and do some poses with the horses. Or maybe something at the skate park. Everybody's roller skating again…"

"I need you to talk to me, Hana. Tell me what's on your mind."

What's on my mind… What's always on my mind, since we came here, since my birthday party? Exhaling slowly, I decide to put all my cards on the table. I'm trying to do better, right?

"Remember when we went to New York last time, and Scar and Hutch went with us?"

"Is that the last time you slept? That's been weeks–"

"I thought Scar might like me a little then." Tracing my nail along the grain in the wooden countertop, I feel so silly saying it out loud. "I guess I was wrong."

Her brow relaxes, and she leans back on her barstool. "I'm not so sure. He's definitely interested in you. It's painfully obvious. I was actually a little worried, because he doesn't seem, I don't know. *Safe*?"

"I'd argue the opposite. I've never felt more safe than when I'm with him." Leaning forward on my elbows, I exhale. "Why does he keep me at arm's length? I've tried to be open, warm…"

"He's ten years older than you, for starters."

"I'm twenty-one!" Exasperation burns in my stomach. I've

never been aggressive, but I've also never felt this way. "I'm not a baby."

Blake walks over and slides the curl behind my ear. A smile softens her features. "You've always been able to get what you want. Scar is protective of you, and he is older. Maybe he thinks you don't think of him in that way."

She picks up the tablet, and I consider what she's saying. In my opinion, I've been very clear I'm interested in him, but maybe he interpreted it as friendship. Maybe I do need to be a little more suggestive.

Glancing at Blake, I sometimes wonder how we came from the same parents. She's dark and curvy and confident. She looks like a woman who can get anything she wants–and clearly she can. I'm waifish, pale and insecure. *Damaged…*

Oskar Lourde is a grown man. He's quietly confident and sure of himself.

"I think maybe he knows I'm not worth the effort."

Blake stops at the door, leveling her gray eyes on me. "I've only talked to him a few times, but he seems intelligent. If he can't see your worth, he's not the man I think he is."

A smile twists through the frown on my lips and the pain in my chest turns to gratitude. Of all the things for her to say, after all I've done…

"Thanks, B. I don't deserve you."

"You just keep getting better. That's all I care about."

"I will."

I promise, I will.

CHAPTER 2

"**T**ALK TO ME, DIRK." I'M IN MIDTOWN MANHATTAN, LOOKING up at the Empire State Building. "What do we know?."

I've been in the city for two weeks, and I'm no closer to finding "Ivan X" than when I arrived. The last time I was here, Dirk traced the blackmail payment Blake made for the porn film supposedly starring Hana to Trip Alexander, their friend and occasional roommate.

Of course, we went after him, but he gave us the slip after dropping a shitload of information that only muddied the waters even more.

Trip claims he's trying to help the girls, but his actions keep putting him in the wrong place with the wrong people. I don't trust him, but Blake is undecided. Hana doesn't remember enough to be a reliable source.

Hutch is right–this case is fucked up. We find answers, but they only lead to more questions. Now Trip has disappeared, and his friend the pornographer-blackmailer seems to have learned how to be a ghost overnight.

"I've got nothing." Dirk exhales heavily in my ear. "After weeks of un-encrypted messages and sloppy trails, Ivan X is suddenly a privacy wizard?" Sarcasm is thick in my partner's voice. "Either he's gone deep undercover, or–"

"He's dead." My voice is grave.

The line falls silent, and I know Hutch's younger brother, our computer-genius partner, is thinking the same thing I am. Still he pushes back.

"I'm hesitant to call it without a body. Why kill Ivan?"

"Trip said we should be asking why everything." I'm thinking out loud.

"Trip said to follow the money."

"I'm going to Gibson's. Someone has to be in charge over there now."

"You think whoever took over Gibson's is the new point person?"

"I don't know. They could transfer the club to a dummy for a little while, until the dust settles, but it's a good place to start. Even dummies come from somewhere." Holding out my hand, I hail a cab to get me to the financial district.

"Watch your back. After talking to Hana, it sounds like her porno was actually a snuff film. I don't like you going into that place alone."

My thoughts are distracted. Dirk is right, but the murder victim in that film can't be the person Hana said it was. It's impossible. With all the drugs in her system, it could've been a dream.

"Scar? Are you listening to me?" Dirk's a good guy. He's not as big as Hutch and me, but he's smart as a fucking whip. He also knows how to handle himself in a fight.

Hell, he knows how to handle himself around brutes and billionaires, which is why his dad nicknamed him the duke.

"Nobody's going to mess with me, Dirk."

"I want to agree with you, but we've seen way too many unexplained deaths lately. Call me paranoid, but I'm tracking your phone."

It takes a lot for me to feel warmth after all that's happened to me. I've got a layer of concrete around my emotions a mile thick, but affection still nudges like one of those sprouts that can't be stopped.

"I'll be careful."

"Text me when you're out."

I'm in a black leather jacket and jeans. My long, brown hair is tied back in a samurai bun, and all the ink on my skin serves a dual purpose–it covers the scars and it tells people to keep their distance.

The cab stops outside unassuming, glass double doors. It could be a store from how it looks at street level, but all the action is below ground. Passing the driver cash, I step out and go around to the alley entrance.

Gibson's is an old, basement bar that flouts the laws, cleans the money, and accommodates the darkest thugs in the unciv-ilized world. It's not the first time I've made this descent into hell. Still, after all this time, I doubt anyone here will remember me.

That was years ago, after Simon sent me from Minsk to New York to be a bodyguard for his brother Victor.

I was pretty messed up when I saw my wrecked body. I wasn't sure what was left for me anymore, and hell, maybe I was depressed. I had no family, no job, no prospects, and now people recoiled at the sight of me. I didn't have a plan, so I accepted Simon's story and did the job he required.

I got to know some of the guys in his employ, but more than that, I got to know what they did and who their bosses were. Then I grew to hate them. I could deal with the rack-eteering, the theft, the money laundering, but I grew angry when I found out they were doping horses. Sex trafficking was the final straw.

Simon threatened my life. He said I knew too much to walk away alive. He said he owned me, but when I found out Victor was a pedophile, I drove to the airport and flew to South Carolina. Simon could rot in hell. I didn't have anything to lose, and I wasn't protecting his brother any more. Victor was lucky I didn't cut his balls off before I left.

Hutch didn't know why I showed up in his office that day. He offered me a job, and I took it. I joined their private investigation firm, and I stayed on guard. If Simon or his minions wanted to come for me, they'd better be fully armed and well-prepared.

Years passed, and no one ever did.

I want to believe they still haven't, but this is too many coincidences. I don't believe I just happened to cross paths with these women who also happened to be mixed up with the Petrovs. Simon is involved in this somehow, and I have to get to him before he gets to me.

"We're not open." A thick, Italian man with dark hair and a thicker accent steps between me and the door.

Bowing up my shoulders, I look down on him from my full, six-foot-four height. "I'm not looking for trouble."

His eyes narrow, and he's not intimidated. "What are you looking for, friend?"

"Petrovich sent me."

He immediately falls back at my lie, lowering his arms and stepping aside. "Why didn't you say so in the first place?"

I don't answer, but he just gave me a shit-ton of information in his retreat.

"No worries." I nod, moving past him into the bowels of the red-velvet club.

It's all shades of burgundy and maroon, from the leather booths to the shag carpets lining the floors and the bar. Heavy curtains hang around the perimeter, I'm sure to hold the cigar smoke that floods the air during business hours.

Smoking is prohibited in all bars and restaurants in New

York City, but at Gibson's it's all about the atmosphere. Whiskey, martinis, high-balls, and cigars. Pretty girls for hire, and who knows what else goes on in the back rooms.

I know what else.

Waiters and busboys are preparing for the night. They don't look up as I cross the empty space to the office, hoping to find answers. Pushing through the painted-black door, I'm surprised to find a young woman in the room.

"Oh!" She jumps and spins around when I enter, her voice between a shriek and a scream.

She blinks up, up, up at me, with black eyes and bleached-blonde hair, and I vaguely recognize her. She's that little girl who was hanging around Blake's friend last time we were here. It takes me a second to remember her name.

"Stormy?" My lip curls. "What are you doing here? Aren't you underage?"

"It's Rainey." She shoves a lock of bobbed hair behind her ear. "I don't know what you mean. I was just getting my coat."

"It looked more like you were going through the desk."

Her brow furrows, and her eyes dart side to side. Her fingers tremble, and the fact she's so nervous puts me on guard. Dirk's words about creative murders drift through my mind.

"You're Hana's friend." She blinks up at me. "What are you doing here?"

"I was looking for Trip." She doesn't have to know the truth, and I figure I'll see what I can get out of her.

Fishing worked with the Italian upstairs.

Rainey frowns, grabbing a piece of fabric that looks like it's made of teddy bear fur. "I told you, I left my coat here last night. I'm just picking it up."

"I know a lie when I hear it."

"Last time I checked, you weren't welcome at Gibson's."

Now I'm definitely suspicious. This girl is way too young to know anything about me.

"Who told you that?" I take a step closer, and she only partially withdraws.

"Greg said the van Hamiltons weren't allowed back in Gibson's." She waves her hand as she talks, closing her eyes and shaking her head. "They got in some kind of fight or something. If you're working for them, you're not allowed here either."

My eyes narrow. Maybe she doesn't know anything or maybe she's covering a slip. I can't be sure. "So you're here for a coat, but you also happen to be sorting the mail?"

"I lost my ID. My fake ID." Her face scrunches as she examines me. "Are you a cop?"

"I'm a private investigator. Who's in charge now?"

She shrugs. "I don't know. I don't know anything."

It's then I realize we've been slowly pivoting this whole time, and she's at the door, which she quickly opens and slips through.

"Fuck," I exhale deeply, watching her run away at top speed, banging into a chair before sprinting up the stairs.

Even if she doesn't know anything, she'll run her big mouth that I was here asking questions. Odds are I've blown our cover, and there's no point in remaining in Manhattan. If Ivan X isn't dead, he'll go even further underground.

Stepping out into the big empty bar, I give it one last sweep, looking for anything I might have missed.

My eyes land on a black door leading to the hidden rooms. I know what goes on back there, and it's all illegal and off the record–and evil as shit.

It conjures a memory living in my head…

You think you're better than me? Victor's words echoed in the small room. *You are me. I'm a dirty old man? You're a dirty young man. I'm a killer? You're a murderer. You'll show me the respect I deserve.*

I grabbed him by the lapels of his coat. *If I were a murderer, you already be dead.*

Freak. His words were the desperate cry of a cornered rat. *You have nothing to live for. No one wants you.*

My response was flat and cold. *Then they'll fear me.*

I step out of the bar into the fading twilight, shaking away his words and how deep they cut me.

I slide my phone from my pocket and comply with Dirk's wishes. It's not affection or any sort of misplaced sentiment. It's my military training. You always check in with your partners. Communication is a lifeline.

Didn't find anyone in charge, but possibly got some info. Heading back to Hamiltown. Home tonight.

I've already hit send when I realize I just called Hamiltown my home. *What the fuck?* It's a decent enough place. It's quiet and I've built a nice house there... *Shit.* Scrubbing my hand over my eyes, I know I've gotten attached. The other thing my sorry life has taught me is love is a liability, a weapon of torture. Attachments are dangerous.

Dirk's reply is swift. **See you soon. Fly safe.**

How long has this been growing? I'll actually be glad to get back and check in with Dirk and Hutch. I'll be glad to be in my own bed tonight.

Then I'll see her.

CHAPTER 3

PEPPER SITS ON THE HEAVY WOODEN BAR IN THE MIDDLE OF HUTCH'S oversized kitchen holding a plastic-spiral bound recipe book from a ladies auxiliary. "Lurlene's making chicken and dumplings for dinner tonight. She said it's the easiest thing because she can use her slow cooker. Y'all should join us because it's always too much food."

"I love Lurlene's chicken and dumplings." Hutch's housekeeper is the best cook. I take the book and slowly turn the pages, scanning the amateur photos and wondering if Scar might be here, too. "You think she'd mind if we came? I hate to make more work for her."

Pepper is Hutch's niece, and he's been raising her since his sister died several years ago. She's nine years younger than me, but we have a ridiculous amount in common.

She rolls her eyes and crosses her legs on the bar. "Lurlene is always happy to have y'all here."

I guess if my sister is Hutch's fiancée, she'll be living here soon. "I'll check with Blake."

Pepper has already moved on to the next item in the middle of the bar. "This chicken does not spark joy."

She sounds like she's reciting a mantra, and I look up to see her holding a polished, pecan bowl with gray moss. In the middle is a colorful, taxidermic hen.

"Thank you, chicken, for your contribution to this house, and now I shall let you go." She holds it out, turning to one of the open, double trash bins hidden in the bar, ready to drop it.

"Hang on!" I catch the display before she tosses it. "Is this your item to throw away?"

Pepper's mouth puckers with a frown, and she slants her dark brown eyes at me. "Whose side are you on? That thing is creepy as–"

"Pepper!" I shake my head. "This was a really popular item last Christmas in New York. I saw one of these at Barney's for eight hundred dollars."

"Barney can keep his dumb chicken. It's creepy, and it does not bring me joy."

"What's all this joy business?" After moving the nesting hen to the top of the refrigerator, I return to my little friend.

Her light brown hair is in the usual pigtail braids, but I notice today they have a little more flair, a little French braid style going on. Her dark brown eyes are accentuated by a touch of mascara. I realize, Pepper's not a skinned-knee shortstop anymore. She's maturing, and I'd better catch up quickly.

"Have you heard about the KonMari method?" She frowns at me, and my nose wrinkles.

I do my best to make my memory work. "Is that the Netflix show with that cute little Asian lady?"

"She's Japanese and her name is Marie Kondo."

"Right!" I smile. "She seems so kind. You like her?"

"She says the best way to find yourself is to get rid of all the clutter in your life. You have to clear the way for the universe to speak to you."

My eyebrows rise, and I nod. "I've always wanted to hear from the universe, but it's never really happened."

"Because you need to tidy." Pepper nods like she's solved all my problems. "Clear the clutter, get rid of the things that do not bring you joy."

Measuring my words, I don't want to attack. "Shouldn't they be *your* things?"

She exhales and her shoulders drop. "That's the hard part. I've run out of things that don't bring me joy."

"What about the things that *do* bring us joy?"

"I haven't gotten to that part."

"I have a recipe for sugar cookies that only has three ingredients." Turning quickly, I open the refrigerator and take out the butter. "That's tidy, don't you think?"

Pepper hesitates, then she nods. "I mean, I guess."

"We'll be so tidy, Lurlene won't even know we've been here." Moving around the space, I open cabinets. "It's just unsalted butter, granulated sugar, and flour."

"That's it?"

"Grab the pure vanilla extract, and we'll be fancy." Reaching for a sterling silver bowl, I look over my shoulder. "Does she have sprinkles? We could be extra fancy if she has sprinkles."

"Sprinkles are not tidy. They make a mess." Pepper giggles, and I love that she's coming out of her funk.

"No sprinkles!" I hold up a wooden spoon. "So we beat the butter, sugar, and flour together until we have a dough." I dump everything into Lurlene's prized mint-green Cuisinart mixer and switch it on.

We're leaning closer as we watch it blend, and I add a few drops of vanilla extract.

"This won't take long," I muse as we wait, hypnotized by the beaters.

"You said you only ate food off a truck," Pepper says quietly. "How did you learn to make cookies?"

"My friend Debbie and I used to make these after parties." I stop there.

Hutch wouldn't like me telling Pepper about my old days in the Manhattan party scene and how we loved eating cookies as we came down off whatever drugs we'd taken. Hutch has only reluctantly agreed to me and Pepper being friends, and I think it's because Blake got pissed at him for calling me a bad influence.

I'm really not...

"You'd have cookies *after* the parties? That's weird. Why didn't you have cookies *at* the parties?"

Chewing my lip, I think about how to answer this in a good-influence way. "They were more like dress-up parties. Not like eating parties."

Jesus, don't even get me started on how we ate–or didn't.

Pepper nods like she understands, but it's clear she doesn't. I flip the switch off on the mixer and carry the silver bowl to the counter where a cookie sheet waits.

"Now we form one-inch balls, roll them in the sugar, and flatten them on the tray."

She follows my lead, forming the little golden spheres and covering them with the sweet granules until they're all done and mushed.

"Ten minutes or until they get gold at the edges." I set the oven timer, and we lean against the counter to wait.

"I think sugar cookies are the tidiest of cookies." Pepper chews her finger, and I smile.

She was younger than I was when her mother died. I was thirteen when I lost my dad, but she was only eleven–and it was her mother. I don't know how to talk to people like real therapists do or counselors, but I care about her.

"Blake was worried you'd think she was trying to replace

your mom when she marries Hutch." Looking down, I hope I'm not overstepping. "She would never do that, you know?"

Pepper hops onto the bar again. "I think Uncle Hutch should get married. Lurlene said he should have his own family."

My stomach shifts, and I feel like I understand all the joy talk now. "You're Hutch's family, too. I mean, I'm no expert, but he loves you a lot."

"But I'm just his niece. I'm not really his daughter."

"No, but he's known you the longest."

Sitting straighter, she points to the oven. "They're turning golden at the edges!"

I get the feeling she's trying to change the subject. Hell, as a master of distraction, I ought to know. "That means it's time to take them out. Then they have to cool."

We're sliding them onto the rack, and she absently notes. "Uncle Hutch said he'll be glad when softball season starts up again, but my softball glove doesn't bring me joy."

"It doesn't?" I'm shocked. "But you're the hardest working short-stop in the little league."

"That was sixth grade. I'm so much older now. I like skating better."

I'm a little sad at this news, but it reminds me why I came here. "I need to take more pictures if I'm going to be ready for my show. Would you and your friends meet me at the skate park tomorrow for a photo shoot?"

"Yes!" She bounces on the bar, eyes dancing. "I can show you my new trick where my feet go up while I hold the side of the ledge... One of the skater boys taught me."

There's the feisty little jock I missed, and maybe this is why she's not so interested in softball anymore. "What's this skater boy's name?"

"Tommy." She leans forward, examining the cookies. I'm about to ask for more info on Tommy when she cuts her eyes up at me. "Mr. Scar got back last night."

My jaw drops, but I recover fast. "How do you know that?"

"He stopped by to talk to Uncle Hutch. They said a bunch of stuff I didn't understand, but he asked how you were doing."

I hold my expression steady, doing my best to hide the fireworks going off in my chest. "What did your uncle say?"

"He said you were good." Pepper's nose wrinkles. "Are you doing good? Your face is all red."

"Of course!" My voice is too high. Lifting a cookie, I hold it to her mouth. "Try one and see what you think."

She takes a bite then quickly devours the rest. "Dang! These are amazing! They're buttery and crispy and chewy… they're like candy!"

Allowing the smile I've been fighting to split my cheeks, I scrub my fingers in the front of her hair. "That means they're perfect."

Rocking side to side on the bar, she eats two more cookies. "Lurlene said it's about time somebody saw that diamond in the rough. I didn't really understand what she meant, though. Who's the diamond? Is it you or is it Scar?"

My mouth is dry, and I feel like ants are on my skin. I need to go. "Maybe you should ask Lurlene."

"I think you're the diamond and Scar's just rough."

I exhale a laugh as my cheeks flush again. "I'm not much of a diamond."

"You should take some of these cookies to him. I think he'll like them, and since he was asking about you, you can say hi."

Looking up, I catch a glint in her eyes, and I'm going to have to be very careful around Pepper. She's smart as a whip.

"You think Scar likes sugar cookies?"

"I think he likes your cookies."

My eyebrows shoot up, and I give her leg a playful shove. "Mind your business."

She exhales a laugh and hops off the bar. "I've got more tidying to do. I'll see you tomorrow at the park."

"Bring your friends." Picking up the remaining cookies,

I wrap them in a paper towel. "Maybe I can meet Tommy. I hope he's a good boy."

"He's good," she calls back. "At skateboarding."

Shaking my head, I quickly clean up our mess, impatience twisting in my stomach. I'm antsy and breathless and excited and I really need to be cool. Taking a few calming breaths, I scoop up the small bundle and head out to the waiting golf cart I use to get around town.

We have a few hours until dinner, and I'm ready to share my cookies.

CHAPTER 4

Scar

STANDING IN FRONT OF THE WALL IN THE OFFICE AT MY HOUSE, I look at the sketches I've made of what we know and what we don't.

"That's some old-school shit." Dirk laughs, studying my wall. "What will you do if somebody comes to the house?"

"Lock the door," I growl, not bothered by his teasing. Seeing it this way helps me think.

"Three seemingly healthy men died of heart attacks." Hutch's deep voice focuses our conversation. "One gunshot victim is missing, and the blackmailer is gone, possibly dead."

"We also have a dead girl and Hana as the target of a blackmail racket and possibly star of a snuff film," Dirk adds. "If you can trust her memory, which I for one, do not."

My jaw clenches at his words. I don't want to cross Dirk, but I don't like him speaking that way about Hana.

"She was right about him being dead." My voice is low, and I hope it doesn't sound defensive.

Hutch joins in quickly. "Blake pointed out she wasn't in the room when Hugh told us Victor was dead. Somehow she knew."

"She thinks she did it." Passing a hand over my mouth, I try to make sense of this nonsense.

"Which begs the question, who would benefit from Hana thinking she's a murderer?" Dirk points to my wall. "I think somebody wanted Hana to take the fall for Victor's death–or at the very least, wanted to turn attention from himself."

"Ivan was blackmailing Blake, so maybe he's the murderer? Maybe that's why he's gone now–he got caught?"

"But he told Blake it was porn." Dirk adds. "He could've raised his price and the stakes by accusing her of murder."

"So we'll operate off the assumption Ivan didn't know he had a snuff film on his hands," Hutch muses.

"If it even is that." Skepticism is thick in Dirk's voice.

"It takes more than one person to make a video." I quietly state the obvious. "Ivan isn't the only person who knows what happened."

"Does Blake still have the link to the files?" Dirk taps quickly on his computer keys.

"It was a QR code." Hutch notes. "She still has the image, but the link is broken."

"Send it to me," Dirk says, still typing. "It's possible I can figure out where it used to be stored and see if that leads anywhere."

"What does Hugh say about all of this?" I look over at Hutch.

"Same as before. He congratulates us on getting the girls out of danger, taking care of the bad guys, and helping get their money back."

"So he's still not talking." I put my hands on my hips, looking up at the wall.

"You think he's hiding something?" Hutch sounds less

like he's asking and more like he's thinking the same thing as me.

"That old man knows more than he's telling us." Like Trip said, I think to myself, *why...*

"You coming over for dinner tonight? Lurlene made plenty for everyone."

Pulling the ring on my bottom lip under my teeth, I think about what he's asking. "Maybe. I need to unpack."

"We'll set a place for you." Hutch's voice is calm, authoritative. He's our leader, but he's not a boss.

"I'll be there," Dirk calls out. "In the meantime, send me that code, and I'll see what I can track down. I still have a bot running, searching for Ivan. If he's alive, I'll find him."

"Ping us if you hear anything," Hutch orders.

We sign off, and I cross my arms, looking up at the wall. One of the dead guys is Hana's father, Charles van Hamilton. The other dead guy is the former owner of Gibson's, who we think killed Debbie, Blake and Hana's friend, although he denied it.

The third is Victor...

Taking out my phone, I quickly tap on the face. *Need to talk to you, sir. Would it be possible to stop by tomorrow?*

I'm respectful to Hugh van Hamilton, not only because he owns the town and he's Hutch's close friend. He's also Hana's uncle.

He despises texts and all the modern technology, but I get a reply from Norris. *Mr. Hugh says he will be available tomorrow morning at eleven.*

I quickly tap back. *I'll be there.*

Hugh had Victor's ledger, he also got it from one of Victor's guys–who he said his bodyguard killed. That old man knows a hell of a lot more than he's saying, and I need him to start connecting these dots. My hope is if I tell him a bit of my story, he'll open up. Then I can take what I know to the guys.

Before he disappeared, Trip told us to ask why Victor went after India van Hamilton and her daughters, but I know they were connected before Charles was killed.

Hugh said Victor was embezzling money from Charles's estate, but I also know Charles was mixed up in the doping scheme Victor was running. They shared a thoroughbred horse, and he was in over his head.

If Hugh knows Simon, many puzzle pieces will snap into place. The only wild card is Hana. Who wants us to believe she killed Victor?

Exhaling a frustrated growl, I want to go back to New York City, but until Dirk finds another lead, it's a dead end. As it is, I've got to stay here for now.

But staying here could be more dangerous for me than walking into Simon's lair.

"Hello?" A soft, female voice I recognize calls from the kitchen, and electricity zips through my chest.

Moving quickly, I shut down the computer and grab my phone. Stepping into the hall, I close the door to the room and turn the key in the lock. Then I put the key in the pocket of my jeans.

"Anybody home?" She calls again, and her voice is like the sweetest music to my ears.

Fuck. I clench my fists and steel myself. I can't be this way with her. I have to be in control.

Clearing my throat, I step into the bright, open kitchen and when my eyes land on hers, all the breath slips from my lungs.

Hana's standing in a shaft of sunlight with her pretty curls piled on her head in some kind of messy way that looks too damn cute. She's smiling like she always does, like she's nervous and confident all at the same time, which doesn't make any sense.

Nothing about her makes sense–in particular the way

she's crawled under my skin and lives in my head rent-free 24-7.

Now she's in my kitchen in cutoff jean shorts and a long-sleeved white sweater. Her pink toenails are exposed in black flip flops, and she does a little wave. She's the best thing I've ever seen, and it makes me want to pack up all my shit and get as far away from here as possible.

I'm not afraid of anything, but this tiny woman with her fucked up past and her sweet little smile is going to be the death of me. I know she is, and I'm walking right into the fire anyway.

CHAPTER 5

Hana

MY HEART BEATS SO HARD, I THINK I MIGHT FAINT. I'M STANDING in Scar's kitchen, and he's glaring at me like he's trying to decide whether to throw me out or ask me to sit down. Now I'm second-guessing everything, including my decision to come over here with a bundle of sugar cookies.

Sugar cookies? Really, Hana? Like that's going to help him see me as an adult. I guess I did take advice from a twelve-year-old.

He's standing in front of me in faded jeans and a black tee that shows off the sleeves of ink running down both his arms, covering the scars I still don't know how he got.

I want to know. I want to know everything about him.

His hair's pulled back in the usual bun, and he's watching me with those cool-blue wolf eyes making my entire body weak. A ring is in his lip. He doesn't always wear it, and when he crosses his arms, his biceps expand and the muscles in his shoulders ripple.

"Hey." His voice is low and smokey.

A smile breaks across my face. "Hey, yourself. I heard you were back."

My voice sounds way more confident than I feel. He's a six-foot-four tower of scary-assed sex, and I want to curl up in his arms and never leave.

"I got back last night." He's watching me like he always does, like he'd kill anybody who touched me, yet he won't touch me himself.

It's so frustrating.

"Did you have a good trip?"

He shrugs, lowering his arms and entering the kitchen, but keeping the large, wooden bar between us. It's the first time I've been inside his house, and I realize his bar looks a lot like the one in Hutch's kitchen. It's the same, rough-hewn wood and heavy metal hardware.

"The trip was fine. Not a lot of answers." Opening the refrigerator, he looks inside then up to me. "I haven't been to the store yet. All I have is beer."

"That's okay!" I wave my hand, stepping forward and placing the bundle of cookies on the bar. "I brought these for you. Pepper and I made them, and she thought you might like some."

God, I want to die. I sound so young and immature, and I want to sound like my sister—confident and strong.

I'm twenty-one. I should've said I'd have a beer. Only, it's too early, and I'm trying to show everyone I'm making good choices.

Looks like I'm stuck with sugar cookies. Thank God sprinkles aren't tidy.

Scar's brow furrows, and he walks over to where I'm standing. Looking up, I study his small nose and lovely full lips I want to kiss.

He opens the paper towel, and a whisper of a smile softens his amazing face. "Cookies?"

"It's a super-simple recipe. When I heard you were back, I really just wanted to come over and say hi."

As I'm talking too fast, he takes one of the pieces and lifts it to his mouth, popping the entire thing inside and nodding. "It's good."

A flush sweeps through my entire body. I'm sure I'm beaming like I just found the cure for dementia instead of whipping up a batch of three-ingredient sugar cookies, quite possibly the easiest recipe on the planet.

He takes another one and bites it in half. "You made these?"

"Pepper and me."

"Thanks."

"So that's all, I guess. I just wanted to come by and say hi and welcome home." And now I'm repeating myself. "Are you going to dinner at Hutch's tonight?"

I don't know where that came from. I haven't even decided if I'm going or if I'm even invited just because Pepper mentioned it.

"Are you?" His brow furrows in a way that makes me wonder what's the right answer.

Two weeks have passed. Is it possible, he's not as interested in me as he was when he left. When he stopped by my birthday party, it really seemed like he wanted to touch me, to hold my hand at the very least. I know I felt something.

He told me I looked really pretty.

Now it feels like he's pushing me away.

"I might. Pepper mentioned it, but I haven't talked to Blake."

"I might be there."

This is it, I decide. I have to go for it. If Blake is right, I have to be completely clear.

Stepping forward, I put my hand on his resting on the bar. He stills at my touch so much I'm not sure he's breathing. I don't pull back. I spread my fingers over his large fist, tracing a line to the ink on his wrist.

"I hope I'll see you there."

His eyes are on my hand touching his, slender and pale, fingers longing to thread. He only nods, that sexy muscle moving in his jaw.

I want to kiss his cheek, but instead, I take my hand away and go to the door. Hesitating, I look back to give him one last smile. His gaze is hooded as he watches me, and he doesn't smile back.

"Maybe I could tidy your room!" Pepper sits on the floor across from me, scooping glass beads from the tray as we play a game of Mancala.

Blake's in the kitchen with Lurlene helping her plate the food, and Dirk and Hutch stand by the fireplace talking quietly.

"Sure. Whatever." I'm not really paying attention to her, I'm straining to hear what they're saying and catching my breath every time a door opens.

When I got back from Scar's house this afternoon, Blake met me at the door to say we were having dinner here tonight. She said Lurlene wanted the whole family together again.

Lurlene isn't a blood relative, but she treats us all like her children. It's one of the things I love about this place. From the first night we were here, she brought us in, fed us an amazing dinner, and made us feel welcome and at home.

I spent a little extra time getting ready for dinner, styling two braids on each side of my hair, adding a touch of perfume behind my ears. I'm wearing my ivory lace Balenciaga shift, which I know only Blake and Debbie would appreciate. It's short and low-cut and highlights my best features–my long legs and my shoulders–while blending with my skin.

My eyes are smoky, and my lips are pale pink and matte. I'm going for "innocent seductress," neither of which I am. I'm not innocent, and I've never been much of a seductress. I'm going to give myself the hiccups with all this stress.

"It's TMZ, I'm sure of it." Dirk's holding a glass of wine, and I think maybe I should slip into the kitchen and get one to calm my jumpy nerves. "It's the only thing that ties them all together."

Hutch looks down, speaking quietly. "We can discuss it at the office. I don't want…" He glances over to where I'm sitting with Pepper.

"Of course." Dirk takes another sip of wine, turning to look at the gas log. "I got my schedule of classes for the fall. I'm only teaching one course, but it's two days a week for three hours."

His older brother nods. "You can manage that easily. How much after-hours prep?"

"Not much."

A light tap on the front door precedes it opening, and Pepper is on her feet at once. "Uncle Scar!"

My stomach flips, but I keep my eyes fastened on the game. I do my best to clean up our Mancala mess without revealing my trembling fingers. I want to seem cool and casual, not flustered or overly interested in who just arrived and how excited it makes me.

"Hey, Shortstop." He lifts her into a hug, and I sit back on my heels watching his large, inked hands squeeze her small back. "What's new?"

She shrugs as he lowers her to her feet. "I'm learning the Konmari Method."

"Is that softball?"

"No, it's about throwing stuff away."

His eyebrow arches, and his amused frown totally melts me. "What do you have to throw away?"

"Exactly." Pepper rolls her eyes.

He's so confused and so handsome in a black, button-down

shirt and dark jeans. His long hair is clean and tied back, and Dirk meets him in the center of the room.

"Hey, bro. Glad you decided to join us."

They shake hands, and I'm sitting on the floor doing my best to breathe normally as I track him with my eyes.

Scar nods. "I can unpack tomorrow."

"It's good to have you back." Hutch gives him a brief hug, squeezing his shoulder, and Scar grips his arm. "None of us should work alone on this case."

"I'll be fine." He turns, and our eyes meet.

My heart squeezes, and heat floods my cheeks as his eyes move down my body and back up again in a blink.

"Hana." He says it as if clearing his throat.

Pepper pops up beside him. "Did you like Hana's cookies?"

"Ah…" He seems unsure how to answer, and I want to die.

Luckily Blake enters the room. "What cookies? I hope you're not spoiling your dinner."

"Hana taught me to make these awesome sugar cookies. They're like candy!" Pepper is talking loud, like she's forgotten to be twelve. "Only three ingredients, and it just took ten minutes."

Chewing my bottom lip, I study my clenched hands in my lap wondering why my life is so ridiculous. Here I am, trying to be a sophisticated temptress, and *cookies*…

"I know that recipe." Blake's voice is quiet as she sits on the sofa beside me. "Was it Debbie's?"

I glance up, and a spear of memory slices my stomach. It's been less than a year since Debbie died, and the pain is still so fresh.

My voice is quiet. "No point in burying it with her."

She puts her hand on my shoulder and presses her lips to my forehead. "I love you, sis. This year has been a shitshow."

No arguing with that. Scar's deep voice cuts the quiet. "Hana's cookies were delicious."

I blink up to see his blue eyes holding mine. He's still

guarded, but just like always, he won't leave me hanging. I almost think he's teasing, but it's impossible to know.

Still, I give him a smile. "I'm glad you liked them."

Lurlene bustles through the kitchen door at that moment, bellowing. "Time to eat. Take your places at the table before it gets cold."

Blake stands, taking Hutch's arm as he smiles down at her. The way he looks at her sometimes is truly pornographic, but I'm the only one who seems to notice. Pepper runs to jump on Dirk's back, and he gives her a piggyback ride to the dining room.

Looking up, I notice Scar is waiting for me at the edge of the sofa. He holds out a hand, and I take it, carefully standing so my underwear doesn't show beneath my short skirt. Why the heck was I sitting on the floor? I really do have to act more mature if I expect him to take me seriously. Blake would never sit on the floor.

"Thanks." I'm a little breathless standing in front of him.

He towers over me, looking down. "Thank you for the welcome home gift."

Everyone is laughing and standing around the table, but we're still by the fireplace. We're so close, my stomach is a cage of tormented butterflies. "I'm glad you liked them."

"I like your hair." His eyes trace the loose braids on each side of my head, and I pray I don't turn red.

"Thank you, again."

He looks down at me with such intensity, I wonder if he sees all the things I want to say in my eyes.

"Are you two planning to join us or what?" Pepper calls, breaking the moment.

"Come." His hand lightly touches my arm, and I want to close my eyes and lean into him.

I imagine stretching up to kiss his cheek, then his lips, then his tongue with mine. Warm energy floods my veins, and I think he would lift me off my feet, so high nothing could touch me. I imagine him wrapping me in his arms and holding me so tightly, never letting go…

Instead I take my usual chair across from my sister, next to Pepper. Scar sits beside Blake across from me, and as the serving dishes go around, I realize this is a terrible seating arrangement. Every time his eyes meet mine, my stomach dips like I'm on a roller-coaster.

I'm not going to be able to eat a thing, and Lurlene's chicken and dumplings is my favorite dish.

"What's all this tidying up, Pep?" Dirk has no problem shoveling food in his mouth.

Pepper wiggles around, and I know she wants to climb onto her knees in her chair. She and I seem to be having the same problem with wanting to have fun and wanting to be taken seriously at the same time.

"She's throwing away everything." Hutch groans, joining the conversation. "Last week I found my old Marines jersey in the trash."

Pepper's eyebrows shoot up, and she shakes her head. "That shirt did not spark joy."

"How would you know that?"

"To be fair, it did have holes in it." Blake's left hand is joined with Hutch's on top of the table, and I don't know how they manage to eat when their hands never part.

It's possible I'm jealous, because I want to touch Scar that way. Stealing a glance across the table, his eyes flicker to my full plate and up to mine again, and his expression darkens. My stomach tightens even more, and now I'm afraid my food might come up. Is he angry?

One minute he's complimenting me and being kind, the next he's glowering at me. I can't read him at all.

"I'll tell you what did *not* spark joy." Hutch grumbles. "Finding my jersey in the trash. I'll be glad when softball season starts again."

"I've decided softball doesn't bring me joy." Pepper makes the announcement, and silence falls over the table.

Everyone stops eating and looks at her, and my little friend appears to shrink in her chair.

"But you're so good at it…" Blake's soft voice trails off, and I know she's doing her best to be friends with Pepper and not interfere.

As the one person who's had time to adjust to this new information, I jump in quickly.

"Pepper's learning to skate. Tomorrow we're taking pictures at the park, and she's going to show me some of her new moves." A small hand grabs mine under the table. Clearing my throat, I add, "I think it's good to try new things, don't you, Hutch?"

Hutch places his elbow beside his plate and leans his head against his hand studying his little ward. "Whatever makes you happy, Pep. But does Coach Perkins know? What about your teammates?"

"Softball season is a year away," Dirk interjects. "I think we should see how Pep's feeling in March, yeah?"

"I guess." Pepper shrugs.

Cutting my eyes over, I give her a wink, and she presses her lips into a smile.

After plates are cleared and dessert is served, Scar stands and thanks Lurlene for the meal. "I'll check in tomorrow," he says to Hutch before starting for the door.

I'm on my feet, hustling after him as the rest of the group hangs around the table talking.

"Hey!" My voice comes out like a yip, so I take a breath and try again. "You know I have that show coming up in New York in a few months–the photography show at the Milo gallery?"

He pauses and turns to look down at me. I swallow air again, and do my best to exhale slowly. He's silent, waiting, so I continue. I got this ball rolling, after all.

"Anyway, I was hoping you might let me take those photos of you. Remember? We talked about it before you left?"

"I told you, I don't take pictures."

"But you really don't have to do anything. I mean, you'll do something. It's not like you'll be sitting there doing nothing." Oh, God, Hana, get a grip. *Inhale, exhale…* "What I mean is, you can do something you would normally do or something you like doing, like a hobby, and I would be there to capture it."

Blue eyes slide from mine to my hair, down to my lips, which tingle. I can't help pulling my bottom one between my teeth and his gaze flickers again to my eyes.

"Please?" I smile softly. "I think you'd make an amazing subject. I'd really like to have you in my show."

He's not smiling. The muscle in his square jaw moves, and I swear to God, one of these days I'm going to lose all control and kiss him.

"I'll think about it." It's all he says before disappearing through the door.

I do not collapse against it.

But just barely.

CHAPTER 6

Scar

I LEAN MY SHOULDER AGAINST THE COLUMN OUTSIDE HUTCH'S FAMILY estate as the door closes behind me. Hana was so beautiful tonight. As she stood there looking up at me, chewing on her full, pink lip, I had to focus all my energy on not touching her.

I wanted to reach out and put my thumb on it, pull it free from her teeth then cover it with mine. I wanted to taste her pretty mouth, lift her off her feet and press her against the wall.

She keeps reaching out, carefully, hesitantly, and I keep pushing her away. How will it feel when she takes me at my word and walks?

Pain like knives slices through my stomach, and I push off the wooden post, staggering down the steps and out the gravel drive to my waiting truck. Why does she torment me this way? What is it about her that won't let me go?

Liability, danger, weakness, all the reasons I have to keep her at arms length push against my temples as I make the short drive home, but they can't keep her out. I close my eyes and exhale a growl. I want to act on these feelings she stirs inside me. I want her in my bed.

Entering the dark space, I don't even turn on the lights. I unbutton my shirt as I walk to my bedroom and pull the garment over my head, tossing it on a chair. Reaching back, I take the band out of my hair, then I shove my jeans off and push through my sheets.

It's been so long, so very long. My cock is hard, and I cover the tip with one hand, sliding my palm around and doing my best to kill this desire. Nothing keeps her out of my mind.

I picture her fair skin marked by my hands, my mouth. I see the burning pink outline of my palm on her ass, the dark red markings of my mouth on her shoulders.

Fuck, that's another thing. How could I be rough with her after all she's been through? I'm a sick fuck, and she deserves a prince. The last thing she needs is a beast like me. Still, I picture the back of her head against my shoulder. I'd drag my palms up her body, her tiny breasts, perfect handfuls, hard nipples in my fingers.

I'd toy with them until she was at the edge, then as I slid my dick inside, I'd take them lower, applying just the right amount of gentle pressure to have her quivering and bucking against my cock. *Good girl,* I'd hold her neck and whisper in her ear…

My soul begs to possess her just once. *Once,* and I would remember everything about her. Like the rings on a tree, she would mark the time in my heart.

Dammit, I throw the covers back and go to the bathroom to grab a washcloth. Leaning hard on the counter, it doesn't take much—two strokes of my fist before my desire for her pulses out of me in hot bursts.

It's a poor substitute for the real thing, but I don't have a choice, not with the way things are, with so many unanswered questions, and the chance at any time she could be used as leverage against me.

I won't let that happen. I'd die before I let anyone hurt her.

Cleaning up, it hits me–for the first time since the fire, I care about something. Truthfully, I care about a lot of things, and I'd better get a handle on it. I have to school my emotions, pay attention to who's watching. I won't let any of them be hurt, especially not Hana.

"Mr. Hugh will be with you in a moment." Norris, the old butler for Blake and Hana's uncle greets me at the door of the van Hamilton estate. "Miss Hana is out by the pool if you'd like to walk around and wait there."

My insides tense at her name, but I can't stop my feet from taking me to where she is. I can't stop any part of myself from wanting to be in her presence.

Blake and Hana came here for protection almost a year ago. Hugh van Hamilton is their father's uncle, but he has no wife or children. Hutch has been the closest thing to a son he's ever had. After the obvious threats were neutralized, he convinced them to stay. It didn't take much convincing, once Blake and Hutch got together. I think Hana likes being here more than their apartment in New York.

From what I've been told, she's healthier here than she was in New York, although now that I see her in a bathing suit, I'm not so sure.

She leans back in a chair, and her long curls are over one shoulder. She's wearing a large hat and dark sunglasses, and in her pale pink bikini, I see the lines of her ribs, the points of her hip bones.

"Have you had breakfast?" My voice is gruff, and she sits up quickly like I startled her.

"Scar?" She turns in the chair, and her slim thighs barely touch. "I didn't know you were coming over today."

"I have a meeting with your uncle. Answer me."

It's a stern order, and she stands, sliding the sunglasses off her eyes. She's not wearing makeup, and her face is young and fresh. Still, her dark blue eyes are too big in her slim face, and they're lined and tired.

"Ask me again." She smiles, her full lips parting.

She has some kind of gloss on them, which makes me want to kiss her even more. Then I want to sit her on my lap and make her eat an entire omelet.

"I asked if you've eaten breakfast." She's so tiny looking up at me, and her nose wrinkles.

"I had a piece of toast with my coffee. I'm not much of a breakfast eater. Unless you're asking me for a brunch date?"

"You didn't eat your dinner last night." I growl, and her glowy smile starts to fade. I'm being an asshole, but I'm angry. "Why don't you eat? You're too thin."

Her eyebrows rise, and she blinks rapidly as pink colors her cheeks. "Some people find it attractive." She's trying to tease, but her voice wavers.

"I've seen starving people. It's not attractive."

"I guess Blake got all the curves in our family."

"If you'd eat, your body would respond. You'll never be healthy if you don't take care of yourself."

"I'm sorry you find me so unattractive." Her voice is sharp, and she snatches up her towel, wrapping it roughly around herself under the arms. "Thanks for stopping by to tell me what I already know."

Her cheeks are burning red, and tears fill her eyes. My stomach cramps at the sight, and clenching my fists, I curse my roughness. I'm so fucking frustrated–of course, I find her attractive. Can't she tell?

I'm pissed as hell and ready to chase after her when a throat clears beside me. "Sorry if I'm interrupting." Hugh's craggly old voice speaks. "Walk with me."

I hesitate, looking in the direction Hana just fled. "I think I should go–"

"You didn't ask, but it's probably a good idea to let her cool off a bit before you try and explain yourself. Hana's a special girl, quick to forgive. Let her sort out her thoughts, and it'll be easier for you."

My shoulders fall, and I feel like a complete asshole. "I didn't come here to make her cry."

"I should hope not." He gives me a tight smile, and we start to walk along the brick path that leads down to the stables. "This thing between you is an unexpected development, but not entirely without merit."

I'm not sure how to respond, so I don't. I look up at the blooming pear trees mixed with weeping willows. The landscaping around the old van Hamilton estate is ancient and enviable. Massive trees mix with blooming shrubs, and they're all established and healthy.

"Norris told me you texted." Hugh carries a cane, but he doesn't really need it. He uses it more to emphasize his points. "Hate those damn things. Sending a tiny message and pretending it's the same as personal interaction. Back in my day, people would visit, sit down, have coffee or a drink."

"It's too early to drink." Although after what just happened with Hana, I could use one.

"So what brings you to me today?"

We pause, and I give the elegant landscape another quick sweep, checking for workers or anyone else who might be listening.

"The man in your trunk." I speak quietly, studying the old man's expression.

"Andre Bertonelli." He nods.

"Italian?"

"He worked for the Petrovs in New York. One of them owns a nightclub, and he had access to their books."

"Gibson's." I nod, thinking this makes sense. "So you never had contact with Victor or… anyone."

I wait to see if he knows about Simon.

"I heard Victor was stealing from my nephew's estate, then I dug deeper and found out he was laundering money for a shell corporation owned by a group of Russians or an oligarch or both. I didn't get far enough, and to be honest, I didn't want to. Such things can be deadly, and I'm too old to chase after gangsters. The girls are out of danger, and the men who were pursuing them are dead. That's enough for me."

My lips tighten, and I nod. He can think that if it helps him sleep at night. He's right–he is an old man, and Hutch, Dirk, and I will handle this.

"Any idea how Victor met your nephew's wife?"

"I believe it was through illegal gambling." The old man straightens with a sniff. "I'm not going to delude myself into thinking I'd have been a perfect parent, but Charles wasn't my son. I had no power over him, and he made poor choices. I only hope I've been able to recover what he lost, and shield my nieces. They're good girls. They shouldn't have to pay for their father's sins."

"I agree." My voice is low, and he nods.

"Hutch will take care of Blake." He studies me, as if he's still deciding. "Hana might have inherited her father's reck-lessness, but she has a sweetness he did not. I think she truly wants a better life."

I don't answer that. I think Hana struggles with demons he can't understand, but I understand them. I know well what it's like to be haunted by the past. Glancing up at the mansion, guilt claws in my chest. Still, I decide to take the old man's advice and give her space. I've done enough.

I need to talk to Hutch. It's time I came clean on how much I know about all of this and how deep my connection to it is– see if he agrees. This can't be a coincidence.

I only hope he doesn't decide I'm a danger to his family and tell me to go.

CHAPTER 7

THE WHITE SHAG ON THE RUG COVERING MY BEDROOM FLOOR IS long and tickles my nose. I'm lying on my side, and my face is hot and red and puffy from crying.

I don't want to cry anymore. I had a bad night, and I couldn't sleep until almost dawn. Then I awoke at nine and decided I was tired of fighting the memories.

Every time I closed my eyes, I was thirteen again and terrified. I was back in my old bedroom too afraid to sleep, pulling the covers tight around my head and curling into a tight ball. I always went to sleep in fear, like I was trapped in a house on fire, and no one could save me. The walls were collapsing on top of me, and no one was strong enough to protect me.

Closing my eyes, I conjured images of him, tall and strong, scarred from the flames only he could fight. He lay beside me, long and lean. He wrapped me in his arms. He covered me with his body, and I slept.

Today, in the bright light of reality, he basically said I disgust him.

Looking down at my body, I pinch the skin on my stomach, trying to make it have rolls. I don't want to be ugly. I don't want to look as sick on the outside as I am inside. Pulling my knees to my chest, I wrap my arms around them and imagine shrinking. I imagine growing smaller and smaller, until I disappear in the long threads of the carpet. I'm Alice searching for the perfect drug to make me invisible.

Closing my eyes, I remember the last time I dropped acid to escape the pain. It flowed out of me like water from a broken vase. I sat on the edge of the balcony, on the roof of our building in New York, and leaned back, holding out my arms as the wind pushed through my hair, blowing it all away to the ends of the earth. Lifting my chin, I was free. I didn't hurt anymore.

The city lights spread out before me like a carpet, and I could walk on thin air. Debbie grabbed my waist and told me not to fall. We were laughing so hard. We could go anywhere, a thousand miles away.

In the beginning I wondered if that's why she died. I wasn't there to hold her waist and tell her not to fall.

It's been four months since I've taken a drug.

Trip's visit was the last time. Seeing him brought back too many memories. Debbie was dead, and I was still alive. All the things I'd done surrounded me. They grew and grew until they were taller than the Empire State Building, heavier than the Great Wall of China. The demons crowded so close I couldn't breathe.

Of course, Scar doesn't want me. He found me that night and carried me back to his place. It was the first time I slept at his side, but I don't even remember it. I only remember waking up here, after he brought me home.

My phone is in my hand, and I scroll to Trip's number. I haven't seen or heard from him since our last visit to New York. The last time I lay at Scar's side and slept like a baby.

Blake said Trip is gone. She said she doesn't know where he is, and she doesn't care. She never trusted him, but he was my friend.

Touching the screen, I watch it change as the call goes out, seconds ticking. Is he really gone?

The screen changes again, and my heart stills.

"Does your sister know you're calling me?" Trip's casual, always so bored with the world tone drifts through my empty bedroom, and fresh tears fill my eyes.

"You answered." I'm lying on the floor holding the phone to my face.

"When have I ever not taken your call?"

"I wasn't sure how much had changed."

"Oh, hell, everything has changed." I hear the clink of ice against crystal, and I imagine he's lying on a sofa in a suit holding a vodka like always. "You're a country girl now, Blake is engaged to a giant, the old gang is shattered… Is this a setup?"

"Are you kidding?" I laugh through the tears. "I needed to hear a friendly voice."

Someone who wouldn't judge me.

"Are you crying?" The question is more bored than concerned, an older brother rolling his eyes at my foolishness. "Did that brute succeed in breaking your heart? He truly is undignified. Did you know he nearly broke my neck?"

"I'm sure you deserved it." I push off the floor, touching the tears from my eyes and wondering just how much nobody told me about our last trip to the city. "I'm so tired of being treated like a baby. I'm twenty-one now."

"Ah, that's right. Sorry I missed it. Happy birthday, a few weeks late."

"Thank you, a few weeks late."

"I'd have taken you out for your first, legal bender, but I guess all of that's behind us now."

Wrinkling my nose, I imagine us being retired from the party scene now that I'm actually old enough to enjoy it legally.

"I miss everybody. Nobody tells me anything except what I'm doing wrong. What's new in the city?"

"I have no idea. I'm taking a break from the madness. It was getting a little too true-crime for my taste. You know I don't like intrigue."

"Don't tell me you're in St. Moritz with your mother."

He laughs loudly. "Good God, I'm not desperate. No, I'm somewhere warm."

"That could be anywhere." I sigh, looking out the window at the blooming crepe myrtles. "I wish I was at the beach."

"Aren't you near one?"

I hadn't thought about it. Now I'm thinking about my pictures. Miranda Beach is less than a half-hour drive from here. I'm thinking of Scar there, in the waves, in my arms...

"Did you hear I got a show? It'll be in a few months at the Milo gallery."

"I did not. That's incredible."

"Will you come?"

"Send me the info, and I'll consider making an appearance."

Pressing my lips together, I trace my fingernail along the edge of the quilt covering my bed. "I need to repay my debts, Trip. I want to start fresh, make up for what I've done."

His voice turns serious. "I don't know if that's possible. Some things can't be undone. You know what happened to Grish."

"I heard he had a heart attack, which is weird. But he wasn't my friend. He only ever talked to Blake." Leaning my forehead against the side of my mattress, I close my eyes. "Who's running Gibson's now?"

"You're asking all the million dollar questions, aren't you?" An edge enters his voice. "You sure this isn't a setup?"

"I don't know how to prove it's not. I told you nobody tells me anything." Exhaling heavily, I rise to my feet, walking to the full-length mirror in my bathroom. "I feel lost, I guess."

"What do they say? If you're at the bottom, things can only get better?"

"Not in my experience."

He chuckles. "Perhaps I'll see you in a few months."

"How shall I say goodbye?"

"Ciao."

He's in Italy… "Ciao bella."

"Chin up. You're Hana fucking van Hamilton."

A smile ghosts across my lips as we disconnect, but I feel even more alone.

I want to do better, but Trip says it's too late. Walking through the elegant bedroom suite my great uncle provided, I change out of my bikini and into a long-sleeved, beige caftan dress. It's Oscar de la Renta, and Debbie made fun of me for dressing like Billie Eilish when I bought it. I argued it's not Gucci.

Eat.

I pull my hair up in a bun on my head and make my way down the stairs to the kitchen. My phone buzzes in my hand, and I look down to see a text from Pepper. ***Can't make the skate park today. Tomorrow?***

I'm actually relieved, even if I know work would take my mind off things. Pepper would help me feel better. She always lifts my mood.

I pause and quickly text back, ***Tomorrow's great.***

Looking up, I see Blake standing at the bar, eyes fixed on her ever-present iPad pro. She's holding half a sandwich, and she's wearing a tight beige wrap-dress that hugs her curves and shows off her full breasts. It makes me want to pull on another layer of clothes.

When I enter, her gray eyes flicker to mine, and she smiles, shoving a dark brown lock behind her ear. "I didn't know you were here. I thought you were doing a photo shoot with Pepper."

"She had to reschedule." I go to the refrigerator and open

the door, looking for anything easy and super fattening. Pizza would be perfect.

"I made chicken salad if you want some. It's in the green bowl. I'm trying to decide what type of cake we want for the wedding. Plain white almond or strawberries and cream. What do you think?"

"Mama would say almond." Pressing my lips together, I pull out the bowl of healthy chicken salad and set it on the bar. Then I pull out four slices of bread and the jar of mayonnaise.

"Mama? Really?" Blake watches me as I add a scoop of mayo to the first slice of bread. "You know, adding mayonnaise will make it bland, and I used my special seasoning."

Her voice goes higher when she says *special seasoning* like it's a tease. I continue adding the extra condiment. Going to flavor country isn't my goal here.

Helicopter sis steps closer. "What's up? You seem a little… down. Pardon the pun."

I put the knife down and take a big bite of sandwich. She's right. It's bland, and I wish I'd listened.

"Hey." Blake reaches for my arm. "What happened? Talk to me."

Lowering the sandwich, I exhale heavily. "I don't know. I'm wondering what I'm doing here. I'm a photographer. I should be in New York."

Her slim brows furrow, and she tilts her head. "I thought you loved it here. You said New York was so toxic."

"This isn't my home." I try another, bigger bite of goopy sandwich. "I don't fit in here. Everything is wrong."

Even as I say the words, they hurt. It's me that's wrong.

Blake presses her lips together like she's thinking, and she walks back around to where she left her iPad. "I think anyone who's been through all you have is entitled to a down day every once in a while."

"It's more than a down day." My voice hardens as anger simmers to life in my chest.

"Okay." Her voice is soft. "You've just seemed so happy here, getting to know people, taking pictures. Carmen loves you, and Pepper thinks you're the greatest.

I know she's right, and the anger grows hotter in my chest. I don't have a snappy comeback, which just gives Blake more room to talk.

"I've been so proud of you." She returns to where I'm standing. "You've been working so hard, and I see it. I really do."

Clenching my teeth, I fight the emotions churning in my chest. They have nothing to do with her. "Not everyone would agree with you."

Reaching out, she places her hand on my cheek. "Not everyone knows you like I do. You're so much more than our old life."

Glancing up, her eyes are glowing. "You're proud of me?"

"Yes." She smiles warmly. "It's okay to feel lost sometimes. I do, too, but we're here. We've come so far. Don't give up now."

Nodding, I leave the sandwich on the bar and start for the door. I'm not giving up, and I'm pissed as hell. I have come a long way, and he's going to see it.

"I'll clean this up when I get back. You're right–about all of it. I've got to take care of something."

CHAPTER 8

MY SHOULDERS ARE TIGHT, AND EVERYTHING THAT HAPPENED today is a lead weight in my stomach. Hurting Hana is the heaviest. The memory of her pretty cheeks stained red with embarrassment, her beautiful blue eyes filling with tears.

Fuck. I couldn't be a bigger dick if I kicked a dog.

Scrubbing my fingers against my eyes, I explain to Hutch. "I can't tell you over the phone. It's not secure."

"Sorry, man, I didn't know taking Pepper to the orthodontist would be an all-day deal. They're doing impressions, and then they want to sit down and make a plan. Didn't they used to just slap braces on us? It feels like overkill." He's distracted but happy. He's always wanted to be a dad.

"I don't know." I'm not happy.

"Shit, I'm sorry. I forget you didn't have this as a kid."

That's putting it mildly. "We need to talk soon. I should have told you all this in the beginning, but I guess I'd hoped…"

I don't finish that sentence because it'll make me sound naïve, which I've never been. I know what I left behind and what could easily bite me in the ass at any time.

"Can you at least tell me what it's about?"

Glancing around the empty house, I don't think my phone is being monitored, but I don't know what might have changed since my slip-up in Gibson's. "I need to fill in the gaps between when you left me at the hospital to when I came here."

I'll be lucky if he doesn't punch me in the face for putting us all at risk. I'd let him, too, even if we're pretty evenly matched. He's two inches shorter, but he's bulkier than I am. Motivation would be the deciding factor, and I feel like I deserve an ass-kicking right now.

"Does something need to happen? Dirk can help get the ball rolling if it's a security matter."

I shake my head. "I don't know. We can decide after we talk."

He can decide if I need to go away for good, if I'm the security threat.

"Damn, I'm sorry to put you off. Want to meet up at the house later tonight?"

Pulling the ring on my lip between my teeth, I know he likes to have his evenings for family time. Still, "I'm not sure it should wait until tomorrow."

"I'll text you when I'm out of here."

Disconnecting, I shove my phone in my pocket and place my palms flat on the wooden bar. If he tells me to leave, I'll have to say goodbye to Hana. Can I do that? Can I leave her here without protection?

Dropping my head, I exhale heavily. At least she'll be safe from me.

Sliding my hand over the bar, I made this piece of furniture. I found the cypress, chopped it up, sanded and carved it, then put it all together. I made one for Hutch as well.

I can make a fucking piece of furniture you'd pay top-dollar for at a store. Why can't I be as careful with people?

A noise behind me puts me on guard. *Shit.* Is somebody breaking into my house? Turning quickly, I'm startled by the sight of Hana standing in my doorway.

I'm surprised. Energy surges in my chest, and I want to touch her. She's breathing fast, and she's dressed in some odd dress-cape-type thing that looks like an enormous, ivory burqa. Still, she's glowing bright.

She closes the space between us like a blonde tornado. Her jaw is clenched, and anger ripples off her in waves. "I have something to say to you."

Lifting her hand she gives my shoulder a hard shove. At least, she seems to put some effort into it. I don't move.

Everything I want to say twists in my chest as my eyes consume her. She's adorable, so spicy with rage. I want to wrap her in my arms.

"Tell me." My voice is low.

"I've only been sweet to you. You have no right to speak to me like you did today. If I were a big girl, you wouldn't tell me to lose weight. There's no difference. I'm trying to get healthy, and I don't need you body-shaming me. I don't need your hot and cold. You're not my boss. I'm a grown woman, and…"

She hiccups as her breath gives out, and a tear spills onto her cheek. I can't hold back any longer. The threat of losing her knots my stomach, and I can't walk away anymore.

Stepping forward, I pull her into my arms. She's so damn small, I completely engulf her in my embrace.

Her body is tense, but I lower my face to her ear. "I'm sorry."

She stills in my arms, and her fingers, which were curled against my shoulders, unfurl.

With every heartbeat, this feels so right. This is where she belongs, in my arms where anyone would have to kill me to hurt her.

I smooth my hand down her pretty curls, pressing my palm against her lower back and drawing her closer. "I'm so sorry I hurt you."

Her hands slide higher until her arms are around my neck, and her voice is soft. "Okay."

The guilt twisting my lungs eases. I squeeze my eyes shut. I want to kiss her, but–

She turns her face, cupping my cheeks with her hands and pulling me down–or am I pulling her up? All I know is our mouths collide, and our lips seal together.

In that instant, everything changes. Her legs wrap around my waist, and I lift her, pressing her back to the wall.

Our mouths open, and a soft whimper slips from her throat as our tongues slide together and curl. Her fingers thread in my hair, and she pulls the ring on my lip with hers.

My fingers grip her ass, cutting into her soft skin, and I drag my mouth along the line of her jaw. She exhales another little moan, and my dick is a rod in my jeans. Tightening her arms around my neck, she stretches her body higher so her mouth is at my ear.

"At last…" she gasps, and blistering fire floods my veins.

She arches her back, and her pelvis grinds against my cock. Her dress is pushed up, and I want to rip off her underwear and fuck her against this wall.

She kisses my brow, my eye, and I chase her mouth, needing the sweet taste of her lips one more time. She's crack cocaine. One hit, and I'm addicted.

Our mouths seal together again, and her fingers scratch through my beard. It feels so good.

My hands slide from her ass to her waist. I want to keep going higher. I want to slide them over her breasts, lifting and squeezing. I want to circle my thumbs over her hardened nipples now pressing against my chest. I want to slide them lower, between her legs, up and down until she's panting and wet, moaning my name. Yes, she is a grown woman, and I want to claim her.

"Fuck," I growl, forcing myself to stop this.

What the fuck am I doing?

Our lips part with a smack, and I take a step away, allowing her legs to lower, her feet to find the floor. Her hands remain clutched in the front of my shirt, but I brace my palm against the wall over her head, keeping space between my body and hers.

"I'm sorry." My voice is gravel. "I shouldn't have done that."

Her pretty eyes flutter open, and she's breathing fast. Hell, we're both breathing fast. I can't tear my gaze from her beautiful face. Her cheeks are flushed and her pink lips are swollen and so fucking kissable.

"Why did you stop?" Her hands remain on my chest, and her slim brow furrows.

"I can't do this."

"You can't?"

She waits for the reason, but I can't tell her why either. I can't pull her further into my world, endanger her with my past. She came here to be safe, and here I am, threatening all of it.

Reaching up, she touches my face with her hand, and I open my eyes to see her smiling like she doesn't care what I say. Her thumb touches my bottom lip, tugs on the ring there, and my insides hum with a mix of adoration and regret, desire and despair.

Curling my fingers against the wall, I push back, going around the bar. The electricity between us is stronger than me, and now that I've touched her, I'm not sure I won't do it again.

She watches me retreat, a little smile curling her soft lips.

Glancing to the side, she crosses her arms. "I accept your apology, but you still hurt my feelings."

"I was a dick."

"Yes, you were." She pokes out her cute lips like she's plotting her next move. "And I think you should make it up to me by doing the photo shoot we discussed. I'd like to drive down to Miranda Beach. Have you ever been there?"

Nodding, I slide my hand along the top of the bar. "It's where I got the wood to make this–and Hutch's."

Her big blue eyes blink wider. "I thought they looked similar. You made them?"

"It was a while ago, but yeah. I found an old cypress tree and cut it up."

"That's perfect. Would you do it again and let me photograph you?"

"It was after a hurricane. I haven't seen cypress down there in years."

"It doesn't have to be that. We can scout around, find something similar and go to work. Forget I'm even there."

I could never forget her presence. Reaching behind my neck, I rub the tension rising from my shoulders. I need to tell her no.

"You can't say no. After what happened today, you owe me."

Glancing up, her hands are on her hips, and a naughty light is in her eyes. It's a big switch from the way she came here, furious and on the brink of tears. She's back to that feisty confidence I can't resist.

I rub my palm over the need twisting in my stomach. I'm ready to do anything she wants. I'm so fucking in over my head with her. I should tell her no, I don't owe her anything.

Of course, I don't. "When do you want to do it?"

"Tomorrow. Meet me at Carmen's shop after five, and we can drive out to the shore."

"That's pretty late."

"We'll get there at the golden hour. Right after dawn and just before sunset the light is diffuse, softer. It makes the best pictures. Sound good?"

It sounds dangerous, but I'm doing it. "Ruth's Rarities, after five."

"See you there."

She heads out the door, and I walk over to watch her drive away. I don't know what tomorrow will bring, but if Hutch doesn't tell me to leave, I'll be at her side or not far from it.

CHAPTER 9

"**O**NCE MORE, PEPPER!" I YELL BEFORE LYING ON MY BACK ON the pavement.

Bracing my camera in both hands, I wait, listening for the noise of her skates to get closer. The moment her hand hits the edge of the pavement, I start shooting.

Pepper flies up the side of what was formerly the public pool. It's now a concrete valley, and her body makes an arc over my head. She does a cross between a handstand and a cartwheel before landing on her skates and flying down into the valley again.

"That was it!" I yell, sitting up fast. Turning the camera over, I quickly scan through the digital images. "I love it!"

The midday sun creates the perfect energy for this high-speed sport. Cassie and Ainsley, two of Pepper's softball teammates, have joined us, and all three girls are dressed in jersey shirts, short shorts, and knee socks. Their skates are candy colors–pink, yellow, and baby blue, and I'm imagining this portion of the show. It'll be a brilliant burst of high-energy color in the middle of my thoughtful black and whites.

I experiment with slowing my shutter speed to create blur, and rolling onto my stomach again, I capture Tommy and his friend Dodge practicing their skateboard tricks.

Tommy's a cute thirteen-year-old with shaggy blond hair tied back in a ponytail. Dodge is a year older, and his light-blue hair sticks out around a black beanie. They do variations of the ollie, but Tommy can laser flip. Dodge can back tail, and I'm capturing all of it with the traffic a blur behind them.

Ainsley leans down beside me. "Exciting."

Nodding, I'm satisfied with the energy, but I want to contrast it with graceful images. "Can you hold the back of the bench and do one of your ballet moves?"

"Sure!" She gives me a big smile and she rolls over to the wrought-iron bench, leaning forward and lifting her leg in a gorgeous arabesque.

"That's perfect. Now you guys have some fun."

Cassie rolls over to her and they clasp hands, bobbing their knees and spinning in a tight circle faster and faster. Their long hair flies, and I'm snapping like crazy until they finally break apart, squealing and falling on the grass completely dizzy.

"Cassie, kick up your feet!" She happily rolls onto her back to comply, propping her back with her hands and holding her skates high over her head. "Perfect–I think we're done!"

Sitting on the bench, reviewing all the shots, I'm so full of light, I could fly.

Part of it is the fun of today, but a big part is the anticipation of seeing Scar in just a few short hours.

Yesterday was so fucking dark. I was so hopeless and overwhelmed, I actually called Trip. I wanted to run away; I almost called my dealer in Hamiltown. Shaking my head, I growl softly at how weak I was.

Blake would've been so disappointed. I would've been devastated.

Scrubbing my fingers against my forehead, I remember my therapist's words. I have to forgive my weakness. My sister is there for me, and the sharp squeals of laughter remind me I also have Pepper and Carmen. Those inner voices are liars. I'm not alone. I do have a place here, and I didn't relapse.

Even more, I found the strength inside me to confront the judgment. I texted my therapist to tell her what I'd done–instead of going back to my old ways, I trusted my strength.

Going to Scar's house changed everything. His arms gave me strength. Kissing him was so much better than any artificial high. Even if he did stop us, his shield lowered, and I saw inside his walls. He needs me as much as I need him.

Convincing him to let me in will take a little more work, but I have a plan for that.

"How's the photo shoot going?" Carmen plops on the bench beside me, holding out a paper cone of fried okra. "Okra?"

"Did you get this off the food truck?" I pop a piece in my mouth before pulling up the photos on my camera, tilting the viewfinder so she can see. "Pepper is really good at this skating thing. Look at her in this one."

I show her the one of Pep with one hand on the concrete and her feet overhead.

"She looks like Tony Hawk!"

I laugh, scrolling through the shots. "She's definitely a superjock."

"You need to hang onto those for a future documentary. She's like one of those Williams sisters or Christina Aguillera. You have the historical evidence right here."

Nodding, I pull my bag on my shoulder. "Hutch and Blake can sort out what to do with their rising star. I've got a gallery to fill. Mind if I hang out with you at the store for a little while? I told Scar I'd meet him there after work."

"He agreed?" Carmen squeals, clapping. "What are you going to do?"

"I'm going to get some lunch." Waving to the kids, I stroll with her to the food truck where I order a large box of fried okra.

Carmen's mother Ruth owns Ruth's Rarities. It's a cute local gift shop filled with jewelry and crafts by local artists alongside quirky gift items and books. I pick up a sequined bag that reads, *You were my cup of tea, but I drink champagne now.*

It's always full of customers, and when we arrive, a group of older women are passing around a copy of the board book *Penis Pokey* and giggling. They end up buying oven mitts that read "Pizza's here" and "Dropping a fresh recipe on your ass."

Chewing my lip, I watch the clock slowly counting down to five, and my heart beats faster the closer it gets. At five exactly, Carmen runs to the door and turns the lock, flipping the sign from *Open* to *Closed*.

"Have to do it fast before another mob of customers shows up," she laughs. "Sometimes I feel like I'll be here all night."

"It's a popular place." I sneak over to the sunglasses area and check my hair, reapply my pink lip gloss, pinch my cheeks.

I wore a thin, white tank top and cutoffs, and my hair is twisted up in a messy bun on my head with a few curls falling around my face. Silver hoops are in my ears, and I'm going for a minimalist look, not trying too hard—just enough.

I'm excited and nervous, and my breath is all jumpy

Carmen is pricing a box of sterling silver jewelry, and I walk over to help her. "You were here when Scar arrived."

"Yep." My friend leans in close, carefully writing the price on the tiny tags in ink.

I can barely fasten the tiny, white price tags to the delicate chains with my wiggly fingers. "He's been here seven years, and he never dated anyone?" She doesn't answer, and I lean forward when I notice her lips twitch. "What are you not telling me?"

"He never showed any real interest in anyone, but he went on a few dates."

My eyes widen, and I'm not sure I want to ask. "Anyone I know?"

"I don't think so?" Wrinkling her nose, she looks up at me. "Have you ever met my mom?"

The chain I'm tagging slips from my fingers, and I blink fast. "He dated your *mother?*"

She shrugs. "She said she couldn't let all that sexy come to town and not go for it. Totally knocked me out of the running. Thanks, Ma. Not that he ever gave me a second look."

I force my brain to think. "She's how much older than him?"

"I guess about ten, fifteen years?"

Carmen keeps talking, but I'm distracted and insanely curious. "Why doesn't your mom ever come to the store? I can't believe I've never met her."

"She spends all her time in Atlanta. She has a boyfriend there." Carmen chuckles. "She keeps saying she's giving the store to me, but I'll believe it when I see it."

A knock on the glass makes my heart jump to my throat, and I look up to see Scar standing outside the door, blue eyes fixed on mine.

It takes me a beat to remember to breathe. "Your mom was right."

"Forget about that." Carmen follows me as I grab my bag and head to the door. "Nothing happened."

I'm glad to hear it, and I think maybe I've gained a little useful information. "Thanks, babe." We air-kiss before I leave. "Wish me luck."

"I'm rooting for you." She gives me a little shove out the door. "Bag him."

The door closes behind me and I hear the lock turn and the shade lower. I wonder if he heard that.

Leaning against the glass, I exhale a soft laugh, looking up at him. "Hey."

He's wearing the usual faded jeans with a heather-gray tee,

and his hair is pulled back in a bun with a few pieces escaping on the breeze. His lip ring is gone, which is a little disappointing. I love his Viking look, towering over me with that intense gaze. I'm already planning out the shots I want of him in my head–the salty wind in his hair, him looking out to sea.

"Ready?" He's not smiling, and I know he doesn't want to do this.

I also know he kissed me yesterday. It tickles low in my stomach, and I wonder what he'd do if I grabbed him and planted a kiss on his full lips right now. I'd have to climb him first, which is not a problem, but we have to catch the light.

"I packed a few tools in case we wanted to stage something."

"Here." He takes the duffel from me, and I chew my lip as I watch his bicep flex while he puts it in the bed of his pickup.

He holds my arm as I climb into the truck. It's sleek, but practical with heavy tires and a step side. He doesn't make eye contact when he climbs in, and I hope I can make him loosen up or at least be less annoyed to be one of my models.

It's a half-hour drive to the beach. His window is down, and the radio plays softly, some old Rolling Stones song.

I finally break the mood. "Busy day?"

His eyes cut to the side, and I give him a big smile. The muscle in his jaw moves, and I want to lean over the console and slide my finger over it. Then maybe bite it.

"Not too bad." Something's on his mind, but Scar has never been much of a talker.

"What are you guys working on–or can you tell me? Is it classified?"

Another cut of those eyes, and my stomach squeezes when a smile ghosts across his lips. "Just dealing with some past business. It's all good, though. Maybe."

Interesting, but I don't have time to follow up. He turns the wheel, and we're at our destination.

Judging by the sun's position, we have at least ninety

minutes before it's too dark, and I hop out as soon as we stop. Rising on my tiptoes, I dig in my bag for another lens, and my entire body lights up when I feel his warmth at my back.

"Let me help."

"Thanks." I exhale, stepping aside so he can grab my stuff. "I think we have enough time to scout out some good locations. I probably should've driven over here earlier, but I was working with Pepper and her friends at the skatepark."

He follows me down the long boardwalk, and I kick off my sandals at the end, plunging my toes in the sand. It's kind of perfect. The sky is slightly overcast with the sun peeking out, and the wind alternates between calm and bursts.

"Come with me." Spinning around, I grab his large hand.

His lips twitch, but he allows me to lead him out to the water, to an abandoned boat turned upside down and hidden in the brush.

"I thought you said I wouldn't know you were here." He's teasing, which is a very encouraging sign.

"Sit." I position him on the boat so he's facing the water with one knee bent. "Look out at the ocean and think of something you really want to do."

Blue eyes hit mine, and my stomach flips. He looks at me like maybe I'm the thing he wants to do.

"You just want me to sit here?"

"Just for a minute. You have a very artistic look going on, and I want to capture it with the light soft." Adjusting my lens, I look into the viewfinder. "I'll take a bunch of shots then we can move on. Do whatever you'd normally do, sitting by the ocean."

He looks down at his hands, and I start clicking. With a deep exhale, he turns his attention to the waves. It's not stormy, but a front is blowing onshore. The waves are growing higher, and his slim brow furrows as if he's considering it.

My finger presses the shutter button repeatedly, and I capture every flicker of expression. I can't wait to get back to the darkroom. I can't wait to be alone to play around with this face and those eyes.

"Look at me." My voice is quiet, and he cuts me a glance that stops my heart. *Click.* "Perfect."

I hope I got that, and if I did, everyone will want a print.

"Let's see about getting some action shots now." I lower the camera and flip through the viewfinder. "Get ready. You're probably going to be approached to model after the show."

"I'm no model. I'm only doing this for you." Standing, he walks to a fallen tree, and I follow him, chewing my lip so I don't smile too big at his confession. *He's doing this for me.*

Stopping at a large piece of driftwood, he digs in his pocket for a knife. I walk around, climbing on a fallen log to get me higher as he squats beside the stump and presses the blade against the trunk.

"Can you make something with it? I'd love to see you work."

"It's too spongy." He rises to his full height. "If you want to see me work, I have a piece of black walnut at the house. Ruth ordered a few bowls for the store."

My chest tightens at the mention of Carmen's mom. "Carmen said you dated her."

He scratches the side of his beard, glancing up at me. "We went for drinks a few times."

"She's a lot older than you." Holding the camera over my face, I study his expression in the viewfinder. *Is he embarrassed? Guilty?*

"She doesn't really act her age."

"It's no different than you and me." *Click.* His brow arches, and now he's smiling. *Click.*

"It's a little different."

"Not really. I don't exactly act my age. Or I passed my age a few years ago."

His hands are on his hips and the wind pushes his long hair

back. My camera clicks several times as I capture his look of bemused annoyance.

Lowering the camera, I scroll through the shots I've taken. "Want to see them?"

He walks over to where I'm still standing on the log. It puts me closer to his height, and I tilt the camera so he can see the viewfinder.

Handing him the device, I point to the black arrow. "Press this, and you can scroll through them all."

He studies the screen, and I study his gorgeous face, the neat beard on his square jaw. The lines of black ink rising from his collar and the fragile tops of burn scars not entirely hidden. I want to touch him. I want to kiss him again.

Lifting his chin, he gives me another rare smile, and heat fills my stomach. "You're really talented. You made me look…"

He doesn't finish, so I supply my own adjectives. "Handsome?" Leaning closer, I arch an eyebrow. "Sexy?"

Wolf eyes flicker to mine, and butterflies explode in my chest. "I look whole."

His words resonate in me. A strong gust of wind blows my hair back, and we're standing so close. I reach out to place my hand lightly on his cheek. It's how he makes me feel, whole, restored, undamaged.

It's time to say what I want. "Are we friends?"

"Yes." He straightens.

"You're kind of like my bodyguard, but I don't remember hiring you."

"Your uncle hired Hutch, which means he hired all of us."

Looking down, I slide my hand to his forearm. "But Hutch said he would never accept money for keeping us safe. Would you?"

The muscle in his square jaw moves, and his lips tense. "I'm not interested in money."

"What are you interested in?"

No hesitation. "Keeping you safe."

"Why?"

I want him to say it's because he cares about me, but he doesn't. Not yet.

So I continue. "Remember the last time we were in New York, and I slept by your side?"

"Yes."

"Can we do that again?"

His brow lowers, and I brace for him to say no.

Seconds pass, and he doesn't.

He's thinking about it, and I want to do one of Pepper's skater jumps.

Instead, I hold my voice steady. "I haven't slept in so long, and I'm just so tired. I know if you were there, beside me, I could get one night's sleep." Blinking up at him, I smile. "Would you do that for me?"

His full lips part, and I imagine what he's thinking. Me in his bed all night is venturing into dangerous territory, a place he can't control. I'm his weakness, and it's intoxicating to think this amazing man might do anything for me.

Lifting his chin, he looks out at the ocean, and I wonder if he's thinking of something he really wants to do. I know I am.

My hand is still on his arm, touching his skin, and it feels so good. I want him so much.

"Please?" It's a soft whisper, and when he turns to me again, I know I've won.

With a heavy exhale, he nods.

CHAPTER 10

Scar

Hutch didn't tell me to pack my shit and get out of Hamiltown. He wasn't even angry I kept my connection to the Petrovs a secret. He thinks it's an advantage.

Standing in his living room, waiting to have dinner with his family, I wish I could agree with him, but he hasn't seen the depth of their cruelty or their complete lack of regard for human life.

He thinks I can serve as bait. I can draw them out of hiding, and we can have them arrested for money laundering, blackmail, embezzlement, murder.

I think he's being very optimistic.

The Petrovs live by the code of no family, no connections. They claim there is no Bratva, but I've waited in the next room as Victor paid off crooked doctors for doping horses. I watched grown men crying, sniveling like pigs as they begged for their lives. I had no mercy for these men, but I walked out when Victor signed the order to sell a child.

Then I found out six months ago what he did to Hana.

Standing in front of the fireplace, my fist tightens as I think of all the ways I've fucked this up. Letting her take those pictures today tops the list. If she puts my face in a gallery in New York, it'll be as good as putting a target on her forehead.

Still, after making her cry, I was willing to do anything to make her smile. She was so adorable climbing all over the trees, sliding her fingers in my hair, holding my hand and ordering me around.

Then when she looked up at me with those big blue eyes and asked if she could sleep in my bed… My jaw clenches. I struggled with telling her no. She's a temptation I'm not sure I can resist, but what better way to know she's safe?

Scrubbing my fingers against my eyes, I can't help thinking she belongs at my side. If it puts her in danger, they'll have to kill me first.

"Don't look so worried." Dirk claps my shoulder, pulling me out of my thoughts. "I think Hutch is right. If they're tracking you, we only have to lead them out of hiding, catch them in the act, and the district attorney can issue warrants for their arrest. It's the best case scenario."

"If they don't kill us first." My voice is low, and I wish I hadn't come here tonight for dinner. I'm a dark cloud over their family time.

Pepper runs into the room, but instead of her usual jump on my back, she puts her hand in the crook of my arm. "Uncle Hutch said I can go to the show in New York. You'll be there, won't you? We're both models. It'll be so cool. I'm putting it on my TikTok."

Glancing up at Hutch, he only shrugs. "I held out as long as I could."

"Thirteen is the legal age for social media."

Pepper gives my arm a sharp pull, talking out the side of her mouth. "Don't mess this up for me."

I shake my head, glancing up at my partner. "I'm sure you know what you're doing."

It's not true. Ever since he proposed to Blake, Hutch has been worried about Pepper's reaction. They both have. I don't think it's a good time to ease their standards, but what do I know? I'm not a dad, and I've got bigger fish to fry.

"I'd better take off." I'd hoped Hana and Blake would be here for dinner tonight, but Hutch said they were having dinner with their uncle.

I'd hoped I could talk her out of sleeping in my bed, not that I want to.

I want to hold her in my arms. I want to kiss her sweet lips and smooth my hands over her wild curls. I want to possess every part of her body, shield her from all harm, make her mine, but I can't promise her forever.

When everything I've done is revealed, I don't know what will happen, but I'll have to pay for my crimes.

Standing in my kitchen waiting for her to appear, I tell myself this is only for safety. It's only so she can sleep, so those deep lines will ease around her tired eyes.

Like either of us believes it.

Like I can have her in my bed beside me all night in the dark, her sweet little body pressed against mine, and not touch her. Everything in me wants her, and I'm lying to myself saying it's all about safety. She couldn't be any less safe with me. My dick twitches at the thought.

The golf cart glides silently into my driveway, and she's here. I sense her presence like the moon stirring the tide. She's in my blood, and I look up to meet her eyes through the screen.

"Am I too early?" Her smile is confident and nervous, that tantalizing combination as she enters my home.

"We're not on a schedule. Does anyone know you're here?"

"I told Blake so she wouldn't worry." She closes the space between us, her head only reaching the center of my chest.

I want to reach down and pull her into my arms. She smells like fresh flowers, and her presence awakens my soul. She lights up my heart in a way that's impossible to overlook. I could see it in my face as I scrolled through the pictures she took today.

I thought my ability to feel this type of emotion had died, but I was so wrong.

She puts her hand in mine like she did earlier, and I pull her to my chest. She's wearing light knit shorts and a beige top. A long sweater is over her shoulders, hanging down to her calves, and her long blonde hair hangs in spirals down her back.

"Did you have a good dinner?" I speak against the top of her head.

"Yes!" She nods, her cheek against my chest. "Norris had filets with baked potatoes and asparagus. I ate everything but the asparagus. But only because I don't like the flavor… and it makes my pee smell weird."

Her voice is so proud, it makes me chuckle. "Good girl."

I give her a light squeeze and release her, still holding her hand, I lead her to my bedroom. It's dark, lit only by lamps situated in the corners. The walls are dark wood, and the king size bed is made with gray sheets and a black duvet cover.

She slides a hand over the soft cotton. "It's very elegant."

My bank account is sizable, but I earned it protecting bad men. I didn't steal it, but I can't help feeling like it's tainted, especially in view of her past with Victor. It's a past she needs to know, and she needs to know what really happened to him, not what she believes.

We'll get there. Hesitating, I study her looking up at me from beside my bed. I want to kiss her. I want to slide the thin sweater off her shoulders and trace my lips from her forehead down her cheek, into her hair.

Instead, I remember I'm going to control myself tonight. "Do you need to wash or brush your teeth?"

Her cheeks flush a pretty pink, and she shakes her head. "I did all that before I left Uncle Hugh's. Or I guess, before I left my house." She glances at the headboard. "He's really sweet, asking about my pictures..."

An awkward silence falls in the room, and I gesture to the bed. "Hop in. I still need to do a few things."

She climbs onto the mattress, and I tear my eyes away from her cute little ass pointed up at me. Her butt is surprisingly round. It feels good in my hands, I want to grip it while she rides my cock, gasping my name. I remember wanting to mark it with my palm, and I clear my throat, sliding a hand over the front of my jeans to calm my raging hard-on.

Without a word, I head for the bathroom to change into sweats and stop these thoughts of fucking her. I brush my teeth and press a cool washcloth to the back of my neck before returning to the bedroom to find her curled in a ball. Her eyes are closed, and her breath is soft. I think she's already fallen asleep, and I decide it's for the best.

She really did come here to sleep, and I need to get my head straight. Yes, I kissed her, and she kissed me back. But there are a lot of steps between kissing and fucking, not that fucking is something we need to be doing.

Sliding my hands through my hair, I tie it back and slide into the sheets beside her. Lying on my side facing her, I'm not sure I'll sleep tonight. The heat of her body and the degree of my longing make it difficult to relax.

The almost-full moon shines through my window, and I lift a curl off her shoulder, threading it around my finger. What would it be like to have her with me always? Hana is beautiful, sophisticated, and talented. She's fragile like a battered daisy.

My anxieties, the risk and the danger, scroll in my mind, keeping me awake. Rolling onto my back, I wish for sleep. I'm tired and my body aches. I'm frustrated with fighting my desire for her.

Reaching up, I slide my hand behind my head, and she

exhales a soft sigh that lights my senses. I'm so aware of her presence.

Her eyes are closed, but she moves closer to me, putting her arm around my waist and her head on my chest. She nestles closer to my side, and the scent of fresh lavender and sugar surrounds me.

Lowering my arm, I wrap it around her back, holding her securely, and the fist in my chest unfurls. She feels so good in my arms. Her body fits at my side like she belongs there, like she's the missing piece.

I won't let anyone hurt you ever again. It's a solemn promise from a man who can keep it.

I will keep that promise.

Closing my eyes, I think of the day she brought me sugar cookies. Who would bring me cookies besides Hana? Shifting slightly, I bring my other arm around her so I can hold her completely in my arms.

Her chin lifts, but her eyes remain closed. The most peaceful smile softens her face, and I close my eyes, drifting into a gentle sleep.

In my dreams, I kiss her. She sits up in my bed and lifts her shirt over her body. She's not wearing a bra, and her tits are round and soft, dark nipples pointing at me. Taking my hands, she places them on her body, and I slide my palms over her breasts, lifting them to my mouth, kissing them and sliding my tongue around the tips as her head falls back with a moan.

My cock is so hard. I'll have to be gentle until she's accustomed to my size, although she surprises me with her knowledge and her appetites.

She's feisty, pushing my shoulders, forcing me to lean against the headboard as she kisses her way down my bare chest. She's not afraid of my scars. She's not afraid of the black ink covering them.

Slender hands clutch the waist of my pants, and I lift my hips, curious to see what she'll do. Her eyes widen at the size of my erection, and a smug grin curls my lips. *Don't worry, angel, it'll fit, and it'll feel so good massaging your G-spot.*

Without hesitation she wraps her fingers around my shaft and starts to pump. Her lips pucker over my tip, and she sucks, making me moan and drop my head back.

"Fuck, yeah," I gasp.

Her hot, wet mouth surrounding me electrifies my mind. She focuses on my tip, using her spit to smooth her hand working up and down my shaft. With expert technique, she squeezes as she nears the top, as her tongue flickers around the edges.

She's too fucking good at this, and I've wanted her for so long, I'm going to come hard and fast, and I want it to be inside her.

"That feels so good, baby girl. " My voice strains, and I thread my fingers in her hair. "So fucking good."

I want to hold her head and lift my hips, drive my cock down her throat, but I don't. "I'm not a baby," she argues, her lips grazing my shaft, and the dream starts to fade.

The shadows dissolve, and my eyes blink open slowly as the ceiling of my bedroom comes into focus. Dawn is breaking outside my window, and this is not a dream. Hana is between my legs sucking on my cock, and a charge of pleasure shoots to my brain.

"Fuck…" Desire lifts my hips, and my shoulders press against the headboard. I'm hard as an iron rod, and Hana's sucking me off like a pro.

Her breasts are bare, nipples taut, and looking down, I watch them graze my thighs. She's my living fantasy, and she pulls me deeper into her mouth, sucking me all the way to the back of her throat.

"Hana," I groan, placing my hands on her head.

I couldn't stop her if I wanted to. Orgasm surges in my thighs, tightening my ass, and I want to pull her onto my lap. She tickles my sack lightly, and fuck me.

"Feels too good, baby," I groan. "I'm going to come."

"Okay," she gasps, wrapping her full lips around my tip and sucking harder.

"Fuck." My eyes roll back, and I'm past control. "Fuck…"

My hips jerk as I surrender to the primitive response. My cock throbs and pulses, and Hana holds me, sucking and swallowing.

Sweat breaks out on my forehead, and my vision blurs. I'm pretty sure I levitate. She gives my tip a few more sucks, and the sensation almost knocks me out of the bed.

"Hana," I catch her hand. "It's sensitive."

She slants her eyes up at me, and my stomach heats. *Perhaps my girl enjoys a little kink?*

Sitting back on her feet, she crosses her arms like she's satisfied at her accomplishment. "How many calories do you think are in semen?"

"Come here," I exhale a laugh as I reach down, catching her under the arms and pulling her to my chest. "What are you doing to me?"

"Something we both want." She's sassy, and I like this change.

Her arms are around me, and her breasts press against my chest. Her head is below my chin, and I spread my palms over her back as I hold her. Tilting my face, I kiss her forehead. Her lips are at my neck, and our bodies are aligned, chest to chest, hip to hip, all the way to our toes.

She wiggles, and my arms relax. Her chin lifts, and she looks up at me with bright eyes. "I slept so good last night. Didn't you?"

"I did." I feel better than I have in a while, relaxed, rested, sated. "Now I'm hungry for your sweet little cunt."

Her eyes flash, and she laughs as I flip her onto her back.

Rising onto my elbow, I press my lips to hers briefly before working my way down to her perky nipples. I spend a few moments on them, circling my tongue over the hardened tips and pulling them with my lips. She moans, threading her fingers in my hair.

I make my way lower, pausing at her navel to kiss and circle my tongue around it, and her back arches higher.

"Mm, your beard tickles." Her sultry tone has my dick tensing up again.

"Get these out of the way." Hooking my thumbs in the waist of her thin shorts, I pull them down, following a path down her hip to hover over her bare pussy. *Beautiful.*

With a groan, I want to slide my tongue everywhere between her legs, suck her clit and make her come long and hard.

My hands are on her thighs, and I'm ready to spread her open like a peach.

In a low, throaty rumble, I exhale, "Just a little a taste…"

With a flash her body goes rigid like she's been shocked. My grip is loose, and she jumps out of the bed faster than I can stop her, scooping up her clothes and holding them over her naked body.

"Hana?" I'm confused, but she seems equally confused, blinking fast as she pulls on her shorts.

"It's okay." Her voice wavers, and she finishes dressing fast, her hands trembling. "I-I'd better get back to the house. If anyone wakes up and finds me gone, they'll think something happened."

"But you told Blake—"

"I didn't tell Norris." She's blinking back tears, pulling her sweater over her shoulders.

What just happened?

"Wait." I swing my legs off the bed, but she backs away from me.

"I'm okay. Really." She's talking too fast, and she is clearly *not* okay. "Maybe you can come over later for breakfast. I'll make lots and lots of breakfast for us, and we can eat it all."

She bolts through the door before I can find my boxer briefs. The screen door slams, and I'm left standing in my kitchen, completely nude, wondering what the fuck just happened.

CHAPTER 11

I DON'T KNOW WHAT JUST HAPPENED.

Only, that's not true, I do know what happened, and it makes my temples throb. Tears coat my cheeks as I drive through the misty dawn. I slept better last night than I have in years, and this morning was the icing on the cake–until it turned to acid.

Fuck you, Victor.

Inhaling with a jerk, a sob clutches my throat. I never saw it coming. I didn't know this would happen with a man I wanted, a man whose body I've craved for so long.

It was all following the plan. Scar's strong arms were around me, and not a single nightmare could break through his protection. When I woke up with his impressive morning wood in my stomach, I went for it, and I got him.

I wanted to make him feel good. I wanted to make him come, and I wanted him to know it was me making it happen.

It didn't take long to have him groaning my name, and even better, he finally stopped fighting us.

He came hard enough to smash the boundary he'd built between us. I was inside his walls, ready to go all the way for the first time ever.

When he looked at me, his blue eyes were no longer guarded. They were full of heat and lust, and so much affection. Fire saturated my body. Then he kissed me.

He kissed all of me. He worshiped me, and it felt so good. I was so ready for it to feel so much better.

Just a taste…

Those words coming from Scar should've fueled my desire. Instead, my body slammed me straight into the past. I was a child, in a black room with a large man taking what he wanted.

"Oh, God." Fresh tears coat my cheeks.

I'm such a fucked-up, damaged person, and it's so unfair—to both of us.

I want to be with Scar. I want him to be obsessed with me. I want him to crave my body, my taste, my scent. Now when I hear those words, everything shuts down. Pain like a knife slices my heart into pieces, leaving me bleeding.

Squeezing my eyes shut, I don't want to be this way. I want to love him completely, but as the understanding grows clearer, the weight in my stomach grows heavier.

Scar has suffered enough. He deserves a woman who is whole and can love him the way he deserves to be loved. He should have someone who will fulfill all his desires.

Parking the golf cart in the garage, I walk slowly to my bedroom suite. The house is quiet and dark, and not even Norris is awake.

Going straight to my bed, I plunge between the sheets, curling into a ball in the cold. It's not the same as being in Scar's arms. I'm alone again, unprotected and afraid, and wondering if I'll ever be a normal person.

My phone buzzes in my hand, and I lift it to see it's a text from him. ***Hutch needs to meet this morning. See you later?***

Touching my eyes with my fingertips, I do my best not to cry. ***You want to see me?***

I hit send, and wrap my arms around my waist, my fileted heart throbbing.

As far as he knows, I went from sucking his dick like a lollipop to flying out of his house like it was on fire. Who wants a crazy person in their life?

Yes.

My eyes heat at his single-word reply.

I don't know what to say, and as the seconds tick past, I decide it's okay not to answer for now.

Embarrassment, humiliation, my beating heart all combine to make it impossible to sleep. Not to mention, I slept so well last night, I'm not tired.

Throwing the blankets aside, I quickly shower and change into leggings and a long-sleeved sweater. I start to wrap my hair in a bun when I catch the scent of warm woods and clean man-scent. Hesitating, I hold my hair to my face and inhale deeply, allowing his essence to relax the pain in my chest.

He said yes. He still wants me.

My shaky insides grasp at that thin shred of hope. That fierce, beautiful man still might be mine.

I dig my camera out of the bag and jog down the stairs. The best I can do with this dumpster fire of a situation is make art. The best art grows out of pain, right?

Norris has a fresh pot of coffee waiting, and I grab a scone off a tray. My uncle's dear old butler must have been awake when I arrived, and he always takes good care of us.

He has an assortment of fresh food on trays all day long, from scones or biscuits and fruit in the morning to little sandwiches in the afternoon. Uncle Hugh's cancer is in remission, and he and I both are trying to get healthier.

Walking down to the basement darkroom, I flip on the

red light to let everyone know I'm working. Placing my sadness away, I try to recapture the excitement I felt when I was taking the photos.

I summon the ideas swirling in my mind with Pepper and her friends at the skate park and Scar on the beach. Inspiration lifts me beyond my past and gives me hope I can make something beautiful from the pain.

Going to the computer, I plug my camera into the hard drive and start sorting through the images. I also take out the film in the back and scroll through the ones I stored for further manipulation.

I like that I can use digital editing on certain photos, but I really enjoy getting creative with lighting and saturation on film. Some of them I'll make distressed or vintage, over-exposed or monochrome.

Debbie knew so many photographers in New York from art school. Two in particular let me follow them as they worked, and they taught me different techniques. They told me about the cameras they used and the lenses and how to adjust shutter speeds.

Blake preferred making money as a model, so she could pay for her clothes and tuition without having to borrow from our mother until she turned twenty-one and her trust fund matured.

I just borrowed money from anyone who'd lend it and drank on whatever tab was open. God, I was such an idiot. Trip has to help me pay it back now that my own trust has matured.

Thinking about money, I remember a certain photographer who preferred the heroin-chic look of the early aughts. He was a total dick to my sister. I think he called her fat, and she never worked with him again.

He'd find Debbie and me some nights when we'd be getting drunk or high, and follow us around, taking pictures that made us look like the nuvo Kate Moss or James King. He was a real asshole, because he would sell our images to Page Six and never give us a dime.

My favorite photographer was an older man. He was obsessed with Blake's 1950s-era pinup curves. She would sit for him, and I would hang out watching him work. He let me in the darkroom where he'd fine tune the hue and saturation so her photos looked like they were taken in the days of Marilyn Monroe or Jane Russell. He taught me the most about light and shadow.

Anyone can take pictures, he'd say, but to make a mark on the art scene, you have to have a vision as an artist, your own personal style.

Starting with the photo of Pepper, I enlarge it to poster-size and add a halo around her feet overhead. Her mouth is set in a firm line, and she's a superhero, flying on four wheels and defying gravity.

Ainsley doing the arabesque is my next poster, and I add a vintage sepia cast to make it look like something from the seventies, roller girl.

Pulling out the roll from the beach, warmth flushes my body when I'm hit by Scar's ice-blue gaze. Moving down the line quickly with my scope, my breath becomes shallow in my chest.

He's a living work of art, and blending him with the turbulent ocean waves, the overcast sky, and the orange twilight makes him appear mythical, my viking prince.

It's possible I'm biased, but I think even a casual observer would stop and stare at him.

My favorite is him on the boat, looking out to sea. Wisps of hair frame his face, and the muscle in his square jaw is pronounced beneath his beard. One large hand is near his cheek, and he's so terribly dangerous and totally fuckable.

I snapped so many images yesterday, I'm just seeing what all I have, and my heart stops when I find one where he's giving me a hint of a grin.

Furrowing my brow, I try to remember what I'd said to make him finally crack a smile. He'd been so impatient with the entire process.

Starting with those two, I blow them up to poster sizes. I add the effects, and in the final bath as the lines solidify and become more distinct, a flutter fills my stomach.

I can usually only hold his gaze for a moment when we're together. It's so intense. But alone in this dark room, I absorb his energy. Looking straight at me, his gaze is hungry and possessive.

His brow is lowered, and the storm in his eyes is elemental, primitive. Powerful. He's poised to consume, his possession complete. I'm lost in his pirate gaze, in the set of his jaw and his straight, white teeth. He's a rock, unmovable, ready to crush anyone who might challenge him.

The ink curling around his forearms and climbing up his shoulders to his neck are flames of black fire covering the damaged skin. Taking another frame, I zoom in on his fingers holding the knife.

Such elegant hands, long fingers with fragile skin, damaged tissue barely peeking out at his wrists. Leaning my face against my own hand, I study his scars up close–injury transformed into art.

I want to know his story.

With a sigh, I'm ready to take a break for the day when my heart freezes at the last three pictures on the film roll.

A face looks back at me, pictures from a night so long ago. *How did this happen? Had I started this roll of film and forgotten it?*

The first is a black purse dropped on the concrete with all the contents spilled out. Lipsticks and theater tickets, a pen and and a powder brush on the ground beside black stilettos.

The next is Debbie looking over her shoulder at the lens, heavy cat eyeliner on point, bleached blonde hair peeping out beneath her black kubanka hat.

Finally, one is of me with my hair in a bun at the nape of

my neck. I'm in a plain white dress, and I look so young holding a cigarette in my fingers. I only held it–I never smoked. I'm
sitting on an iron bench, blue eyes glassy.

My chest heaves, and I realize this is one of the nights I've
forgotten. So many nights I don't remember, when Debbie and
I would do stupid, reckless things.

A full-body cringe forces me to turn away, but a flash of
memory grips my attention. Closing my eyes, I press my back
to the wall. She was supposed to protect me, but something
went wrong. I was lost.

Flickers of memory, images flashing like a moving train
through blinds. I'm in a dark room with old men sitting around
me. One is at my feet, and it's the same old torment–hands
touching me, a mouth on my skin. I'm paralyzed, holding the
torch, staring at the body on the floor.

"He's dead." The whispering voice is female now. *Is it
Debbie?*

A man is holding a camera, but he's not like me. He's film-
ing everything.

Cold sweat breaks out on my arms, running down my
torso. A silver cup is in my hand–I gave him his final commu-
nion, his final rites.

Pushing back on the table, I spin away, slamming off the
lights and jerking the door open. I'm out of the darkroom and
running up the stairs, away from what I did.

CHAPTER 12

Scar

"**Y**OU LOOK RELAXED," HUTCH QUIPS AS I ENTER THE OFFICE.

"Fuck off." I don't feel relaxed, not after the way Hana bolted from my bed this morning completely freaked out.

She went from sexy vixen to terrified child with the flip of a switch–or the touch of my lips–and I've been mulling over it all day.

I want to find the man who did this to her, dig him up and kill him again. *Slower*.

"So you're relaxed, but not completely?" Dirk jokes, leaning back in his chair and placing his foot on the desk. "That sucks."

"I want to find these fuckers."

"Now you're speaking my language." Hutch walks to the filing cabinet behind his desk and takes out his beretta, turning it to the side. "After what you told me, sitting still feels like a mistake."

"Going after Simon's organization without a plan would be

the mistake." My tone is grave. "Those guys don't get caught, and if they do, they walk."

Hutch lifts the shade on the glass front door. It's just the three of us–him, Dirk, and me–and we typically don't get walk-in business. "Simon Petrovich thinks he can order hits, blackmail our girls, steal from them, but you know their organization. We can draw them out and break this ring. I'd like to bring Louie into our circle if you trust him."

Louie Jackson is a police sergeant in Brooklyn Hutch has known since he retired from the military and got his private investigator's license. He helped us the last time we were in New York when we had a dead body on our hands.

I exhale heavily. "It's been seven years since I was in their circle. They're so paranoid, they're always changing how they do things."

"They still operate out of Gibson's."

"It's true." I remember the day I went there. "If it hadn't been for Rainey, no one would've questioned me."

"Rainey." Hutch, growls softly. "She's a kid, and she knows all of us."

"What do we know about her?" Dirk taps on his laptop, and the young girl's face appears on the screen.

"She's a party girl, close to Natasha, friends with Blake and Hana–with all of them." Hutch says. "She's very young."

"They all have fake IDs," I note.

"Hana's show would be the perfect cover." Dirk's still scrolling. "We could make it appear she and Blake are in the city alone, then see what comes out of the woodwork to find them. Hana owes money all over town, she's racked up gambling debts, she's in the snuff film."

The objection is on my lips, but Hutch beats me to it. "Blake wouldn't like us using Hana as bait. Anyway, they all know Blake and I are engaged. No one would make a move on her."

"All the more reason to think they would go alone. You'd dare anyone to mess with your fiancée."

"I'd dare anyone to hurt Hana."

Dirk sits up in the chair, leveling his hazel eyes on me. "Right, but we want to catch these guys, don't we? You two are the perfect tools for catching them."

"Then let me do it. Don't put the girls at risk."

Hutch's voice is thoughtful. "Hana's already at risk if they believe she killed Victor."

"Hana didn't kill Victor." My tone is final, and his green eyes flicker up to mine.

"Or if she was involved in his death–"

"She wasn't involved."

He exchanges a glance with his brother. "It sounds like you know more than you're telling us again."

I let that pass unanswered. "I think you're overestimating our chances against these guys. Simon has a tight-knit, highly trained group of thugs with a lot of money backing them. We're three men."

"Three motivated men with military training, police connections, and an insider's knowledge of their network." Dirk gives me a wink. "I'd bet on us any day."

My jaw tightens. I'm still not convinced it's enough, and I won't risk Hana being hurt again.

Hutch crosses his arms. "I think our odds are better than you give us credit for. You should know from our days in the military, a quick, strategic unit can be very effective against a slow, bloated organization that thinks it's invincible."

Nodding, I think through what I know of my old boss. "If we knew what he wanted, perhaps we could give it to him."

"Are you able to detect any kind of pattern in all this?"

"No." I shake my head, frustrated.

"It doesn't matter what they want." Dirk's voice has an edge. "If we cut off the head, the body will die."

Exchanging a glance with Hutch, I slide my hands in my pockets. "That's one way."

Kill Simon.

"I think it's the only way." Dirk's gaze glitters with confidence.

He's charming and smart as a whip. He's also the youngest of our group, which makes him a deadly motherfucker. Dirk won't hesitate. Like his computer programs, it's all ones and zeros, black and white.

"Let me see what I can find out before we set anything in stone." The last thing I want is a war where I might be taken out and Hana could be left unprotected.

Hutch is right about learning from our military days. I learned things are not always so cut and dried, and nobody wants a pyrrhic victory.

"I'll wait for your report." Hutch picks up his keys. "You coming to dinner tonight?"

"Not tonight. Thank Lurlene for me."

I have business.

Pulling out my phone, I send a quick text to my girl. *Still working. Sorry.*

Gray dots precede her answer. ***Will you be at Hutch's?***
No—don't worry.

Funny how quickly my mind took ownership of her. It happened the moment I saw her, the moment her blue eyes captured mine. I don't believe in love at first sight. I still don't, but something shifted when she touched my arm.

Her fragile heart, so damaged but still fighting so hard, reminded me who I am and what I fight for. She's the beautiful face of their victims, the ones marred by what they did, and it's what drives me to this day.

Reaching above the door to my home office, I take down the key and unlock it. A gray, metal box is hidden behind a stack of books. Inside is a device I put away long ago—a disassembled phone from the days when phones were not so smart they had to be destroyed to protect your location.

Reassembling it, I take the old-school black cord and plug it into the wall. I slide a small chip in the back and power it on for the first time in seven years.

I put so much effort into disabling this device, hiding it in a metal box as if that would keep them from finding me.

As if I didn't know they always would.

As if I didn't keep this phone knowing one day I'd be here, placing this call from the only number he'll accept.

It rings once and Simon's voice is on the line. "And he's back."

An invisible fist grabs my stomach at the sound. We haven't spoken in nearly a decade, but I can tell he hasn't changed. He's the same heartless thug he always was, surrounded by evil, protected in his bubble of dirty money and corruption.

My tone is low, equally cold. "I'm not back." My hatred for him and his entire web of crime has only grown stronger, burnished into steel after this morning with Hana. "I want to know what you want."

"I'm confused." I can see his cruel smile in my mind. "You called me."

"I'm not playing games, Simon. This isn't about a horse, and it isn't about money. So what is it?"

"It's always about money, Oskar. However, in this case you're right. Other factors are involved. Much has changed since you deserted your post. Perhaps if you'd fulfilled your obligations—"

"Doping, murder, embezzlement." My jaw grinds on the words. "I put up with a lot, but when you started hurting kids, I was out."

"Taking all your knowledge with you. Do you know why I let you live?"

"Because none of your assholes are strong enough to take me out?"

He scoffs. "A well-timed bullet would take you out. I let you live because I find you interesting. Every move you make intrigues me."

His words make my skin crawl, but I'm not buying it.

"You've never been interested in me. You want something, so I'll ask again, what is it? Charles van Hamilton's debts don't warrant all of this."

"Charles van Hamilton was an annoying gnat, a foolish liability. He lost again and again, bigger and bigger, yet he wouldn't leave the game. Ultimately, he had to be removed."

"So you had him murdered, and Victor proceeded to siphon off the money he owed you."

"Victor siphoned off thousands. Charles owed me *millions*." Anger enters his tone. "Now Victor is dead–my brother, my *pakhan. That* cannot go unanswered. Justice must be served–an eye for an eye, blood for blood."

"And Debbie Desayda-Rice?"

"I don't know Miss Desayda-Rice."

"She was murdered by your nephew."

"My nephew had his own entanglements. I have no interest in that situation."

"What's your interest in Hana?"

"Hana van Hamilton belongs to me. Charles pledged her to me as payment." His tone is flat, but my insides are raging.

I've fought this decree before.

"Hana is not a slave. She's an American heiress. You can't claim her like a thoroughbred or a painting." *Or a forgotten little boy.* "Her disappearance would be noticed."

"You should know, there are many ways to collect what belongs to me."

The fire simmering in my blood leaches into my voice. "Hana does not belong to you."

It's a thinly veiled warning, and silence lingers between us on the line.

"Interesting." An evil grin is in his voice, and his one word alarms me more than a sniper's bullet.

"Scar?" I hit the End button at the sound of her voice.

Returning the phone quickly to the metal box, I place it behind the books and shove the key in my pocket.

"Hana?" I step into the hall and close the door.

Our eyes meet, and my chest tightens.

Seeing her for the first time since this morning hits me hard. She's been on my mind, but after speaking to Simon, her presence in my kitchen with her blue eyes wide, looking so small and sweet and vulnerable, every protective urge in my body roars to life.

Adrenaline is in my veins, and I close the space between us. She looks at me with so much trust, I'm ready to kill anyone who tries to hurt her.

Taking a beat, I swallow the ferocity under my skin and gentle my tone. "You okay, baby girl?"

"I'm not a baby." Her voice breaks as she steps into my arms.

Warmth replaces the adrenaline in my blood, and I surround her with my embrace. Her cheek is against my chest, and I hold her, giving her my strength, willing her to have as much as she needs.

"You're right. You're not a baby." Lowering my face, I press my lips to the top of her head, inhaling her fresh scent of flowers and sugar. "You're still a lot younger than me."

Moving her head against my chest, her defiance makes me smile. "I've lived so much already."

Closing my eyes, it's true. "I won't treat you like a baby."

Stepping back, she looks up at me. Mist shimmers in her eyes, and I reach out to slide my thumb over her smooth, ivory cheek. Her skin is porcelain, absolutely flawless–on the outside.

"Can I sleep here again?"

"You can sleep here anytime you need to."

Her cheeks relax, and her full lips press into a smile. "In that case, I'll sleep here every night."

Satisfaction is in my chest, and I nod. "Whatever my lady needs."

"My Viking prince." She gives me a little wink, but my smile darkens.

I'm no prince.

Hana is curled up in my bed looking at her phone when I enter the room, showered and with my teeth brushed. We crossed a bridge last night, but when I touched her, it went up in smoke. I don't feel right charging back in again, as much as my body hungers for her.

Blue eyes flicker to me when I get closer, and I'm gratified by the way they widen then darken with interest.

I'm in thin gray PJ pants, no shirt, and I do my best to sound neutral, not like I'm ready to devour her in those tiny shorts and thin cotton tank that does little to hide her small breasts and peaked nipples.

"How are you feeling?"

"I'm okay." Her voice is quiet, and her eyes track my movements. "How are you feeling?"

Sliding between the sheets, I lean on the pillows propped against the headboard facing her. "I feel like you're in my bed. I want to touch you, but I want you to feel safe more than anything."

Blinking down, her pouty bottom lip disappears into her mouth. Discarding her phone, she puts her small hand in mine, lifting it to her face and sliding her cheek against it.

"From the first day we met, I knew you would keep me safe. It's like my own body has betrayed me by not trusting you."

Turning my hand, I cup her jaw with my palm. She's so beautiful, and the demons of my past are so much closer than they've ever been.

"Your body will protect you." I remove my filthy hand from hers. "I'm not a good guy."

She slides her palm over my chest, higher to cup my neck. "I'm not a good girl. I don't know your past, but I know you're a good person. Only a good man would do all you've done for me, expecting nothing in return."

Reaching out to kill the light, I slide lower in the smooth

sheets. She moves closer, placing her cheek on my chest and wrapping her arm around my waist.

Lifting her small hand in mine, I kiss her knuckles. "Tell me about that night."

Her chin dips, and her fingers tighten around mine. I know she knows what I'm talking about, and with a deep exhale, she begins the story.

"When Blake was sent to boarding school, Debbie was my only real friend. Of course, I had other friends—Trip and Rainey. Natasha, but she was always competing with me. So it was Debbie and me." She pauses, and I slide my hand to her shoulder, holding her. "But Debbie wasn't Blake. Blake would never have done the things Debbie and I did."

I gaze out the window into the moonless night. "What did you do?"

A soft sigh. "I don't remember."

Why does she say that? "Are you afraid to tell me, or do you really not remember?"

She hesitates, silent, and the *scree* of the cicadas fills the silence between us. Spring is coming, new life, rebirth. Hope attempting to bud in my chest—what is she doing to me?

When she speaks, her voice is traced with guilt or maybe it's shame. "Debbie and I would take turns roofieing each other."

My jaw clenches, but I hold judgment. "How old were you?"

"Sixteen…" Her voice lowers when she confesses. "Fifteen."

Closing my eyes, a pit is in my stomach. "Why would you do that?"

"I don't know why Debbie did it. I remember I felt free, like I could do what I wanted and fuck everyone who had a problem with it. I was so stupid."

"You were angry."

"Maybe. We said we did it to be wild, to laugh at what we did when we were high and the way people responded to us."

"You could've been arrested."

"We were careful. We'd watch out for each other, but one night we were separated. That's when it happened."

She hesitates, but this is where we need to be. This is where I'll get answers.

Still, I proceed with caution. "Did anyone else know you did this?"

"Of course, Trip knew." She hesitates, thinking. "Maybe Natasha, but she and I had stopped speaking by that time. Greg was around, but I don't know how much Debbie told him or how much he cared. He never seemed interested in me. He was always talking to Blake."

I'm making mental notes while at the same time, holding her close. My reckless girl, so broken and damaged, so angry, fighting her pain and searching for meaning.

"Tell me about the night you were separated."

She sniffs a deep breath. "It's only been coming back recently and only in flashes, but I'm sure some of them are real memories."

"Tell me about the flashes."

"I'm in a dark room—one of those rooms in the back of Gibson's." I know the ones she means. "A group of old men is there, and one is on his knees in front of me."

She shivers, and I lift my other arm to hold her closer. My palm is on her back, and I slide it up and down. "It's okay. You're safe with me—it's a memory. It can't hurt you now."

Her chin bobs, and she clears her throat. "I don't know how much of this is true. Blake gets angry when I say I don't remember, but I'm really not sure—"

"I'm not angry." I give her another squeeze, and the tension slowly eases from her body.

She trusts me.

"So the man at my feet would touch me the way Victor would, while the others watched." Her voice goes quiet as if she's embarrassed. "He never did more, because he said I wasn't his. He said I had to be intact."

Her voice thickens, and she moves her hand from mine to her face. Whispering, she continues. "I didn't want to respond to his touch, but I couldn't help it. He said it was because I liked it." Warm tears are on my chest. "But I didn't like it."

Fury blazes in my chest, and closing my eyes, I breathe slowly. *Inhale, exhale…*

Again, I think the way he died was too good for him.

"You are not filthy." My voice is throaty. "Your body responded the way it did because you're human. You were abused."

Her knees rise, and she cuddles closer at my side, wrapping her arm around my waist. "In the darkroom, I remembered that night. Victor was there. He was lying on the floor at my feet… The voice said I killed him."

Silence wraps around us, and her breath is hesitant. She's so vulnerable.

I don't want to push her, but very gently I urge, "Whose voice?"

"I don't know." She sounds so tired.

"You didn't kill him, Hana."

"You don't know that." Her voice breaks.

"I know." Another warm hug. "Sleep now, angel. You're safe with me. I will always keep you safe."

I might not be a prince, but that's a promise I can keep.

CHAPTER 13

Hana

SLEEP SURROUNDS ME LIKE A LONG LOST FRIEND, A WARM BLANKET, soft and comforting. Scar's strength radiates into my body, and talking to him about my past actually helps me put away what happened. It's separate from me now; it can't hurt me anymore.

In his arms, the voices lurking in the shadows, the ones that make me feel so gross, the ones that say I'm worthless, grow smaller until they disappear, puffs of smoke driven away in the wind.

I will always keep you safe… His words are warm liquid in my veins.

He will keep that promise, and the more I'm around him, the more pieces of my heart he steals.

Lying on his side facing me, his arms encircle me, defending me against the bad. His eyes are closed, and his chest is at my cheek. Clean soap and warm man-scent flood my senses.

I carefully slide out of his embrace so I can see him. With

the light of dawn growing at the edge of the horizon, his straight nose, high cheekbones, and square jaw are cast in a golden softness. He says he's no prince, but he certainly looks noble with sleep gentling his features.

He treats me with so much care, but I have the distinct feeling I might give him care as well. When we're together, he smiles–I actually heard him chuckle once. The memory warms my heart.

He's utterly breathtaking, a bit terrifying, and completely gorgeous.

And I want him so much.

My mind returns to yesterday morning, and our sexy wake up. He was mine for a little while, before it all went to hell. I want him to be mine again.

Taking the cup off the bedside table, I sip fresh water, then I lean forward and press my lips to his strong brow. Feathering my kisses lower, I touch his cheek, and he exhales a soft noise. I slide closer, and I'm pleased to notice he's hard and ready for me.

Reaching down, I slide my hand over his impressive bulge. He wakes at my touch, a large hand moving to cover mine.

"What are you doing, Hana?" His voice is thick with sleep– or is it desire?

I'm pretty certain he still wants me. "I want to be with you. Would you want to be with someone like me? After what I told you?"

His brow softens, and he pulls me beneath him, holding me down and bracing his masculine frame on his elbows. "What are you talking about?"

I lift my hands to his broad shoulders, studying my pale skin against his dark, inked muscles. "I've done stupid things. I've made bad choices." Regret pinches my stomach. "I'm nothing to be proud of, but I'm loyal. My love is true."

"Any man would be lucky to have your love, but I'm not any man. I've done things…"

Every beat of my heart fills me with longing. He's holding me down, and it feels so good.

Blinking fast, I meet his wolf eyes. "Maybe we can make something better together?"

Touching his sexy square jaw, I lift my lips to his. He doesn't pull away or tell me to stop. He lowers his face to mine, and our mouths open. Our tongues slide together, and heat blooms between my thighs.

His mouth moves mine, drawing me higher as a bubble of desire rises in my chest. His cock is steel pressing into my stomach, and I exhale a soft moan when he moves his kisses into my hair, grazing my ear, his beard scuffing my neck.

He pauses, and I hear the tension in his voice. "Is this too much?"

Lifting my legs, I wrap them around his waist. "It's not enough. I want you inside me. Please…"

Once more our eyes meet, and his simmer with barely re-strained desire. "I don't want to hurt you, angel."

"I believe you." Reaching up, I pull his lips to mine. I want him so much.

He lifts his torso, catching the hem of my tank top. I arch my back and help him slide it over my head. His eyes land on my bare breasts and linger. One large hand cups the side, and I feel self-conscious.

I lift my arms to cover my nudity, but he stops me, catching my wrist and taking it to his lips for a kiss. "You're so beautiful."

"Not too thin?"

A rare grin curls his mouth, and he shakes his head. "You're always so beautiful to me."

Lowering his face, he pulls a hard nipple into his mouth, sliding his teeth across the sensitive peak then flickering his tongue against it quickly.

My back arches, and I exhale a *Yes…*

I want more–all of him. An ache throbs between my legs, and I know it can only be filled by him.

Fumbling my hands to his waist, I push against the cotton pants he wears to sleep. His hands cover mine, and he pauses once more. "Are you sure?"

"Yes." I'm nodding impatiently, squirming beneath him as tendrils of orgasm curl in my thighs, centering in my core. "Yes…"

I'm chanting as he discards his pants quickly, reaching for a condom from the side drawer. Licking my lips, I watch as he rolls it on, thinking how I had that sexy cock in my mouth yesterday. I remember the sounds he made when he came, and I want him inside me, making them again.

His warm palm slides up my thigh, holding my ass, and his eyes are focused on guiding the tip into my glistening core. I have no idea how this will feel. I know from the stories it will hurt, and I also know it will get better.

A fish is trapped in my stomach, and it's flipping wildly as his dick nudges, pressing its way into my body. It's soft and insistent, and since I didn't tell him, he doesn't know to go slow.

Spreading his chest over mine, with one swift thrust, he tears through my virginity, and my eyes go wide. It hurts like a motherfucker.

"Oh, shit!" I gasp as my fingers curl against his shoulders, nails breaking the skin.

He freezes. His head lifts, and he doesn't move.

His eyes hold mine, and his brow furrows. "What's wrong?"

I'm blinking fast, doing my best to breathe through the sensation of tearing skin. "I didn't expect it to hurt so much."

"Is this your first time?" Confusion is in his deep voice, and he holds still, not moving his massively erect cock seated fully inside my core.

I force my fingers to unfurl. I want this experience, this memory with him. I want to be his forever. "You're my first… this way."

"Oh, fuck." He lowers his face again, and I feel him start to withdraw.

"No." Tightening my legs around his waist, I hold us together. "Please. I want this. I want you to be my first. I want this memory to be yours."

Cupping his cheeks with my palms, I guide our lips together again. I move my hips and his dick slides into me again. The pain has eased, and I want him more than ever.

Strong arms wrap around my waist, and he pulls me tighter against his chest. "You still want to do this?"

"Yes." I wrap my arms around his shoulders.

"I need to move."

Closing my eyes, I nod, molding my naked body completely with his. "Okay."

The space between my thighs no longer feels torn. It doesn't feel like much of anything. Adjusting my hips, I try to see if it will hurt again when he starts to move.

"Fuck, Hana." He groans, and a shudder moves through his body. "You're killing me."

"I'm sorry." I have no idea what I'm doing, since this is my first time. I only know that when his hips rock this time, it's a new sensation. "Oh…" I gasp, squeezing my thighs around his waist.

"Am I hurting you?" He sounds like he's the one in pain.

"No…" I clutch his shoulders with my eyes squeezed shut. "Keep doing that."

It feels like ridges moving against my insides, awakening parts of me I didn't know existed.

"Fuck me," he groans as his hips pick up speed. "You feel too good."

"What is that?" I gasp as his cock hits deeper.

Something he's doing touches a part of me I don't recognize. It provokes an urgent need, pleasure almost like I need to pee or I'm going to burst involuntarily into operatic singing.

"Fuck, it's so good." His mouth covers mine in a consuming kiss.

My eyes close, and my mind zeroes in on the place where

we're joined. His cock drives faster, deeper, hitting that spot, sending bursts of sensation all the way to my toes.

This new orgasm is different. It climbs into my lower belly, provoking me to pump my thighs. I'm riding him as he's thrusting into me.

Our mouths break apart, and my back arches as I let go with a loud moan. His large hand cups my ass, drawing me closer to his hips and he goes even deeper, impossibly deep, then he holds with a sexy, low groan.

Wrapping my arms around him, I press my cheek to his skin as his cock pulses, as I feel him finish with a shudder. His hand slides from under my ass to my lower back, and we hold each other so close.

Gradually, our breathing slows to normal. My eyes are hazy, and I'm wrapped around his long frame like a vine. I never want to let him go, but he moves, once again kissing my shoulder, my neck, lifting his face to meet my gaze.

Now his expression is completely relaxed. He's different than I've ever seen him—not angry or guarded, but curious and open. "Why didn't you tell me you were a virgin?"

"Was I?" My brow furrows. "I didn't know if I was or not."

"Yes." His forehead drops to my shoulder, and he exhales a laugh.

It makes me laugh, and the result is he glides out of my slippery core. "Oh, shit." I exhale a snort, and he shakes his head looking down.

"You should've told me."

"You might not have done it."

"Damn right."

"But I wanted you to do it." Now I'm smiling, tracing my finger along the line of ink on his shoulder. "So I'm glad I didn't tell you."

"I never want to hurt your sweet body." His hands are on my waist, and I'm surrounded by him, full of him. I'm in heaven.

"Good news, from what I understand, it shouldn't ever hurt again now that we've done it."

He shakes his head, and I love it when he smiles. "What will I do with you?"

"Hopefully a lot more of what you just did." Reaching for my phone on the bedside table, I hold it above us. "I need to document this very important moment in my life."

"Hana," he groans.

"I'm a photographer, now stop being grumpy and smile at the camera."

"I'm not smiling at the camera."

"Then don't." I snuggle close to his shoulder, getting my cheek next to his. He's looking away, so I kiss him. "At least look at it."

"Where do I look?" It's more complaint than cooperation, but the glint in his eyes tickles my stomach.

"Look at me."

He does, and I get one shot before he sits up quickly, discarding the used condom. "Let's get you cleaned up."

In a sweep, he lifts me in his arms. I toss my phone on the bed before wrapping mine around his neck as he carries me to the bathroom. He walks to the back corner, sitting beside the sunken, jetted tub, and switches on the water. I expect him to leave me here while it fills, but he doesn't.

He stays with me on his lap, looking into my eyes. "If I'd known, I'd have tried to make it better for you."

Holding his neck, I think about this. "I'm not sure how you could've made it better. It was always going to hurt the first time."

His beard scuffs my skin as he kisses my neck. "I might have figured out a way to make it hurt less."

The water rises higher, and I tilt my head to the side, studying his face and wondering if it's possible I'm in love with him. I'm pretty sure I am. *How long have I been here?*

My voice is quiet, and I slide my thumb across his cheek. "I never believed I could have something wonderful."

His expression changes, and he looks down at my nude body in his arms. "I never knew to dream of you."

Brushing my nose against his, my smile melts into a happy kiss on his lips. "What happens now?"

He kisses me briefly before lifting my legs and gently lowering me into the warm, swirling water. His expression is dark, and he doesn't join me in the tub.

"I don't know." It's the last thing he says before leaving me to return to the bedroom.

CHAPTER 14

HER BLOOD ON THE SHEETS CHANGES ME. POSSESSION BLAZES INSIDE me at the thought of what this means.

Mine. Like a primitive drumbeat, it thuds with every beat of my heart.

She gave this to me, but she has no idea what I've done, who is entangled in my past. She has no idea my connection to the man who hurt her. Even if I ended it, I'm worried she won't understand. How can she understand, coming from her life of privilege, how little voice I had in my fate?

Surviving the fire, regaining my strength, moving to America, even knowing Hutch all played a role in my ability to walk away. Saddest, but perhaps most fundamental, was my belief I had nothing to lose. I agreed with Victor–no one cared or would care for me, so when it got to the point I couldn't stomach anymore, I didn't care if they assassinated me.

Then she wobbled up that gravel driveway outside Hugh van Hamilton's estate.

We've got to have a serious conversation. Soon. I can't do it with her in my tub buzzing with afterglow and asking me what next.

Her blue eyes are so bright and trusting, she's so open and ready to heal and grow together. What kind of bastard would I be to crush her still-damp wings with the truth?

I need to unfold the story in a way that will help her understand my lack of choices, as I understood the choices she made. Life is not as straightforward as we want it to be. Desperation leads to all sorts of bad decisions.

Carrying the soiled sheets to my laundry room, I take down fresh ones and remake the bed, then I return to the bathroom where Hana is quietly sliding a beige, natural sponge down her creamy-smooth arm.

"How are you feeling?" I sit on the side of the tub.

Her blue eyes flicker up to mine, and she gives me a tentative smile. "A little sore, but the water feels good."

"Good." I lean forward to kiss her lips, and before I can straighten, her hand catches my cheek, holding me a beat longer.

"What are you doing?" Her voice is back to shaky confidence, and I take her hand in mine, pulling it to my lips for a kiss.

"Just cleaning up. I'll drive you back to your uncle's place when you're ready."

Nodding, her chin drops, and she seems sad.

Tension twists in my chest, and I touch her chin. "What's wrong?"

Her slim shoulder rises, and she tilts her head to the side. "I don't know. I guess I thought we'd spend some time together now that, you know… *we did it*. But I guess it is the middle of the week."

The tension grows tighter, and I realize how wrapped around her little finger I've become. I can't leave her this way.

"I need to work, but I could take you with me. Want to tag along?"

Her eyebrows lift, and she seems happier. "I can bring my camera, and while you're in the office, I can take more pictures."

"Sounds good." Leaning down, I give her another kiss on the lips. "Get dressed, and you can be my shadow."

Seeing her happiness makes me happy, even though I'm acutely aware of all the potential landmines of taking her to the office, considering we're still working out our plans for Simon.

"You won't even know I'm there," she chirps.

"Where have I heard that before?"

She stands, and I pull down a towel, wrapping it around her body. Her arms are pinned at her sides, and I lean forward, parting her lips with mine and sliding our tongues together.

It feels so right having her in my house, in my bed, holding her this way, kissing her. We made love, and she didn't bolt–she didn't even seem panicked. I'm not sure if it means she trusts me or if it's something else, but I feel like we've taken a big step forward.

"No fair," she pouts.

"What?"

"You've got my arms all pinned, so I can't touch you."

"If you touch me, we won't leave the house."

Her eyes slant, and she gives me a naughty grin. "What's wrong with that?"

"You're playing with fire, angel."

"I'm not afraid of fire."

"Sounds like we're perfectly matched." I give her another quick kiss, fighting the urge to lift her off her feet and carry her back to bed.

I seem to have the urge to carry her everywhere now, which is ridiculous.

"Come on. We'll swing by your uncle's, grab a bite to eat, then head to my office."

"*Now* you're relaxed." Dirk's teasing greets us as we enter the office.

I flip him the bird, but Hana bounces over to where he's sitting with his feet up, balancing a laptop on his thighs.

"How can you tell?" She's light and teasing as well, and the fist in my chest is gone.

I guess my partner is right. I'm completely relaxed.

Dirk leans forward on the desk, speaking like he's unraveling some great mystery. "You see, his brow is typically lined *and* his jaw is clenched. Now, the jaw is relaxed."

"Ahh, I see." Hana nods, crossing her arms, and gazing up at me.

She's fucking adorable, but I shake my head. "Glad you two are having fun."

We stopped by Hana's uncle's on the way here, and she changed into jeans and a thin sweater that hangs over her hands. It's so thin, I can see the camisole underneath, and I confess, it's doing it for me. Her long, spiral curls hang down her back, and her lips are glossy pink.

Norris made omelets, and Hana made a big show of eating a whole one, pointing out it was made with two eggs and cheese. I traced a curl off her cheek wishing I hadn't been such an asshole to her that day at the pool. My gorgeous girl has navigated enough abuse in her twenty-one years.

I want to make the next twenty-one—and more—as painless as possible.

"I have news." Dirk announces, and I slide my finger over the touchpad on my computer to wake it. "Natasha is the new manager at Gibson's."

Straightening, I meet his eyes, and he nods. "Not sure what that means."

"I'll tell you what it means." Hana declares, snatching our attention. My breath stills waiting for what she's about to say.

"It means *I'm* never going there again. As if it weren't bad enough, now Natasha's in charge? Gag."

My shoulders drop, and Dirk exhales the breath we were both holding. "Damn, Hana."

"What?" She looks from him to me, confused, but he's quick to salvage our slip.

"You know what hit me the other day?" Standing, he walks to where she's leaning against Hutch's desk. Her eyebrows rise as she looks up at him. "You're going to be my little sister in a few months."

"You're right!" She smiles brightly. "I guess I hadn't thought about it either. I'm going to have two big brothers."

"Hot little sister." His eyebrow arches, and he gives her a flirty grin.

All my good feelings evaporate, and the fist is back. "Knock it off."

My voice is more of a threatening growl than I expect, and Hana's eyebrows shoot up.

Dirk laughs, wrapping his arm around Hana's shoulders. "What? You don't like me noticing my sexy future sister-in-law?"

Hana's eyes flicker from him to me, and she steps from under his arm, walking straight to where I'm about to go off like a fucking volcano. *What the fuck is wrong with me?*

"Thanks, Dirk." Her voice is soft. "But I'm off the market."

Hana slides her hand up the side of my arm, almost like she's calming a wild animal, which I imagine is what I look like. I'm stunned by the murderous urges surging in my chest.

"Dude, breathe. I was only joking." Dirk holds up both hands, but his eyes are sparkling as he laughs. He's got my number. "I have to say, I like what you're doing to him, sis."

"I'm not sure I like what you're doing to him." Her voice is quiet, and she watches my face. "You okay?"

I do take a breath, passing a hand over my brow and forcing a smile. "It's all good."

I want to pull her in for a kiss, but I'm not trying to piss all over her.

"I'm going to take some pictures, okay?"

Nodding, I clear my throat. "Sure. See you in a bit."

A hint of a smile curls her cheeks. "Okay."

She heads out the door, and Dirk's eyebrows rise. "This is good. I like it. Did you tell her what we're working on?"

"No." I look down, conflict raging in my chest. "I'd like to tell her about my past first. I don't want to surprise her with all of this then tell her she's bait. We have time."

"I think Hana and Blake will really help us. They're cool and they're smart. And they're well-connected in the city."

He's right, but my cave-man insides can't let her go. "I still don't like putting Hana at risk."

"I don't either, but we'll never be far away. She'll be protected."

It gives me an idea. Going to the metal cabinet, I pull the top drawer open and quickly work the combination on the lockbox inside. "Tell Hutch I have the beretta."

"Any particular reason?"

"No point in being armed if you don't know how to shoot a gun."

"All true." Dirk nods. "So you're doing target practice?"

"Teaching."

"The only thing I've ever shot is a camera." Hana wrinkles her cute nose at me as I explain the basics of the firearm to her.

"Your sister took Hutch's gun last time we were in the city, and I'm pretty sure she didn't know what she was doing." *She shot the wrong guy.*

"Weren't you there?" Her brows furrow, and I shake my head.

"She was with Hutch. I was looking for someone else."
Ivan X.

Hana's jaw drops, and she grabs my arm. "Did Blake shoot Grish?"

"No." Shaking my head, I think about what happened to him.

Frustration simmers in my chest because I haven't been able to figure out that piece of the puzzle. I'm very familiar with the Petrovich method for disposing of individuals who know too much or who have become problematic.

What I don't understand is why Simon's nephew was disposed of like a mark.

"So it really was a heart attack?" Hana's blonde head tilts to the side. "He was so young. I guess it was something he didn't know about. I had a friend once who collapsed while playing basketball, and he had no idea he had… I can't remember what they called it."

"Aortic stenosis." My voice is quiet, and she smiles.

"I think that's it! How do you know?"

The standard operating procedure is to explain the sudden heart attacks as congenital when the real cause is a lethal dose of drugs.

"Back to your lesson."

We're in a vacant field facing the woods at the edge of a new subdivision just outside Hamiltown. It's a popular place for local kids to sneak away for the keg parties, because it's somewhat secluded. Nosy old ladies like to call Hutch to break them up.

I've set up a target forty paces away, one twenty paces, and one ten.

"It's good to understand how the gun works at different ranges." I sit behind Hana on the side of my truck, situating her body in front of me, between my legs.

"When you handle a pistol, it's not like in the movies. You

can't simply pull the trigger over and over and hit something. You have to focus."

My arms cover hers, and both are outstretched in front of us. "Look down the site at the target and exhale slowly."

"Okay." She tilts her head, and I feel the breath leave her body.

"Now."

She pulls the trigger, and *POP-POP-POP!*

The gun fires repeatedly. One shot might have hit something, but her hands fly up, and her knees bend as she shrieks. If it weren't for me behind her, holding it, the beretta would've sailed out into the field.

"Shit!" She looks at me, shaking her hands before pressing them to her cheeks. "I didn't know it would jump like that. It's so loud!"

Swallowing my laugh, I nod. "That's why we're doing this. You shouldn't wait until you need to use a gun to know how it feels."

"Jesus, my whole insides are shaking." She exhales a laugh, turning to look out at the target. "I don't think I hit it."

"Doubtful."

"I guess I'd better try again."

"Ready when you are."

She does a full-body shake like a boxer, and I grin watching her. When she sees me, she steps between my thighs, leaning into my chest.

"Why am I learning to shoot a gun again? I can think of other things we could be doing."

My dick twitches, but I give her a nudge. "First this, then that. Now come on."

"Okay." With a grumble, she presses her back to my chest again.

She does a little wiggle of her ass against my crotch, and my dick surges more.

"Concentrate," I grumble, although I'm ready to bag this and throw her in the truck.

She makes a pouty noise and straightens her arms, gun in her hands. Before she lifts it, her face turns, and she kisses the side of my jaw.

It completely kills my focus. "Hana…"

"It's like in *Star Wars*. A kiss for luck."

She's too damn cute, and I can't argue. I want to kiss her. I want to say fuck this, I'll do all her shooting for her, but I need to know she can protect herself if something happens and I'm not there.

The thought twists my stomach, but it strengthens my resolve. "Eyes on the target, exhale slowly."

She does what I say, holding the gun straight ahead, allowing her breath to release, then she pulls it. This time when the shots ring out, one after the other, her weapon doesn't fly out of control. It remains steady, leveled directly on the target.

Lowering the gun, her eyes are focused straight ahead. "I think I hit it that time."

Taking the gun, I slip it in my holster as I walk out to where the target is pinned to a stack of wood. Small, black holes are all over the outline of a torso, and satisfaction warms my belly. They're not focused like a marksman's would be, but they're good enough to fend off an attacker.

"Not bad at all." I hold up the large sheet of paper for her to see.

"Wow." Her eyebrows rise, and she carefully touches the bullet holes. "I'm a badass."

"Let's try the closer target."

We spend about an hour practicing. When she's ready to try it without my help, I step away, taking a bag of sunflower seeds from my glove box and popping a few in my mouth.

"Show me what you can do."

She gives me a determined nod before turning to face the target. Lifting her arms, she lowers her cheek, aligning her gaze on the site. Her torso detracts as she exhales, and she fires the shots without flinching. Good student.

"I'll get it." Shoving the gun in the back of her jeans, she takes off the short distance to retrieve the target then brings it to where I'm sitting, spitting out shells.

The shots are clustered around the center of the drawing, and my eyebrows rise. "That's really good."

"What are you eating?" She steps between my legs, pulling my hand open.

"Sunflower seeds–want one?"

Her lips twist, and she nods. "Sure."

Taking a black and white shell from my hand, she puts it in her mouth then bites down, chewing several times before her nose wrinkles and she starts to cough.

"Oh…" She turns away from me, coughing and spitting. "Why would you eat that?"

"What the hell?" I scoop the bottle of water off the ground and hand it to her. "You don't eat the shells."

"Why didn't you tell me?" Sticking out her tongue, she swipes the hard fragments away, still coughing and sputtering. "That's awful."

"You've never had a sunflower seed?" Her lips press to the side, and she has a bit of shell on her chin. "Come here."

She returns between my legs, and I'm ready for Plan B. "You're an excellent shot for a Park Avenue princess."

"I'm no princess." Her chin lifts, and she tries to be sassy.

I flick the fragment away then lower my face, tracing my lips along her jaw. "Is that so?"

"Yes." Heat fills her tone as her hands slide along my waist, finding their way beneath my shirt. "I'm a bad girl."

"You are?"

"Mm-hm." Lifting her chin, she whispers in my ear. "Now show me how to eat a sunflower seed."

"I have to get more out of the truck."

"I'll come with you."

CHAPTER 15

Hana

'M STRADDLING SCAR'S LAP IN THE CAB OF HIS TRUCK, WATCHING AS he puts a sunflower seed between his full lips. His square jaw moves as he cracks it in half, then he takes out the heart with his fingertips.

"This is the part you eat." He holds the small kernel between us.

Licking my bottom lip, I gaze at him. "That was hot."

His brow furrows, and he gives me one of those rare grins. "Was it?"

I lean down and slide my tongue over his long fingers before covering them with my lips, taking the seed out of his grasp with a little suck.

When I sit up, his blue eyes have darkened. "That was hot."

His voice is husky, and desire zips through my veins.

"You think so?" I rest my arms on his shoulders, and I want him to kiss me.

This entire afternoon, I've been burning up with lust. I

don't know why he wants me to learn to shoot, but I won't argue if it means I get to stand with my back against his chest while his warm breath tickles my neck and his cock nudges my ass.

My patience is not great, and I lean forward to slide my nose along his cheek. He smells so good, like warm woods and clean soap. "We're pretty secluded out here, you know?."

Large hands slide up my thighs, scooping my ass forward on his lap. "Why do you think I brought you here?"

"To learn to shoot?" I lift my face, so it hovers just above his.

"Yes." He lifts his chin and kisses my mouth. "How are you feeling?"

"Like a badass."

That gets me another low chuckle, and a thrill races to my core. "I love to hear you laugh."

He kisses me again, and this time our lips part. His tongue slides against mine, and my body ignites. Heat floods my core, and I exhale a whimper.

"I love to hear you moan." His beard scratches my face as his lips move into my hair, kissing behind my ear. "You smell so good. I want my mouth all over you."

"I want that." I gasp, leaning back and quickly whipping the thin sweater over my head. Just as fast, I strip off the silk cami I'm wearing under it. "I don't know why I wore so many layers."

"So I wouldn't have to kill every man who looks at you." His rough growl is against my breast as he pulls a tight nipple between his lips.

"Oh, fuck," I gasp as pleasure races through my stomach.

He's right, that sweater is too thin to wear alone, but the possessive turn he's taken since we slept together is very gratifying. He apologized for overreacting to Dirk, but after the shit I've suffered, I don't mind having a massive bodyguard ready to fight off unwanted attention for me.

His mouth moves from my breast to my shoulder, up to

my chin, and I cup his cheeks as I kiss him hard, with all my passion. Scar makes me feel so safe and so sexy.

My tongue curls with his, and his hands move to my lower back, sliding over my bare skin. He rocks my crotch over the bulge in his pants, and heat sparkles through my legs.

"Feels so good," I sigh. "I want you inside me."

"I didn't bring a condom, but I'm clean. Hutch likes us to get tested regularly, even if we're not with anyone."

Sliding off his lap, I unbutton my jeans, pushing them down my hips, leaving me in only my lace thong. "I think that's a good policy."

I climb onto his lap again, covering his mouth with mine. Our kisses are ravenous and hungry. I pull the hem of his shirt, and he whips it over his head. Next my hands drop to his waist, fumbling with the button on his jeans.

He slides them down his hips, and his massive erection springs free, long and hard and extending up to his belly. I lean down to run my tongue up the length of his shaft to the tip.

It jumps and he exhales a low groan, fisting his hand in the side of my hair. "As good as that feels, I want to be inside you, too."

Sitting up straighter, I lick my lips, studying his dark eyes. "I want you to make me come."

Lifting me off his lap with ease, he turns me so I'm facing the windshield, and orders gruffly, "Lean forward." I do as he says, and gasp as his tip nudges my core from behind. "You're already so wet."

With a swift thrust he glides fully into me, and my palms slam against the dash. "God, yes," I moan.

One arm wraps around my waist, and his beard scratches my back as he arches forward, kissing his way up my spine. "Lean back, baby."

I do as he says, arching my back against his shoulder, and his hand goes between my thighs, sliding up and down and circling my clit. He's deep inside me as my hips start to rock. It feels incredible. I moan as he kisses the side of my neck, breathing hard beside my ear.

"Ride me, baby." His fingers massage and tease my clit, and his cock is hitting that place inside me again.

"Oh, shit, you're doing it."

"That's my girl," he whispers in my ear. "So beautiful. Come on my dick."

My eyes squeeze shut, and I grip the back of his neck as my body arches higher. Pleasure floods through my stomach at his words, at the sensation of fullness. His arm that was around my waist moves higher, his rough palm sliding over my breasts, squeezing and pinching my hard nipples. It's all too much.

Orgasm races through my legs, summoned by his hand vigorously massaging my clit as his fat cock drives into me. My thighs start to tremble, and my inner muscles grasp and pull as I break with a loud moan.

"Oh, fuck," I whisper as I shoot through the stars.

This feeling is unbelievable. Bucking my ass, I grasp his hand as the sensations become too powerful. I'm so sensitive, and our fingers thread together as his ass lifts from the seat.

He groans in a way that curls my toes, and I'm flooded with another burst of hot pleasure knowing he's coming with me. I feel him pulsing, and I feel the slippery wetness of our orgasm on my ass and thighs.

Falling back on his firm chest, I turn my face to kiss his neck. His coarse chest hairs tickle my skin, and his lips press to the top of my shoulder before moving to my neck.

"Beautiful badass." He kisses my cheek. "I need to stock up on sunflower seeds if this is what they do to you."

"It's what you do to me."

"It's what you do to me." His strong arms wrap around my waist, and I wrap my arms on top of them as joy pulses through my body with every heartbeat. "You're changing me."

With a smile, I rest my cheek against his jaw. He's changing me.

Carmen is behind the counter flipping through a catalog when I enter Ruth's Rarities. Scar said he needed to return the gun and check in with the guys, so I walked down the three-block Main Street of Hamiltown to where my bestie works.

"This bag does not spark joy." Pepper's voice comes from behind one of the rows.

Carmen doesn't even look up from her post. "Then don't buy it."

I peek around the corner at my little friend sitting on the floor, sorting through sequined bags with catch phrases on them. "What's going on here?"

"I brake for dad bods? Seriously?" Pepper cuts her eyes up at me then shakes her head dismissively.

I shrug. "Some ladies like that, especially when you've been married for a while."

"I don't think that's true."

"It's true," Carmen yells from the front. "It's one of our top sellers."

Pepper's eyes roll so hard I think they might get stuck, and I wonder if her objection has anything to do with her lack of a dad, but I keep it to myself.

"I don't think Blake agrees with this." Pepper looks up at me, then her brow lowers. "You look different."

"I do?" Stepping back, I go to the counter where Carmen is working.

My friend looks up, and her eyebrows rise. "You're glowing." Her voice drops, and she leans forward. "You did it. Tell me *everything*."

"What did you do?" Pepper nearly makes me jump out of my skin. "Was it that bologna facial I saw on TikTok?"

"Ew!" My nose wrinkles, and I try to imagine what the heck…

"Good lord, Pep," Carmen cries, "Don't do facials you see on TikTok. Especially not any that involve bologna. Gross!"

"It looked like that horror film…"

"Leatherface?" Carmen shakes her head. "Kids these days. Just because some idiot does something on social media doesn't mean you all have to do it. Just say no."

"You sound like an old grandma," Pepper grumbles.

"And you sound like a little Japanese lady."

I'm biting my lip and doing my best not to laugh at them. I'm so light and happy, and I know it's because I've been getting the most amazing sleep followed by some pretty amazing orgasms–which I have no intention of discussing in front of Pepper.

Our little friend pulls her phone up and looks at it. "Uncle Hutch said I have to meet him at the office now." She walks over and puts her arms around my waist, and I like how even though she's twelve, she still has moments when she acts eleven. "Are you coming to dinner tonight?"

Wrapping my arms around her shoulders, I give her a squeeze. "I'm not sure. I haven't talked to Blake today."

"You don't have to come just because Blake's there. I miss you."

"I miss you too, Skater-girl." Planting a kiss on the top of her head, I give her a little nudge. "You should see the pictures I took. You look like a superhero."

"Maybe I can see them on Saturday? You said I could tidy your room."

She looks up at me, and I tweak her nose. "It's a date, but no throwing away my stuff without asking."

"I'll make a pile and you can decide what you think. Bye, guys!" she yells, running to the door.

It closes with the ringing of a bell, and I exhale a laugh. "She's already anticipating a non-joyful pile of my stuff."

"I think she just likes saying *tidy* or *this doesn't bring me joy.*" Carmen imitates Pepper's voice. "Now, tell me everything!"

"I don't know what you're talking about."

"Do not do me like that. You had sex with Scar, and I want all the details. Is it big? Oh, I know it's big, I've seen him in sweats. Does he have any special moves? How many times did you do it?"

A laugh bursts through my pursed lips, and I shake my head. "I'm not telling you any of that! He'd kill me."

"You can tell me *some* of that."

"I'll tell you he is very good at it."

"Of course he is."

"And very caring…." I think about our recent ride in the truck. "And a bit of a dirty talker."

"Oh… Nice." Carmen's eyes widen, and I snort a laugh.

"You are so crazy."

"Well, I have to get my kicks somewhere. My dating apps are turning up a whole lot of nothing. The quantity is there, but the quality is not. Then I watched that *Tinder Swindler* documentary the other night. Now I don't trust anybody."

Leaning on the counter, I look at the catalog she was holding. It's for signs and other store supplies. "What about Dirk? He's handsome and charming and very smart. Not to mention, he's loaded."

She purses her lips and shrugs. "He never seemed interested. I don't think he thinks of me that way. You know he went to school in New York and all. I think he's more into girls like you."

"Like me?" My brow creases as all the fucked up shit I've done flickers through my mind. "I don't think so. Maybe he just needs a little encouragement."

"It won't make a difference." She clicks through stock items on the computer, and I tilt my head to the side.

My eyes narrow at her indifference. "Is it possible *you're* the one who isn't interested?"

"I don't know what you mean."

"You don't like Dirk! What's wrong with Dirk?"

Shaking her head, she exhales a gasp. "Nothing is wrong with Dirk!"

"But you're not interested in him. Why not? Tell me." I scoot closer to her. "What did he do?"

"It's more what he hasn't done. Why is he still in Hamiltown? He's not Hutch. Hell, Hutch is practically the mayor, and he has Pepper and now Blake." Carmen's voice rises. "Dirk went to school in Manhattan! Why would he come back to this little Podunk when he could have the bright lights of the city? I've never even been out of the state except to go to Atlanta for market."

Pressing my lips together, I'm not sure what to say. "Maybe he likes the small-town vibe?"

"Exactly." She taps her finger on the counter. "I want to see things. I want to travel. I want to go to New York City!"

Her voice rises, and I nod. "Well, that settles it. You're coming with us to my art show next month."

A shy smile curls her lips, and she shakes her head looking down at the counter. "No, that's a family thing. I couldn't impose–"

"You're my best friend. I need all the moral support I can get. Do you know how cutthroat the art world in Manhattan is?" Putting my hand on my stomach, I close my eyes dramatically. "I get nauseated every time I think about it."

I'm laying it on pretty thick, especially since I'm feeling really great about the photos I've taken, but the thought of being back in town with only Blake as a buffer between Natasha and the old crew makes me cringe.

"Having you there would bring me joy."

"Am I really your best friend?" Her voice is high.

"I mean, yeah. Blake's my sister and Pepper's..."

"Pepper," we say at the same time.

Carmen's entire face lights up, and she claps her hands fast. "I'll go!"

"And we can go to Magnolia Bakery and the Top of the Rock and get hamburgers at 5 Napkins…"

"Maybe I'll meet an unattached billionaire, and he'll ask me to be his nanny. Then he'll fall in love with me, and we'll get married…"

"Easy there, what about that swindler?"

"Oh right, speaking of strange men, so I was in Steamy Beans this morning, and Wilma said a handsome stranger was in town. She said he was well-dressed and very attractive."

My eyebrows rise. "Is he still here? What happened?"

"She said he was asking a lot of questions about the town and the original families."

Uncomfortable prickles skate across my skin. "He was asking about my family?"

"Don't worry. He's probably some historian from one of the colleges or somebody who did ancestry dot com and thinks he's from here. A long-lost cousin or something."

"Does that happen a lot?"

"Not really."

"Okay…" I think maybe I'll share this information with Hutch or Scar. "I'd better take off in case I have a dinner date."

"We need to do a girl's night. Don't forget your old pal Carmen now that you have a massively hot new boyfriend."

"He's not my boyfriend." Although, I'd like to think of him that way.

"Whatever. Girls' night."

"I'm in!"

Scar wasn't at dinner tonight. Hutch said he was working on their case, so it was just Blake and Hutch, Pepper, Dirk, and me chowing down on Lurlene's amazing pot roast. I wish

Scar *had* been there to see me clean my plate.

Carmen's story about the stranger in town was on my mind, but I decided to save it for Scar. It's possible it was just some local historian or genealogist, but after our impromptu trip to the makeshift firing range, I'm not so sure.

Back at the house, I quickly wash my face and brush my teeth. I slip into my usual knit shorts and tank and grab a small bag as I head for the door.

I'm at the top of the stairs when Blake stops me. She's in tan palazzo pants and a matching long sweater, and her dark hair is loose down her back.

"You've been spending every night out." Her voice is quietly concerned.

"I–um…" My eyes drop, but I decide I'm not ashamed. Lifting my chin, I meet her worried gaze. "I've been spending the night with Scar."

"Oh." Her brow jumps, gray eyes studying mine.

I know she loves me. I know she's my self-appointed mother, and I do love her for it even if it's unnecessary.

"It's okay, B. He's really sweet to me."

Her full lips press together, and she gives me a brief nod. "I only want you to be well and happy."

I give her a quick hug. "I'm both of those things. So much. I promise."

She doesn't answer, but I don't wait. I dash down the stairs, out into the night, and hop on the silly golf cart I use to get around our tiny town. In minutes, I glide up to Scar's house.

His kitchen door is unlocked, and I don't know if he expected me to come tonight or not. We didn't discuss it, but he did say I could come here any time I needed him. I wonder if he knows how much I've grown to need him.

Stepping through the screen door, into the empty kitchen, I notice an unopened bag of sunflower seeds on the bar, and a thrill flutters through my stomach. I've never thought about sex as much as I do now, since I've been with him.

Scar's always been dangerously tempting, but now everything he does is like a little seduction.

The light is on in his bedroom, and I quietly make my way to what has become my sacred space, a place where I can sleep and make love without fear… Only he's not here.

I touch the bathroom door, and it falls open to reveal him holding a towel, fresh out of the shower, completely nude.

My lips part, and I can only gaze at him, tall and sculpted. His long hair is wet, and his ass is perfectly defined, like a tight square. The muscles on his back are long and striped with ink curling from his neck to his waist, hiding his scars.

His beauty hits me so hard, my eyes warm. This man has pledged himself to me, and I feel so unworthy of his devotion.

Blue eyes meet mine, but he doesn't smile. He doesn't move, so I step closer.

"Can I touch you?" My voice is quiet as a whisper.

"Yes."

I can barely breathe as I carefully place my fingers on the tiny fragments of skin not covered with black. His eyes track my movements in the mirror, and I follow the seams of tissue holding him together.

"Are you embarrassed by them?" My eyes flicker to his. "I would be."

"Do you find me ugly? A monster?"

"No! Not at all!" I answer so fast, meeting his eyes, and they soften.

Turning to me, he places both hands on my upper arms. "My scars tell me how strong I am. They tell me I can survive the fire." His voice is gentle. "I'm proud of my scars."

"You're the most amazing person I've ever known." I want to wrap my naked body around his and love him. I want to take away his pain the way he's taken away mine.

Lifting my shirt over my head, I unfasten my bra, letting it fall before wrapping my arms around him again and pressing our skin flush.

I'm standing behind him. We're facing the mirror, so I can see the effect I have on him. My hand slides lower, and I circle my palm over the top of his erection.

"Hana…" He exhales a low groan, turning to face me.

Leaning down, he cups my face in his broad hands, pulling my lips with his, swiping my tongue with his. He lifts his chin to study my face, blue eyes sliding from my brows to my cheeks to my mouth.

I place our palms together, studying the difference in size, the curls of ink along his wrists, the length of his fingers. Folding them together, I hold his knuckles to my lips, kissing them each gently before guiding them to my breasts. I wish they were bigger for him.

He doesn't seem to mind. His hands slide along my breasts, lifting them from the sides and pinching my nipples. He slides his hands around my back, lifting me firmly against his chest.

His face drops to my shoulder, and he inhales deeply.

Lifting my arms, I wrap them around his neck, holding my body flush against his. Heat pulses through my veins with every beat of my heart. "I want you to be the only man to ever touch me."

A noise like a growl rumbles in his chest. Threading my hand into the side of his long hair, I lift his face. Ice-blue fire burns in his gaze, and I place the tips of my fingers lightly to his cheeks, I stretch higher to press my open mouth to his.

It doesn't take more. Strong hands move down my body, cupping my ass and lifting me onto the bathroom counter. It gets our faces closer, and puts his hardened cock at my belly.

Wetness floods my core, and my body is desperate and needy. Since our first time, I haven't felt afraid or shut down. I hope it means I've learned he's different, special.

I definitely want this man, this feeling. His mouth is at my ear, pulling and biting, and echoes of desire pulse through my veins.

"I want to be the only man to touch you. I want you to be mine."

"Yes..." I slide my hand down to cup and tease his erection.

A drop of precum is on the tip, and I lean down to lick it, swirling my tongue around the tip and edges.

"Fuck," he groans, lifting my face. "Take off your shorts."

Hopping down, I quickly discard them and my underwear so I'm standing nude in front of him.

"Your pussy is bare."

It's a valid point, considering what happened. "I guess I wanted to be ready in case..."

He touches my chin, studying my expression. "In case?"

"In case we might try again?" My voice is tentative.

He inhales deeply, and his wolf eyes slide closed. It reminds me of an animal scenting the air. "I want that more than anything, angel. I want you screaming my name, your juices all over my beard. I want to smell you when I sleep."

My breath quickens, and I imagine him taking me that way–him, the man I love.

"I want it, too." I want everything with him, but I'm afraid it might go bad again. "What can we do?"

"I have an idea."

CHAPTER 16

Scar

HANA HAS BEEN ON MY MIND SINCE WE LEFT OUR MAKESHIFT FIRING range in the woods, since she tried to eat a whole sunflower seed then blew my mind in the cab of my truck. We're getting serious, and I can't keep putting off the inevitable conversation.

Still, when she showed up in my bathroom, gazing at me like a work of art, touching my scars, tracing my ink with her fingertips, all thoughts of breaking the mood flew out the window.

Now she wants to try again, and all I can think is I want to give it to her. Even if my hands are filthy, I can do this for her. I can do it for us.

I want to be the one to help her heal, to lead her back to whole. I want to be the only man to touch her. Always.

Walking to the large bathtub recessed in the corner of the suite, I switch on the water, sitting on the side of the oversized jacuzzi as it fills. She climbs onto my lap, completely nude, her bare pussy teasing me with its proximity to my cock.

Wrapping her slim arms around my neck, her soft lips trace a line from my jaw to my ear. "I can do this." Her voice is sultry and low. "I'm obsessed with you."

Shit, her sexy words make my erection weep. I want to bend her over and fuck her hard, but I'm not a selfish bastard. I know accomplishing this will take us to a new level, and I meant what I said, I want to hear her screaming my name as she comes on my face.

Sliding my hands over her ass, I kiss the top of her shoulder. I'm not sure if it's obsession or devotion I feel for her–or a combination of the two. "You're the most beautiful thing I've ever seen."

Holding her hand, I guide her into the warm water. Her back is against my chest, and I lean against the built-in headrest, sliding my hands down her soft arms until our fingers curl together.

Her curly blonde hair is a messy pile on her head, and I kiss the exposed skin at her neck. Her faint, floral scent is in my nose, and holding her this way provokes all the caveman instincts I've been wrestling with since the first time we were together.

"I never enjoyed bathing." Her soft voice is soothing music. "Now I never want to get out."

"I love the sound of your voice." Lifting my chin, I inhale the side of her head. "I love your scent."

My eyes close. This feeling expanding in my chest is fucking terrifying. I realize for the first time in my life my very existence is threatened by the thought of anything happening to her.

Like slippery soap, she rotates in my arms so her stomach is against mine. Her small breasts rest against my chest, and at half my size, she fills every space in my soul.

"You make me feel like I've never felt." Her eyes meet mine, deep blue and so round.

"How do you feel, beautiful girl?"

Her eyes glisten. "Like I'm worth saving."

Lifting my hands from the water, I cup her face. "You are worth saving for so many reasons. Not just for me."

Lowering my lips to hers, our tongues chase, lips pull, my erection grows, and I need to be inside her again. "Do you still want to do this?"

"More than anything." Holding my shoulders, she moves higher on my chest, then with one even glide, her knees rise, and I'm fully sheathed in her hot little core.

"Fuck," I groan as she continues to move, riding my cock up and down as her lips trace a line from my cheek to my ear.

"I couldn't wait," she gasps, and I'm right there with her, so close to the edge. "Make me come again."

Reaching down, I cup her ass, groaning as I lift her off me. "Hold the sides of the tub."

She does as I say, and I lift her easily, so she's sitting on my hands. She's out of the water, and I pull her closer, keeping my eyes on hers.

"I won't hold you down. I'll stop whenever you say."

Her pussy hovers in front of my face, and I watch her expression for any signs of fear. Her tongue slides out to touch her bottom lip, and our eyes are locked.

Placing her hands on the sides of the tub, she braces her weight, and she moves forward carefully, thin brows furrowed.

Lowering her slowly, her pussy lips are right at my mouth. My beard tickles her skin, and she freezes. I stop.

"You're in control, Hana."

She blinks a few times then nods as I guide her to my mouth. My stomach tightens, and I turn my head to kiss her inner thigh. She's warm and damp from the water, and I'm ready to make her feel so good.

Returning to the center, I slip out my tongue, touching her lightly, finding my way to her clit. Her eyes close, and she inhales sharply.

I slow down, moving my lips to her thigh again, kissing the crease of her leg.

Her lips part, and she whispers. "It's okay… It feels good. It's you. I want you."

Carefully, I begin again, tracing my tongue gently over and over, going deeper with every pass, curling my tongue in her warm little cunt. A moan rises from her chest, and I keep my eyes on her face, watching her expression.

Her eyes squeeze shut, and her full bottom lip slips between her teeth. She's not afraid, and my movements grow more ravenous. Using my lips, I pull her skin. Moving lower, I test her wetness. She's right there, and I move my face higher, circling that little bud with my tongue as it grows harder, sucking it as her hips drive forward on their own, leaving my hands.

She tastes like clean water and ocean air, and as she rides my face, her juices coat my chin. She's out of my hands, gripping the top of my head as her narrow hips buck frantically.

"So good," she gasps. "Oh, God."

Pink rises in her cheeks, touching the tops of her breasts, and a new surge of emotion rises in my chest–pride. She trusts me. She's made it through her fear.

She's completely mine.

"Oh, fuck." Her voice breaks, and her hand shoots forward to the wall behind my head. She takes one more quick grind before she breaks into shudders. "Oh, shit, oh, shit, oh…"

Her thighs tremble, and I lick her again, causing her ass to jump. "Oh, no, it's too much."

A smile breaks across her face, and I watch as she breaks into a laugh, sliding down into the water. Reaching up, she pulls my mouth to hers. Our teeth click because I'm smiling, too, which I've been doing a lot lately.

She's given me another first, and in doing it, she's stolen another stone from the wall I'd so carefully constructed around my heart.

"That was amazing," she sighs. "I can't believe it felt so good."

Gathering her in my arms, I slide my thumb over her full lips. "You're amazing." I kiss her temple, then her cheek. "I never want you to be afraid when you're with me."

"I never am." She traces a finger along my brow. "I've only felt completely safe, since the first day you kept me from falling."

I'll always keep her from falling.

Lying on my back in the bed, I watch the ceiling fan turn overhead as I hold her in my arms. We made love again after she came in the tub, and as my orgasm raced through my body, it felt as though our souls united.

I wasn't sure where she left off and where I began.

We didn't talk anymore before she fell asleep. Now her face is at my chest and her arm wraps across my waist. Turning to the side, I study her profile, her small upturned nose, her soft, curly hair.

A little snore rumbles from her lips, and I smile (*again!*) as I lightly trace a curl away from her cheek, watching the way it wraps around my finger.

It's a dangerous game pretending we're perfectly safe here, no threats, no one closing in on us. If we follow Dirk's plan, I'll have to leave her alone with Blake, and I'll have to face the terror such a prospect evokes in me.

My palms get sweaty and my breath is shallow. I've got to prepare her more. She'll never be as safe alone as she would be with me, but maybe I'll be able to focus when the time comes. I need her to feel as confident when she's alone as she does when I'm with her, and she won't if I'm not.

I'm pleased by how quickly she learned to handle a gun. She's a good shot, and tomorrow, I'll teach her hand-to-hand techniques. Filtering through my thoughts, I make a plan. It's the only way I can calm my anxiety about what lies ahead.

In this time we've spent together I've also seen her for the woman she's becoming. She's not a baby. She's not a helpless little girl. She's smart and strong, and I'm proud to watch her emerging from the past, spreading her wings, and being brave.

I like to think I'm a part of her growth.

"You are worth everything I've done and will do." My voice is quiet as I slide the soft curls back and forth in my fingers. "Part of letting you fly is trusting your wings."

She exhales a soft noise, and I close my eyes, doing my best to take my own advice, drifting asleep to the sound of her steady breathing.

CHAPTER 17

Hana

SCAR INSISTED WE COME TO UNCLE HUGH'S STABLES IMMEDIATELY after breakfast. I walk over to the stall where Training Day, my uncle's prized stallion stands with his head over the dutch door, curiously watching us.

"How's it going, Trainey? Wishing someone would take you for a gallop?"

Behind me, Bear is arranging hay in a pile at one end of the small stadium. It's a cool morning, but sweat glistens on his muscles, which bulge and flex every time he lifts a bale. He's wearing a thin, white tank top and gray sweatpants, and his long hair is tied up in a bun. It's very inspirational.

Straightening, he motions for me to come to him. "Ready?"

"For a roll in the hay? Yes, please!"

"Focus, Hana."

He made me wear workout clothes–capri leggings and a jog bra–and when I get to where he's standing, breathing hard he lifts my hand in his.

"This is the correct way to make a fist." He curls my fingers, placing my thumbs outside them. "Don't hold onto your thumbs. If you hit something, you'll break them."

"Ouch." I look up, and his face is so close to mine, I give him a little kiss.

"Hana." He scolds, but a smile curls his lips.

It's all the encouragement I need. "In case you forgot, I had a real breakthrough last night in the bathtub. That was some serious personal growth going on, and I don't just mean your penis."

An actual laugh escapes his lips on an exhale, and I grin as warmth spreads through my stomach. "I noticed. It was very gratifying."

"Gratifying?" I arch an eyebrow at his stuffy word-choice. "I was hoping we'd do a little more *gratifying* personal-growth, face-riding this morning."

His expression resumes its usual focus. "After your lesson. If you're a good girl."

Pressing my lips together, I like the way he says *good girl* all sexy and low, like it's an order. "Yes, sir."

Wolf eyes flicker to mine in a way that makes my knees go liquid. "You're making it hard to focus in those sweats, giving me bedroom eyes."

"Come here."

I hop over to where he's standing, and he turns me so my back is to him. His cock is at my back, and I detect a bit of a rise. "I like this lesson already."

"If someone comes up behind you, threatening you, what would you do?"

"Scream and run as hard as I can for as long as possible."

He releases me and crosses his muscular arms, which are on full display in that wife beater.

His full, kissable lips press into a line as he nods. "If they haven't grabbed you yet, that's the perfect plan. Running away is always the best defense."

"Yay! Lesson done."

"But what if he grabs you before you're ready?"

"I'm dead."

"Hana." It's a low growl, and I shrug. "I mean, look at me. I'm not the buffest person in the family. The best I can hope for is a head start."

"That's why we're doing this. Now, come here."

Once again, I'm wrapped in his strong arms, my back against his chest. I want to melt, but I don't want him mad at me, so I focus. His strong arm goes around my shoulders, and his warm breath skates over my neck, sending yummy chills down my spine.

"If you're grabbed, I want you to think *SING*."

"Oh, like in *Miss Congeniality?*"

"What?"

"The movie with Sandra Bullock? Where she's an FBI agent, and she has to go undercover at the beauty pageant? It's so cute. They have this whole makeover part–the bikini wax is hilarious."

"I need you to focus."

"Sorry." I clear my throat. Of course, he hasn't seen a Sandra Bullock movie. "Okay, *SING*. Let's do this."

"Solar plexus, Instep, Nose, Groin."

"I'm not really going to do that to you, am I?"

"It's okay, I'll dodge. I want you to practice it so if it happens, it's instinctive."

"I don't know if I can actually try to hurt you."

"I told you, I won't be there." He releases me. "Now, I'm going to come up behind you and grab you fast. Get ready."

I don't point out that him telling me to get ready sort of defeats the whole purpose. I suppose the sooner we get this over with, the sooner I can seduce him in my darkroom.

"I've got you now," he growls, wrapping an arm around my neck.

Closing my eyes, I jam my elbow back into his stomach as fast as I can.

"Ow! Shit! Oh, my God!" Bending forward, I clutch my elbow, squinting my eyes against the pain. "I think I broke it!"

"What the hell?" He walks to where I've collapsed on a bale of hay, holding my arm.

"It's like hitting a brick wall." I rub the spot where I hit his abs as the pain gradually fades away. "Why do I have to learn all this anyway? You're always with me."

"What if I'm not? What about when you're in New York for the show?"

"Wait–you're not going to be at my show?" Sadness hits *me* in the solar plexus.

"Of course, I'll be at your show." He sits beside me, putting a strong arm around my shoulders. "But I'm sure there will be times when we're not together."

Looking up at him, all the sadness washes away. "You're worried about me. That's so sweet."

"It's not sweet. It's realistic. I'll get you a can of pepper spray."

"You big faker. You are so sweet." Turning to step into his chest, I trace my finger over his cheek as he inhales deeply. "Stop acting impatient and come with me to the darkroom. I want to show you the pictures I took of you."

Scar stands speechless in front of the poster-sized photos of him on the beach. My stomach is so tight, I can't breathe. I want him to say something, anything. Instead, he places both hands behind his neck. It's a sexy pose that has me reaching for my camera.

"You are truly an artist." His voice is hushed, and he walks down the line, inspecting all the poster-sized prints I hung to dry.

Embarrassment heats my face. I don't have an answer for that, and I feel all squishy inside. It's such an amazing compliment.

"A photographer once told me we're not God; we don't create our subjects. If we're good, we find the spark of life inside and capture it."

"You captured it." His voice is quiet, and he pauses at the prints of Pepper and Ainsley. Then he returns to the images of him on the beach, shaking his head. "You're the first person who found the spark in me."

I'm not sure whether to be happy or sad he would think this. "I made something for you."

Going to the table, I take out a wallet-sized print of the photo I took of us in bed, our first time together. Despite his running away after one shot, it came out really well. My eyes are shining with a happiness I didn't know I possessed, and his gaze is intense and broody, but so full of love.

"You can put it in your wallet or a frame." I'm suddenly self-conscious at my presumption. "Or not."

He takes the photo and studies it silently. My throat is so tight, I feel a little queasy. Finally, he glances up at me. "I'll keep it with me always."

I don't know why that makes me want to cry. Exhaling a little laugh, I tilt my head to the side, thinking of the question I've always wanted to ask. "How were you burned?"

He takes a beat, then in the darkness, he tells me.

"I was with Hutch. We'd just finished our last tour together—when he was still a Marine. We were driving back to the base when we came upon a restaurant fire. It was a remote location. The people had done all they could to get everyone out, but a little girl was still inside."

"So you ran into a burning building to save a little girl?" I can't hold back anymore. Stepping forward, I wrap my arms around him, placing my cheek against his chest. "You're a real hero."

His body tenses, and I lift my face to meet his eyes. "What's wrong?"

"I did something brave—some would call it foolish. It doesn't make me a hero."

"Isn't that what real heroes always say?"

He shakes his head as if to argue, and I step closer.

"You're a hero to me."

He still seems uncomfortable, but I know what he's done for me.

"You say I found the spark in you, but I only captured the way you were looking at me." Sliding my hand up his chest, I clutch the thin tank with my fingers. "Come down here."

His brow relaxes, and he leans down for my kiss. Our lips part, and his tongue slides against mine. It lights the flame simmering beneath my skin. Curling my fingers in his shirt, I drag him closer until my butt hits the table.

I'm ravenous, needing all of him. Sliding my hand down, I cup and massage the erection growing beneath his sexy as fuck sweatpants.

He groans as my fingers move inside the fabric to his bare skin, no underwear. "Will your uncle hear?"

"I have the light on. No one bothers me when I have the light on." His chin lifts, and he looks towards the door.

"I don't know."

Hooking my fingers in my yoga pants, I quickly slide them down my legs. "Please fuck me," I beg.

Even in the dim light of the darkroom, I see the desire flare in his eyes. Closing the space between us, he lifts me as easily as if I weigh nothing, and in a few steps my back is to the wall.

His hands move under my panties to my drenched core, and he slips a finger inside, moving the side of it back and forth over my humming clit. I exhale a moan, loving every aggressive touch of his hand.

"Why are you so wet, beautiful girl?" His low groan thrills me to my core. "Tell me."

"Because I want you to fuck me. I need you inside me. Please." The words come out in a rush, and his lips seal over mine.

His beard scrapes my skin, and his tongue invades my mouth. Gripping his neck, I kiss him back with the same force, curling my tongue with his, devouring him with the same level of eagerness.

He lowers his pants, and my belly tenses. I want him so much, I actually ache. The tip of his cock nudges at my core, and I lift my knees. His hands grip my ass, and in one swift move, he glides fully into me.

"Oh, fuck, yes," I moan.

My fingers curl against his shoulders, and I suck his tongue as I pull his ass closer with my heels. He's impaling me against the wall, and it feels so fucking good.

Another groan strains from his throat, and our mouths break apart. "You feel too good, angel. I can't hold back…" His voice breaks, and a flutter squeezes my core.

Arching my back I ride him. I'm on fire, a column of need, and he's inside me pumping, stroking my orgasm higher.

Pushing with my thighs, I find his rhythm and match it. My eyes roll closed, and the heat in my pussy begins to tingle and build into pleasure.

As if driven by primal need, I claw at my top, ripping it over my head to free my breasts. His mouth clamps on a hardened nipple, and I let out a loud moan as electricity ricochets through my insides.

I'm trembling, fluttering, coming undone in the most intense way. I move faster, gripping at his shirt, needing his skin against mine. His mouth moves higher, climbing to my shoulder, and when his teeth bite my skin, the orgasm explodes in my belly.

"God, yes," I cry as my eyes roll shut.

Our thighs are slick, and I hear him coming as well. He pumps once more then stiffens, holding inside me and jerking slightly. He lifts his chin as if to howl, and as his cock pulses, flooding me with his come, another shimmer of orgasm tightens my insides.

Stretching higher, I slide my tongue from his collarbone to his Adam's apple. Salt fills my mouth, and I hum with satisfaction.

My pussy is throbbing. His taste is in my mouth, and I'm surrounded by the rich scents of sandalwood, sweat, and desire.

We're fused together, breathing heavily, stunned and satisfied by our hunger and our passion. His large hands still hold my ass, and he levels his eyes on mine.

He blinks once, and a slow grin curls his lips. My beautiful monster, my gorgeous hero.

CHAPTER 18

Scar

H UTCH PACES THE OFFICE LAYING OUT THE PLAN, BUT I'M distracted. The only thing I can think about is Hana, loving her, being with her.

I'm like a teenager having his first sexual experience. I can't get enough of her, and I can't think of anything but how soon I can be inside her again.

"So next week they'll stay at their mother's apartment in the Andover building." Hutch slides his finger over his iPad. "Dirk booked us rooms in a hotel around the block under assumed names. We'll have to be careful with our comings and goings so we're not detected."

"What?" My attention snaps to him at once.

"Glad you could join us," Hutch quips, but I'm not in the mood for teasing.

"Why are they going to New York next week? Hana's show isn't for another month."

"They have to meet with the gallery curator. Apparently, it

takes weeks to prepare for these things. They want to see what she's got, arrange the rooms, create marketing materials. Blake said they're actually starting a little late, but it's a small gallery."

Fuck. My chin drops. I still haven't talked to her about our plan, my background. "When are they expected to be there?"

"Blake said Monday. They're taking Hugh's private jet."

"Does Hana know?"

"I have no idea, but I expect Blake will discuss it with her."

I still have time…

Hutch continues. "It's the perfect opportunity to see if anyone comes sniffing around. It's a low-key affair; no one will expect us to be there. Not a lot of publicity like the night of the opening. If someone's going to make a move, this is a great time for it."

"And by *move*, we mean…" I'm on edge, feeling like I'm playing fast catchup.

"Hell, I don't know. It could be anything. Retaliation for Greg's death? Another blackmail attempt? Hana owes money all over town."

"If it's blackmail, why not text?"

"They tried that last time, and it didn't work." Dirk's voice is thoughtful. "Maybe they'll try kicking it up a notch, cornering them in a back alley."

The suggestion makes my throat tight. I need to get her that pepper spray.

"It could be something as simple as menacing eye contact." Hutch shrugs. "It's a fishing expedition."

I don't like it.

The bell dings above the door, interrupting our meeting, and a well-dressed man steps into the office. He has light brown hair and large brown eyes that seem familiar to me, but I can't quite place why.

He's fit like an athlete, and he glances from me to Hutch then to Dirk, who stands from where he'd been reclining with his feet on the desk. "Can we help you?"

"I'm sorry, I was looking for Hutch Winston?"

Dirk glances at the two of us. "What's this about, friend?"

I shift in my stance, crossing my arms over my chest. This guy isn't tall. He might be five-ten, and he's clean cut. He could be a lawyer or some other white-collar type.

"It's about his sister, Judy. I have reason to believe we might… share a daughter?"

My eyebrows shoot up–I see it now. The big brown eyes.

You could hear a pin drop. I glance at Hutch, who looks like someone threw a pan of ice water in his face.

Dirk continues, like a silent bomb didn't just explode. "And you are?"

"Teal Masters." He holds out a hand to Hutch's brother. "Are you Mr. Winston?"

"I'm Dirk Winston." Dirk's brow arches. "Teal Masters… I recognize that name. You play ball?"

The guy's chin dips, and he grins as if he's embarrassed. "Shortstop for the Brooklyn Cyclones. I'm surprised you've heard of me."

"I have friends in Brooklyn. I guess Judy did, too." He looks over at Hutch. "This is my brother Hutch. Judy was our younger sister."

"The Brooklyn Cyclones?" Hutch's voice is careful.

"Minor League Baseball." The guy holds back, which leads me to believe he's not dumb. "Judy did some freelance work for the team, mostly marketing and stuff. She was a good friend."

"So you were friends?" I can sense the protective heat vibrating off my friend.

"We palled around." His eyes drop to his shoes. "One night we were out drinking, and I guess we had a little too much. I didn't think anything of it. I definitely wasn't angry, but she disappeared."

"Nobody disappears." Dirk's voice is quiet, but even he has an edge now.

"She didn't come into work again, and I guess I got

distracted by the new season. Time passed, and before I realized it…" His voice lowers. "A lot of time had passed."

"So you never called her." Hutch crosses his arms, and I wouldn't want to be on the receiving end of his older-brother rage.

Teal seems to understand his position. "Hey, I'm not looking for trouble. Judy never called me either, and when I started looking for her, I found out she'd passed. Then one of the guys said he heard she'd had a baby. I just wanted to know if there's anything I need to know or do…"

"Where are you staying?" Hutch isn't interested in his bullshit, and I can't say I blame him.

"I'm over in Miranda Beach."

"Good." Hutch levels his gaze on him. "Stay there. You start poking around, asking questions, and the whole town will be talking. I don't want that for Pepper."

"Pepper?" The guy looks up at him. "That was my mother's nickname."

A low growl comes from Hutch's throat, and Dirk crosses the room, taking Teal by the arm. "Let's go for a walk. I don't like you, but I'm less lethal than he is."

Teal's brow furrows, and I know he wants to say more. He wants to defend himself, but Dirk knows his brother better than any of us. Dirk was here when Judy passed, and he knows how hard it hit Hutch. He also knows how protective Hutch is of Pepper–we all are.

The door slams shut, and I look at my friend. His nostrils are flared like a raging bull, and I consider calling Blake. She's the only person he'll listen to when he's like this, which is saying a lot.

Still, it would take too long for her to get here, and I can't let him go off this way.

"I don't know anything about family." My voice is low, and I clear my throat. "I was dumped in the fucking tundra at ten and left to figure it out."

Hutch cuts his green eyes at me. "That fucker is not you. Not by a longshot."

"Still, it takes a lot of courage to face your past. I think Pepper would want to know her dad came looking for her." My voice is grave, but I speak from the heart. "I would've wanted to know."

My friend's jaw grinds, and his eyes slide closed. "If he hurts her… If he breaks her heart or makes her hope for something he can't deliver–"

Nodding, I understand his concern. Hutch loves Pepper like his own daughter. She's been his since Judy died when she was nine. Even before that, Judy lived with him full-time, so he was there when Pepper was a baby. Now that Judy is dead, Pepper is all he has left of his sister.

"You've always made good decisions. I know you'll handle this right."

"I have no idea how to handle this. I have no idea what I'm doing almost all the time when it comes to Pepper." It's the most vulnerable I've ever seen him, and fuck, I don't know what to do with that–or what to tell him.

"Talk to Blake." It might be a cop-out, but still… "She's a woman; she's been Pepper's age. She lost her dad when she was young. For that matter, you might talk to Hana. She and Pepper are really close."

His brow furrows, and he nods. "I didn't trust Hana at first, but I was wrong about that. She might be a good place to start."

"Hana's come a long way." Even I can hear the pride in my voice. "She'll help you."

Exhaling a low groan, he scrubs his fingers over his dark brow. "Like we have time for this right now."

"Maybe Carmen can help while we're in New York. Or Lurlene?" I'm grasping at straws, because I understand him being focused on Blake but also worrying about Pepper. "If you need to stay behind–"

"I'm not sending Blake to New York unprotected."

"Dirk and I will be there, and I think Hana's the main one we need to focus on." As much as I hate to say it.

His jaw clenches, and he looks down. I'll talk to Blake. I'll think about it and let you know.

"Don't worry. I won't let anything happen to your lady." Gripping his shoulder, I give him a tight smile. "Or mine."

CHAPTER 19

Hana

I'M HANGING OUT IN THE STORE WITH CARMEN WHEN DIRK WALKS through the door. We both straighten, and I hop over to give him a hug.

"Hey, bro! Are you behaving today?"

His brow is furrowed, and he seems distracted. "There's a fellow outside I'd like you to meet."

Twisting my lips, I'm not sure what to make of that response. "Is he a cop?"

"What?" Dirk blinks at me, and I shrug.

"I asked if you were behaving, and you want me to meet some man?"

The bell rings on the cash register, signaling the end of Carmen's transaction. A small group of tourists ambles out the door, and she walks over to where we're standing.

"Hey, Dirk, what's up?"

The store is empty, and he glances over his shoulder before

leaning closer. "I've got this guy with me, Teal Masters. He says he's Pepper's dad."

"Pepper's dad!" Carmen's eyebrows shoot up, and Dirk lifts his hand.

"Keep it down. We don't want the whole town talking."

"It's only us here, Sherlock." She cuts her eyes at him, and I think she's right. Carmen and Dirk are too snarky for their own good.

"I love his name." I try to diffuse the tension. "Teal Masters–it's like a painting or an actor."

"He's a minor-league baseball player."

"That explains a lot," Carmen quips.

"Would you talk to him, Hana? You know Pepper as well as anyone. Feel him out, get an idea what he's up to. I told him about you."

My eyebrows shoot up, and I look from Carmen back to Dirk. "Sure. I mean, I'm glad to help, but I don't know what I could possibly do–"

"Come on." Dirk takes my hand, and I wave to Carmen as he drags me out of the store.

Waiting outside on the sidewalk is a very handsome man. He's wearing a suit, and he's about the same height as Dirk, maybe a little shorter.

He has a quick smile with a charming, deep dimple right in his cheek. He has a square jaw, and his sandy brown hair is a little shaggy and floppy. But what seals the deal are his big brown eyes–just like Pepper's.

"Oh, yeah." I nod, speaking softly. "He's her dad."

"Teal, this is my future sister-in-law, Hana van Hamilton. She and Pepper are close, so I thought you might want to talk to her." Dirk steps back. "I'll wait here with Carmen if you want to take a walk."

Teal seems stunned, and I confess, I have no idea what Dirk is expecting to happen. Still, I cross my arms and start walking slowly. Teal joins me, and we stroll down the few blocks comprising downtown Hamiltown.

"Van Hamilton," he notes. "So you're one of the founding families?"

"I guess so," I shrug with a little laugh. "I was born in Manhattan and stayed there until I was twenty. We've only recently moved here, and before that, I'd only visited a few times. My uncle Hugh is the real deal."

He frowns up at me. "Dirk said you're close with Pepper?"

"Yeah, we kind of hit it off from the start. We have a lot in common. I lost my dad when I was about her age, and our families tend to be very… overprotective of us."

We've reached the end of Main Street, and I look down the hill to the left, where the softball fields are located. "Let's walk over here."

Following the road to the baseball diamond, we stop at the chest-high fence, and Teal leans forward, resting his forearms on top.

"I always loved the game." Glancing up at me, he arches an eyebrow. "At the end of last season, I tore my ACL for the second time."

"Ouch!"

"Yeah, I'm out. I could do rehab, but it's a long recovery. I just don't have it in me to try again at my age."

"So you came here?" I confess, I'm not happy to hear he's only in town because his career ended.

"I know, you're thinking cocky bastard." He nods, reading my expression. "But it's a scary feeling to lose your reason for living. I started going back through my timeline, thinking of people I'd lost along the way. Judy stood out above the rest."

I think about how I've only recently found my purpose. Who am I to judge Teal Masters?

Exhaling softly, I nod. "Everyone has regrets. It's never too late to try and make up for your mistakes. At least I hope not."

Pushing off the fence, he straightens, facing me. "Would

you go to dinner with me? You could tell me all about my daughter, swap regret stories…"

Blinking fast, I shake my head. "No, I'm sorry. I'm sort of… seeing someone."

Even though we've never officially defined our relationship. Scar and I are a thing, right?

"I didn't mean to offend you." He holds up his hands. "I only thought it would be nicer to talk in a restaurant, sitting down with food and wine. Why is it easier to talk with a glass of wine?"

He exhales a laugh, and remorse permeates the air around him. My empathy is at an all-time high, and I reach out to squeeze his forearm.

"I'd really like to help you. And I love Pepper so much." Chewing my lip, my eyes dart up the hill to where Scar's office is located. "Let me talk to my boyfriend, and I'll let you know what he says. If not dinner, we could meet up at Steamy Beans for coffee?"

His expression brightens slightly. "I'll send you a text. Then you'll have my number if you want to reach me."

Walking through the foyer at Uncle Hugh's, I can't help thinking about Pepper and her dad, and wondering how in the world I might be helpful in that situation. Teal seems nice enough, but I know all of us are hyper-focused on keeping that little girl safe.

Maybe dinner would be a good idea. I could grill him and find out his intentions, if he really means to be a dad to her or if he's just satisfying some biological curiosity.

Sliding my phone out of my pocket, I quickly text Scar. **Dirk introduced me to Teal Masters. He invited me to dinner.** Hitting send, I chew my lip, reconsidering my hasty dismissal. I can be a private investigator, too.

My phone dings, and I look down to see Scar's reply. *Not tonight. Need to talk. I'm heading your way, then maybe tomorrow we can all have dinner?*

His possessiveness makes me smile, and a surge of anticipation at seeing him so soon heats my stomach. I love how just the thought of seeing him again is like a hit of dopamine straight to my brain.

I like that idea. See you soon.

Sliding my phone into my pocket, I walk to the kitchen, where Blake is pouring a cup of coffee. "Hey, I'm glad you're here. We need to talk."

"Everyone needs to talk these days. What's on your mind?"

She gives me a little smile-frown. "I don't know what that means, but I'm talking about your art show. Jill called from the gallery, and they need us to come in for a planning meeting. I told her we could be there on Monday. Will that give you enough time to prepare?"

My stomach jumps, and nervous jitters race through my limbs. "I think so? What do I need to do for a planning meeting? Will it just be me?"

I'm talking too fast, and Blake puts her mug on the island, closing the space between us. "Of course not, I'll be there with you. Don't worry. I've seen what you've done, and the prints are gorgeous."

"Thanks." I blink up at her, feeling self-conscious. "I wish I had more of you."

"What you've got is amazing. They're going to love them all. I really like the ones you took of Scar. They're passionate and exciting." She pauses, giving me a sly smile. "Speaking of, I walked down to check on you the other day, and it sounded like you were having a little passionate excitement."

"I don't know what you mean." I try to act coy, but I can't hide the smile splitting my cheeks. "I'm very professional."

Blake's smile melts into affection, and she pulls me in for a hug. "Yes, you are. I was worried you might have trouble when it came to, you know… because of what happened."

Nodding, I trace a nail along the wooden countertop. "We had a little hiccup starting out, but he helped me work through it. He's helped me so much."

"Well, that's good to hear. I was worried his past might be triggering for you." She exhales, shaking her head. "It was a little for me. It's still hard for me to think about, but Hutch vouched for him. I guess, if Hutch trusts him…"

"What are you talking about?"

My sister's gray eyes flicker to mine, and her slim brows lower. "That he was Victor's bodyguard?"

"What?" The word escapes on my last breath. Clutching the bar, my head goes light.

Blake catches my arm, and I manage to stay on my feet. "He didn't tell you? It's why we're pretending to go to New York alone. They're hoping we might draw out the rest of Victor's crew."

He didn't tell me. Shards of glass rip at my chest from the inside. He was there? He protected that demon?

"Hana, are you okay?" Blake gives my arm a little shake.

Swallowing the bile in my throat, I shake my head, holding onto the counter as I take a step back. "I'm okay. I'll be okay. Really. I just remembered, I need to do something."

She doesn't believe me, but I can't stand here anymore. Catching the door jamb, the wall, I make my way to the stairs. I need to be alone.

"Jill said they'd like to know your theme—if you have one." Blake calls after me, but roaring is in my ears.

I can't seem to breathe, and the staircase feels like it's stretching higher the more I climb. Finally, I'm on the landing, and I just make it through my bedroom door when my lungs give out. I don't turn on the light. Dropping to my hands and knees, I crawl to the corner beside my dresser. It's a narrow, dark space.

It's how I would hide when Victor would come to my room.

Pressing my forehead against my knees, I squeeze the sides of my arms, drawing into the smallest version of myself.

No one can stop him. No one is stronger than him. A shudder rattles my chest at the memory of my childish words.

Someone *was* there. Someone protected him.

Scar was the reason no one could stop that demon.

Scar was the monster protecting him.

A sharp inhale rips through my lungs, and a sound like a wounded animal echoes in the empty space. It's part wail, part audible gasp. It's my heart, breaking into pieces.

"Hana?" The deep voice drifts to me from the door, and I let out a little yelp before clapping my hand over my mouth.

I was always bad at hiding.

Heavy boots sound on my dark wood floors, then they're muffled by the fluffy white rug. I squeeze my arms harder, doing my best to grow smaller.

"Hana, where are you?"

I don't answer, and he stands in the center of the room, waiting.

Seconds tick past, but I don't move.

He exhales deeply, speaking into the emptiness. "Blake told me you know about my past." A heavy pause, the sound of movement. "I never wanted you to hear it that way. I wanted to tell you myself, but I kept waiting for the right moment."

More silence.

Heavy silence.

Impermeable silence.

Only his voice, saying my name.

CHAPTER 20

I HEAR HER BREATH TREMBLING IN THE DARK. I HEAR HER SILENT TEARS, and I don't want to leave her. I want to sling every piece of furniture out of the way until I find her. Then I want to hold her in my arms, protect her from the truth. I want to dry her tears, absorb her sadness.

But I put it there. She wouldn't be in this place if it weren't for me.

I should have told her.

I didn't want to tell her.

I didn't want it to be true.

But it is.

I taught her to trust me, then I ripped it all away. without any warning. I was so consumed by her light, lost in learning every part of her body.

When she gave me everything, I actually wanted to believe we'd erased the past, it was only us and nothing else existed.

It was never only us, and I knew I was playing a danger-ous game.

So I force myself to give her space. I will my boots to move, to walk away from the sound of her sorrow, tearing out my insides and leaving them at her feet.

Rocks are in my throat, grinding out my voice. I place the can of pepper spray on her nightstand and pull the door open.

Looking back one last time, I summon the only words left to say. "I'm sorry."

Such a feeble offering in the face of my mistake.

Blake isn't in the kitchen when I return. I arrived with the can of pepper spray, all prepared to come clean, and she merely glared at me and walked out the room.

She didn't have to say a word. I knew what had happened, and I knew she was right to be angry with me. I should have told Hana about my past, my connection to Victor Petrov, be-fore I ever touched her the first time.

I should have given her the choice to be with a man who would protect someone like that.

Continuing out, I walk the grounds to the stables. The quiet beasts lean their heads over the doors of their stalls, and I walk to the small stadium where I tried to teach her self-defense.

My body warms at the memory of hers in my arms. She kissed my cheek. She scrubbed her little ass against my cock. A growl rises in my throat when I remember how happy she was, trusting me completely.

I had planned to tell her that day. If I weren't so caught up in my lust, consumed with wanting her, afraid she might walk away, I'd have spared her this pain, spared us both.

Clenching my fists, I walk away from the site of these re-cent memories. I understand the old ways of self-flagellation. I think I'd feel better if someone kicked my ass right now. I've never felt so deserving.

The black thoroughbred slips his long nose over the stall door, and I pause, sliding my hand down his shiny face. For a time, I behaved like a beast, going and doing whatever I was told.

Until I broke out of my cage and ran to this town.

"I heard Blake fussing at Hutch about something you'd done." Hugh's gravelly chuckle greets me. "I have a stable manager, and a bodyguard. I could possibly use a driver."

"As far as I know, I haven't been fired yet." I glance up at him, forcing a tight smile.

"That's good. The girls have a tendency to overreact at times." Using his cane, Hugh walks closer to where I stand. "I suppose we all do."

I reach up and scrub behind the horse's ear. "He's a beautiful animal."

"His running days are over, I'm afraid."

I have a feeling I know the reason, and my mind drifts to what he just said. "Why do you have a bodyguard? Hutch checks on you regularly, and he's close enough if something happens."

The old man's eyes level on me. "This isn't your first visit to my stables."

"I was here just the other day–"

"You were here seven years ago, before you started working with Hutch Winston."

Tightness grips my stomach, but I can't deny it. Even back then, when I wore long-sleeves and suits to hide my more distinctive features, I was still too tall to blend in with the scenery.

"Yes." It's all I care to say.

"My nephew Charles had a horse he occasionally kept here, Shadow of the Moon. You brought a doctor to see him." Distaste is in the old man's tone. "Is that what they call them? Doctors do good, but that man seemed intent on evil."

Shame burns in my neck, cementing what I already felt about myself. "I was his security detail. Victor Petrov's brother Simon gave me my orders."

"Your orders." Hugh nods, and we walk slowly up the path

to the big house. "It was not a military position from what I could tell, so it must've been something else."

He stops at the edge of the driveway, where my black truck is parked. "It was something like servitude."

The old man's lips tighten, and he lifts his chin. "I don't judge a man for his mistakes. I judge a man for what he does to make up for them. Hutch trusts you. You've made an enormous impact on my niece. I believe there's more to you than meets the eye. I hope you don't let me down."

With that, he carries on, swinging his cane as he strolls to the front door.

My eyes float up to the window of Hana's room, and grief aches in my chest.

I don't want to let him down, but how can I make this up to her?

CHAPTER 21

AT SOME POINT, I CRAWLED FROM MY HIDING PLACE BETWEEN THE dresser and the wall and into my bed. My old friends were waiting, lurking in the dark corners of my mind, swiping their cold hands at my ankles as I tried to sleep.

Kicking my feet, I curled into a ball under the heavy blankets, pushing back on the whispers that I would never be free, I could never trust anyone, I only attracted demons and liars.

I wrapped my arms around my knees and tried to sleep in a tense ball, back in that house on fire, searching for safety.

Finally, the glow of sunrise lit the edge of the horizon. As it rose higher, the shadows receded, and a fist of anger rose in their place.

Yes, I'd been dealt a bad hand. I'd been abused. I grew up afraid, going to bed every night not knowing who might enter my room.

I'd also left that behind. I'd spent months in therapy. I moved to this town, got away from the people who kept me in the dark. I've worked so hard, and I have come a long way, dammit.

So I trusted someone who lied to me. He wasn't my boyfriend. He barely told me anything about himself–other than he isn't a hero.

He's not.

And I've learned to stand on my own.

My gallery show is coming up, and I have friends who care about me, who are counting on me. I'm wounded, but I have to be strong now. I know how to shoot a gun. I know how to escape an attacker–run like hell and scream my head off.

It's time to be my own hero.

Throwing back my blankets, I go to the armoire and take out black leggings and a sleeveless chambray shirt. I'm going to eat breakfast, and I'm going to stand on my own two feet. Maybe I did love him, but like my sister said, I've come so far.

My hand grazes something cold on my nightstand as I head for the door, and I almost falter in my newfound determination.

A can of pepper spray sits on my nightstand.

Breath hiccups in my chest, and I cover my mouth to hold back the sob. Tears sting in my eyes, and I blink fast.

It hurts.

It hurts so much. Oh, God… I'm not sure I can do this.

A sinkhole where my heart should be opens. The soil crumbles and tries to drag me down, but I close my eyes and grip the doorknob.

"Come on, Hana," I whisper shakily.

A tremor is in my voice, but I tighten my stomach muscles, preparing to fight. Closing my eyes against the pain, I picture a bird, one of those little chicks pecking and fighting so hard to get out of that shell, struggling to survive with wet wings and ugly scars.

"Come on," I urge. "You have to keep moving."

Pushing my feet to move, I step out the door. I take one

step, then another, then another until I'm moving faster. I will face this day, and I will keep moving forward.

It's the only thing I can do, because I'm not giving up.

"This is amazing!" Pepper's voice is hushed, and she walks along the line of prints hanging on the line in my darkroom. "I look like a professional skater!"

The door is open, and the white lights are on. My insides are quiet, numb, but I wanted to keep my tidying date with my little friend. She wanted to see her photos.

I was afraid to come down here, but I took a deep breath, swallowing against the invisible hand squeezing my throat.

Someone has been here. All the prints I'd made of Scar have been taken down, and I assume stored. I'll check in with Blake about that later.

"You're a natural athlete, Pep." My voice is quiet. "Everything you do is impressive."

"Everything except English." She turns pouty.

"What are you talking about?"

"Ms. Ingalls said my writing is stilted and mechanical. She said I don't give good examples from the text, and it's like reading a recipe."

"Dang." My eyebrows rise. "That's pretty harsh. Have you told Hutch?"

"No!" She makes a face at me like I've lost my mind. "He made straight As in all his subjects. You think he wants to know I'm an idiot?"

"You're not an idiot." I give her the slant eye. It's just the two of us in the room, and she's flipping through a stack of prints I plan to take with us on Monday. "I think he'd be happy to help you or get you a tutor if he knows you're struggling. Not everybody's born knowing how to do everything."

Wrinkling her nose, she looks up at me. "It sure seems

that way. Ainsley makes *A*s in all her classes, and she's good at sports, too."

"She's not as good as you." I put my arm around my little buddy's shoulder. "I've never seen anyone play ball the way you did last year, not even professionals. If there's an award for Little League players, you should've got it."

Pepper shrugs, and she points to the photo I took of Ainsley doing an arabesque behind the park bench. "She's prettier than me, too."

Frustration twists in my chest. I remember these days she's experiencing so well. "When I was taking pictures, it looked like you were having a lot of fun. Isn't that the most important thing?"

She doesn't answer, so I continue. "It also seemed like Tommy and his friends were pretty impressed with your skating skills. Not that it matters what other people think."

"Everybody says that, but it *matters*."

Taking a beat, I hand her a photo of Tommy sitting across from her. He's holding a slushie with a red straw spoon towards her, and her head is tilted back laughing.

"It feels that way sometimes, but I'll tell you something I learned the hard way."

She takes the photo, studying it. When she blinks up to me, she's really listening now. I say a little prayer, then I continue with what I'm thinking.

"If you spend all your time worrying about what other people think, you'll miss out on all the amazing things happening around you."

Her lips twist, and my stomach sinks. I can't tell if she got what I was trying to say.

"Wow. This is amazing!" She pulls a print from the stack, and my breath catches.

All my emotions surge to the surface.

"Yes," I manage to whisper, tears heating my eyes.

She's holding a photo of Scar on the beach. It's one of the

ones where he's looking dead-on at the camera, and the intensity of his gaze would make anyone's knees weak.

Only he was looking at me.

"Mr. Scar can be really scary looking." Pepper's voice is thoughtful. "But he's always been really sweet to me. And to you!"

She looks up at me with a bright smile, and I know everyone is thinking the same thing. They all think he and I are together. Pepper's not ready to understand how complicated adult relationships can be.

I've got to get out of here.

Blinking away from the photo, I catch her hand. "Aren't we going to tidy my room?"

"Oh, yeah–let's do it!" She heads out the door, and I don't look back before switching off the lights.

Pepper sits in the center of my bedroom holding up a pair of wooden Dutch shoes. "These clogs do not spark joy."

"That's the truth." I'm sitting at my desk holding a pen. "I wouldn't wish the pain of those shoes on the meanest person in the world."

For a beat, I think… *Maybe.*

"What do we do with them?" She holds the clogs up, examining them. "They look authentic, like something out of 'It's a Small World.'"

"Maybe give them to a theater group?"

Poking out her lips, she nods. "Carmen's taking an improv class in the fall. Maybe she can take them with her!"

"Carmen didn't tell me she's taking an improv class in the fall!"

"Maybe you should spend more time with your friends." Pepper makes a disappointed face, and I laugh.

"I plan on doing just that, starting now."

Turning to my desk, a long checkbook is in front of me, and I scroll through the names on my phone. I'm looking for three in particular, and as I see one, I write a check for the amount I think I owe. I'm not completely sure, but I plan to get Trip to help me when we get to New York. He says I can't repay my debts, but I can sure as hell try.

Walking slowly to where I'm working, Pepper leans against my chair. "What are you doing?"

"I'm doing something that brings me joy."

Pepper's nose wrinkles. "Writing checks? I thought people hated writing checks." Leaning closer, her eyebrows rise. "That's a lot of zeroes."

"I owe a lot of money."

"What did you buy?"

Pulling my bottom lip between my teeth, I can't tell her the unedited version. "Clothes, food… party stuff."

"Must've been some party."

"It was." I shake my head. "I thought the bigger the party, the better I'd feel, but it didn't work."

Confusion lines her face. "But if you owed so much money, why did they keep letting you borrow more?"

"Because when you owe people money, they have power over you."

Big brown eyes blink to mine. "Like they can tell you what to do?"

"More like they own you. Don't ever borrow more than you can repay."

"But if you can repay it, why borrow it?"

Leaning back in the chair, I exhale a deep sigh. "You are a very smart girl, Pepper Winston. I don't ever want to hear you say you're not."

"I guess." She walks to where a small pile of baggy dresses and clear plastic shoes lies in a pile. "I wish I was more normal. Maybe if my mom were here, she could tell me things. Like maybe she was bad at English, too."

I watch her slide her finger down a sequined sheath dress hanging in my closet, and I get an idea.

Taking out my phone, I send a quick text. *I can do dinner tonight. Meet at Slim Harolds?*

It only takes a moment for him to reply. *Sure—7?*

It's a date.

"I'm really glad you decided to meet me. I guess your boyfriend doesn't mind?" Teal gives me a half-smile. "I can't say I wouldn't mind if it were me."

He's wearing nice jeans and a light-blue, long-sleeved button-down. I still haven't broken the big-city habit of dressing up to go out, so I'm wearing a long-sleeved, black sheath-dress and nude stilettos. My hair is down, but I've pulled the top back in a barette.

"I don't really have a boyfriend." I poke my straw in the margarita he bought me.

"It's okay, I understand." He's holding a beer. "It's like a safety thing? Wanted to be sure I'm not a creep first?"

"Something like that." My insides are heavy, and I'm having second-thoughts about doing this.

I really want to be in my pajamas, curled up on the sofa eating ice cream and watching movies with my head in Blake's lap while I cry. The only problem is Blake spends all of her nights with Hutch these days, and I need to do this for Pepper.

The jukebox is playing an old Buddy Holly song loud enough that we have to shout. Slim Harold's is a knock-off of a Myrtle Beach club from the 1950s called Fat Harold's. It's vintage style with chrome high-top tables and red-leather stools. Betty-Boop-style murals decorate the walls.

Older couples like to shag-dance on the sawdust-covered dance floor in the back of the room, and a waitress rolls up to take our order in a dress so short her ruffled, boy-short underwear shows.

"What should I get?" Teal wrinkles his nose as he peruses the menu.

"I know it sounds weird, but the thick-cut bologna sandwich and mac and cheese are really good. It's sort-of their signature dish."

He gives me a skeptical look and orders a grilled cheese and coleslaw. "Never been much for the processed meats."

"Are you're a vegan?" I take another sip of my drink.

My goal tonight is to find out everything I can about this guy for Hutch. We all love Pepper, and after everything she said today, I'm not letting Teal near her until I'm sure he'll only boost her wobbly, pre-pubescent self-esteem.

"More like vegetarian." He sips his beer. "I got into it when I was in training. People talk about how much protein is in meat, but you can get just as much from beans and rice."

"I think they have red beans and rice on the menu." I look behind him on the wall, and my stomach drops when Scar enters the crowded bar.

"They do, but it has sausage in it, which kills the deal." Teal is talking, but I'm not paying attention.

I blink down to the table fast, taking a long sip of my drink. My hands are shaking wildly, so I tuck them under my thighs on the high stool. My eyes heat with tears I will *not* shed in public, but my heart beats so hard it hurts. *What is he doing here?*

My date frowns at me. "Are you okay?"

Leaning forward, I catch the straw with my lips and take another long sip, doing my best to calm my breathing.

"I'm good." I am *so* not good. "You wanted to talk about Pepper?"

"Yeah…" He glances over his shoulder, then back at me guzzling the last of my margarita with a loud slurp. "That was fast… Do you want another?"

My hand is already up, but I'm ducking behind Teal, doing

my best to signal our waitress without drawing attention. It doesn't work.

Scar's wolf eyes land on mine, and his brow lowers when he sees I'm not alone. His frown tightens, the muscle in his jaw moves, and pain flashes from my chest to my toes.

"Another round for both of us." Teal smiles at our waitress, and I do my best not to hide under the table. "I don't know where to begin asking questions. What's she like?"

My insides are roaring, and I wish the waitress would hurry up. Only one thing will kill this pain right now, and it's more tequila. "I'm sorry, what?"

Teal's brow quirks, but he pretends not to notice my distraction. "What's she like? Pepper. Is she girly or tom-boyish? Does she like bologna sandwiches?"

Taking a deep breath, the alcohol is finally entering my bloodstream, and I manage a smile. "She's one of the best athletes I've ever seen."

"Really?" His entire face brightens, and he leans forward on his stool. "What does she do? Swim? Volleyball? Track?"

"Softball! She was shortstop for Stinky's Snow Cones last season."

He emits a staccato laugh, pride twinkling in his eyes. "You don't say?"

"I guess we know where she got her talent now. Although lately she's been into skating… Oh, and that KonMari Method. Have you heard of that?"

"Is that the little Japanese lady on Netflix?"

"Yes, and she's driving us all crazy."

He smiles so big, hanging on my every word, my heart softens in spite of my internal distress. He's so hungry for everything I'm telling him, and hope nudges in my chest for this reunion.

Our waitress is back, placing fresh drinks between us along with our food. I thank her and quickly grab my margarita, taking another long sip. Scar is still watching us from the bar, and it's like burning heat on my skin. I'm not sure how much lon-ger I can take this.

My stomach is in knots, and I can't eat right now, which triggers a whole fresh set of emotions. Maybe if I keep drink-ing, I'll be able to manage something.

Teal sips his beer before taking a bite of his sandwich made with thick, Texas toast.

He nods at my dish. "That looks more like Spam than bo-logna. I won't blame you for not eating it."

"It's really good. My stomach is just kind of jumpy."

Lowering his sandwich, he gives me a flirty wink. "Am I making you nervous?"

I'm about to tell him not in the slightest when a large, dark figure appears at my side. "Masters, right?"

Scar's deep voice slices through the loud music and my insides.

"That's right." Teal straightens, and to his credit, he does his best to appear bold. "You were at the office today. I didn't get your name."

"Oskar Lourde. What are you doing with Hana?"

Chubby Checker sings loudly about wanting to twist again like last summer, and couples are on the floor twisting and shag-ging. The alcohol in my blood turns my pain into anger, and I hop off my stool, catching Teal by the wrist.

"Do you feel like dancing? I love this song—let's dance."

"Yeah." He glances back at Scar. "Excuse us."

I'm ahead of him, walking fast, and when we reach the floor, it's too crowded to do anything but stand close together, holding hands and sort-of bobbing in place.

Teal's face is close to my ear. "What's up with that guy?"

"Just ignore him."

"That's not easy to do." The song ends, and "Rock Around the Clock" starts up, provoking a loud cheer from the sur-rounding dancers.

I'm buzzy and ready to show Scar he doesn't own me. "Isn't this fun?" I shout, smiling up at Teal.

He smiles back, but his eyes dart around the club. I know he's keeping an eye on my ominous bodyguard. "That guy looks like he wants to kick my ass."

"He won't," I shout, shaking my head. "Tell me, Teal, are you planning to make your daughter a lot of empty promises then drop some horrible secret on her and break her heart? Because if you are…"

"I don't have any horrible secrets." He studies me a beat. "I really didn't know she existed until a few weeks ago, so it was more dropped on me. The last thing I want to do is break hear heart… But are we still talking about my daughter?"

"Do you want to take her back to Brooklyn?"

"No–I mean, unless she wants to visit. I'm not looking to move her from a place where she's happy. I really want to get to know her. Maybe you can help me?"

"Of course!" My voice is too loud as the song fades out, and I decide I'd better put something in my empty stomach besides tequila. "Let's eat."

"Good idea."

We're back at the table, and I wobble a bit climbing onto my stool. Picking up my sandwich, I take a big bite. Salty, grilled bologna with American cheese hits my tongue, and it actually tastes really good.

Leaning forward on the high table, I cover my mouth with my hand. "I think I drank my margarita too fast."

Teal gives me another wink and that cute, dimpled grin. "Don't worry. I'll make sure you get home safely."

"Her safety is my job." Scar's low growl makes me jump back and almost slip off my stool.

He catches my arm, easily keeping me in my seat, and his warm, clean scent surrounds me. Pain slithers around my broken heart like vines, but I fight it.

Jerking my arm from his grip, I cut my eyes at him. "You're off duty."

"That's not your call to make, Hana." He says my name softly, and something new is in his eyes, something like the pain I feel at the sound of my name on his lips. "You didn't hire me."

My eyes burn, but I clench my teeth. "Leave me alone."

"You've had too much to drink. I don't like it."

"I don't care what you like."

"Sorry." Teal slips off his stool, and walks around to stand between Scar and me. His head only reaches Scar's shoulder. "The lady asked you to leave her alone, so if you don't mind. I'll be sure she gets home."

Scar leans closer, getting in Teal's face. "I'll be sure you get her home."

With that he turns and stalks back to the bar. The crowd parts like the Red Sea to let him pass, and I exhale a soft growl. "He's got a lot of nerve."

"I think I shat my pants." Teal chuckles, returning to his chair across from me. "That guy is huge and scary."

"I'm sorry. My uncle hired Hutch to protect my sister and me almost a year ago, and some people don't know when their services are no longer required."

He glances from me to the bar, where I know Scar is still glaring at us. "It seems like there might be more to the story."

I take another big bite of my sandwich, and tilt my head to the side. "I'm kind of ready to call it a night. Is that okay?"

"Sure, I can drive you home."

We settle up with the waitress, and I follow Teal out to his slate-gray Audi sedan. It's a nice car with soft, leather interior, and we make the short drive to my uncle's house. Glancing in the side mirror, I see Scar's black truck following a few car-lengths behind us, and the pain twists in my stomach again.

Teal pulls into the long circular drive, and when we reach the front porch, he pauses. "Thanks for coming out with me tonight. I meant what I said about meeting Pepper. I really want to know her."

Taking a moment, I study his brown eyes. He seems sincere, and based on the way he acted tonight, I have no reason to assume he's a jerk. He even did his best to stand up to Scar for me.

"I'll help you, but only if you promise me you're not going to ditch out on her."

"I wouldn't have come here if that's what I wanted to do." He exhales a laugh. "Besides, now that I've met everybody, I think I'd have a group of really pissed off people on my tail if I did something like that."

"You would, trust me."

"I don't want to surprise her or scare her. Will you help me?

"I have to go to New York for a few days, but when I get back, maybe we can meet up at the skatepark? If you don't mind waiting?"

"I'll be ready when you return." I'm about to get out when he catches my hand. "Seriously, thanks, Hana."

Pressing my lips into a smile, I lean back and give him a brief hug. "You're really nice. I think Pepper will be happy her dad cares about her, and who knows, maybe you'll get to see her play ball."

"I'd really like that."

CHAPTER 22

Scar

MY HANDS TIGHTEN ON THE STEERING WHEEL AS I WATCH THEM from the end of Hugh's long driveway. She leans in towards him, and possessive fire blazes in my chest. *Would she kiss that guy? Has she moved on that fast?*

I spent the day going over our plans for New York, mapping out the proximity of our hotel to their apartment, researching the quickest ways in and out of the building. Dirk hacked into traffic cams around the block so we could monitor vehicles and foot traffic.

This distance between us is a gnawing pain I can't escape. I slept like shit last night, and I don't expect tonight to be any better. I really wasn't expecting to find her out at Slim Harold's with Pepper's long-lost dad.

That guy had better watch himself. First he shows up all cocky looking for Pepper, threatening Hutch's happy home. Now he's taking out my girl, buying her dinner, drinks, dancing with her.

My breath exhales on a growl. If she doesn't get out of that car in the next sixty seconds…

The door opens, and her long, silky leg emerges to step on the soft gravel in needle-thin heels. Is he going to let her try and walk to the house by herself?

I'm ready to get out of my truck and walk up there when the asshole jumps out of the driver's side and runs around to hold her arm.

Molten anger surges in my stomach when he touches her. They stop at the door, and he's smiling at her like he wants to kiss her. If he knows what's good for him, he won't dare approach her lips.

Hana pats his arm, and my fist relaxes when she goes inside and closes the door. Teal hesitates a moment, looking after her with his hands in his pockets, then dashes down the drive, into his sedan.

As he leaves, he has the nerve to wave at me. I do not return the greeting. What kind of a name is Teal Masters? It sounds made up.

Several minutes tick past, and I watch the light in her window, her shadow moving around the room.

Dirk thinks it's best for us to fly separately into the city to avoid being seen together as much as possible. I agree, but I need to talk to her again before we go, even if she doesn't want to see me.

I need to know if she's planning to see anyone besides the gallery people. I want to be sure she remembers all the things I taught her and that she packs the pepper spray.

Stepping out of the truck, I slowly make my way up the driveway and in through the back door. It's late, and only the dim night lights are on throughout the house.

My boots thud softly on the thick carpets as I climb the stairs to the second floor, making my way down the hall to her bedroom.

I tap softly, and she makes a little sound for me to enter.

I'm sure she thinks I'm Blake or perhaps Norris. When the door falls open, my breath stills in my lungs.

She's standing in front of the large armoire with her pretty hair piled messily on her head, wearing those sleep shorts and thin white tank I remember so well. It's a punch in the heart.

"Oh!" Her voice is high, and her hands tremble. Still, she lifts her chin, doing her best to seem confident–like she always has. "What do you want?

My arms ache to hold her. "I was worried you couldn't sleep."

"So now you care if I can sleep?" Her tone is defiant.

She has no idea how much I care. "Hana, I know you're angry with me, but I–"

"You're right I'm angry with you. No, I can't sleep, but I'm not the weak little girl I was before. I don't need you."

"It's true. You don't need me." I'm not sure she's ever needed me, but it doesn't change how I feel.

Silence expands between us, and I have no right. Still, I ask. "Did you kiss him?"

Her lips part, and she blinks quickly like she's stunned. "You have no right to ask that."

"I know." My voice is quiet.

"What you should have done was tell me the truth from the first day you knew who I was."

"It's true. I wanted to find the right time."

"We were together every day for almost a year. You could have told me many times."

"I was a coward."

Anger flashes in her eyes, and her voice sharpens. "You're not a coward. You ran into a burning building! Why did you hide that from me?"

"When it comes to hurting you, I can't do it."

"You hurt me by not being honest. I trusted you. Now all I can think is what else are you hiding?"

I can't answer that question. More silence.

"Were you there?" Her chin wobbles, and it takes all my strength to stay where I am and not go to her. I've lost that privilege. "Did you stand in the shadows and watch while he tortured me?"

"No… fuck no." Clenching my fists, my jaw grinds. I shake my head, gazing at my boots. "So many times I've wondered, maybe if I *had* been there, would it have happened? Could I have saved you? I'll never know."

"What I know is you let me believe you're someone you aren't."

"I told you I wasn't a hero."

"You are not."

It's a deeper cut than I can manage standing here at her feet. "I won't see you again before the trip. Will you remember what I taught you?"

"I'll remember who I am and who you are."

Nodding, I concede that's fair. I have to earn her trust again, and it won't be as easy the second time. "I'll never be far away if you feel afraid or in danger. I'm there."

"Goodnight, Mr. Lourde." Her tone is clipped, and I nod.

"Goodnight, beautiful girl."

I'm in my truck in Hugh van Hamilton's driveway with a bag of sunflower seeds on the console. It's an experiment in torture, but I crack the shells and spit them in a cup, then I eat the kernels.

I let my memory play back the day she didn't know what she was doing, when she sat on my lap confused and so damn cute.

My eyes squeeze shut, and I wipe my palm over my brow as I anticipate another sleepless night. Pain torments me, but I can't break free from this need to be close to her, to be sure she's not in danger.

She has every right to be mad at me. I know I fucked up not telling her everything, but I need her to know I hated Victor as much as she did. More, if that's possible.

I haven't decided whether to tell her everything I've done, but I need her to know that much.

Stretching my legs, I push my head against the headrest. I've got a long night ahead of me, but I'm not going anywhere.

CHAPTER 23

Hana

"IT'S REMINISCENT OF SARAH ANN LORENTH AND OLGA FLER with the dreamy lighting and the inclusion of natural elements." Jill Weams has my prints spread all over a large table in the center of the open Milo gallery space.

My head is spinning, and I've never felt so overwhelmed and elated. She's comparing me to fine art photographers I could only dream to be as good as.

Blake wanted to come with me, but I told her I needed to start taking care of myself. I wanted to do this on my own. Now I'm wishing she were here.

Jill is intimidatingly tall with ultra-fair skin and stick-straight, platinum-blonde hair. Her dark brown eyes are focused like an eagle, and she's wearing black slacks and a long-sleeved black turtleneck. She's the ultimate Manhattan glamor girl turned art curator.

"Would you consider enlarging any of them to life size?" With long, elegant fingers, she plucks the photos of Pepper and Ainsley from the stack. "In particular these of the girls on roller skates?"

"Yes!" I hate how small my voice sounds. "I think I can find the supplies I need at Blick and get them done easily."

"Nonsense." She waves her hand. "We have a darkroom here at the gallery and everything you need to do your work. The space is at your disposal."

"Thank you." I'm blinking fast, trying to keep up.

The small gallery is a maze of towering white walls covered in the work of their current featured artist, giant Monet-like pastels of dreamy, impressionist fields of flowers.

"These of the softball players with the donuts are adorable. They call to mind Magda Piwosz, but I'm just thinking of marketing. Truly you have a distinctive style all your own."

"You think so?" Cautious confidence fills my tone. "It's my first show. Only Blake and Jacque Carlisle have ever seen my photographs."

Jill's eyes flash. "You worked with Carlisle? Next to Annie Leibovitz, he's the quintessential fashion photographer of our day."

"My friend Debbie took his class at art school, and he did a session with Blake."

"I'd pay money to see that." She's speaking offhand when suddenly she inhales a sharp breath. "What is this?"

Sliding the photos of Scar from the stack, she places a hand flat against her chest. "Who is this model? I haven't seen him in any of the major circles. He's incredible. Did you discover him?"

My lips part, and pain echoes in my chest when I think of the first day we met so long ago. It was definitely a discovery.

"My uncle hired his business partner to be Blake's bodyguard, and we sort-of met that way."

"He's stunning. Look at the ferocity of that profile. I love what you did here with the saturation and the barest hints of blue and silver. At first glance, I thought it was black and white."

"Thank you." It's the best I can do with my heartbreak still so fresh.

Simply thinking about Scar is enough to prompt an explosion of pain so fierce it steals my breath.

"All of these should be oversized. They'll stop viewers in their tracks." Stepping back, Jill crosses her arms, seeming lost in thought. "The theme is perfect: *Memory*. How do you feel about starting in the front with the children then working our way through the images of the older girls, mid-gallery, followed by the ones of your sister with the horses, ending with this gorgeous man. Yes?"

She turns to me with a smile, and I nod. "It's actually how I arranged them in my mind."

"Perfect. It's going to be tremendous. We'll have the whole town buzzing, but you don't need to worry about that. I'll take care of everything." She slips her hand into the crook of my arm, and we walk slowly across the scored concrete floors. "You just focus on the final pieces for the show, and call me if you need anything or have any questions at all."

"Thank you so much, Jill." I take her card, air kiss, and step out into the breezy afternoon.

We spent all morning composing my art resume, which was embarrassingly light, and a biography along with samples of my work to send to media outlets and art influencers around the city.

Documenting my lack of experience nearly had me running all the way back to Hamiltown. *Who am I to have an art show at the Milo Gallery?* But Jill was so kind, reminding me that everyone starts somewhere. I mentally noted they usually start in art school.

Now I'm exhausted and hungry, and I need to get from Chelsea to our apartment on the Upper East Side.

Hesitating outside the gallery, I scan the throngs of pedestrians passing quickly, walking with purpose to lunch dates or meetings or the office, knowing somewhere in the crowd either Dirk or Scar is following me.

Deep in my bones, I know it's him. The magnetic pull between us remains so strong, I can't help glancing over my shoulder as I wait at the crosswalk, scanning the faces surrounding me. I know he's there. I can feel his eyes on me the way I always could, only they used to make me feel warm and loved. Now I feel injured and alone.

The wind pushes strands of hair in my eyes, and I hold them back. For a moment, I almost see him, wolf eyes watching from the shadows. Black ink curling from his collar down to large hands clenched into fists.

He's still there, protecting me, and I decide I need to move. I've never liked taking cabs, and I didn't arrange for a car. Glancing down at my Filas, I can walk sixty blocks. It's only three miles.

The red hand changes to a white figure, and I cross the street, headed north, letting the fresh air and exercise ease this fist he put in my chest.

At the next stop, I send a quick text. ***Are you still in Italy?*** Hitting send, I cross the street with the crowd.

We're in front of the Empire State Building, and I have to remember to look both ways before crossing. Out of the hundreds of one-way streets on Manhattan Island, they decided to make this intersection two-way. *Jesus.* This is why those old movies have people getting hit by cars here.

I look back to be sure he remembers, which is ridiculous. For starters, I don't see him, and of course he remembers. My phone buzzes, and I read quickly.

Is the little bird sneaking out of the nest again? Trip is such a dick, I think, tapping out my reply.

I'm in the city prepping for my show. Are you here?

Continuing through Midtown, if Trip's in the city, he'll be at his mother's place, which is two floors below our apartment. It's perfect, and I won't have to say anything to Blake.

Indeed, and I heard from dear old Rusty the van Hamilton sisters are in the building.

Rusty is the ancient elevator operator in the Andover, where we've all lived since we were children.

Only for a few days. I need your help.

I'm making good time, and I feel the tightness in my chest loosening. I guess that old advice about getting exercise for depression is true. Only, when I'm depressed, I never feel like exercising.

Does Blake know you're talking to me?

Rolling my eyes, I keep it short. *Blake doesn't need to know. I'll see you tomorrow evening.*

I'm not giving him the option to put me off. Trip was there when I got myself into these messes, and he's going to be there when I hand over the money to get myself out of them.

A light sheen of sweat coats my upper lip, and my hair is frizzy around my head when I reach the building. I'm sure I smell like a wet dog, but I couldn't care less.

Pausing at the front door, I cast one final look over my shoulder. We both needed the walk, I think.

"Miss van Hamilton, welcome home." Our doorman tips his hat as I skip into the large, marble foyer.

"Thank you, Cyryl."

Rusty waits in the elevator, his gray hair yellow from cigarette smoke. "Miss Hana, it's good to see you again." His voice has only gotten scratchier with age.

"Thanks, Rusty. I'm working on an art show at the Milo." Leaning against the elevator wall, I can't help a grin. The bubble of excitement in my chest won't be denied.

"Miss Blake told me. She's so proud of you."

Warmth pulses through my veins. "She set it up for me, you know? For my birthday? I can't believe she thinks I'm good enough to pull this off."

"You've always been my favorite sisters." He holds the

doors open when we reach our floor. "Maybe I can get the night off to see it."

"I would love that!" I give his shoulder a squeeze. "You're my favorite elevator guy."

Our apartment is four doors down, but before I touch the door handle, it opens.

"Hana! My goodness, I didn't think you were coming home tonight." Mama is on the other side wearing a formal gown and vintage fox stole, complete with head and tail.

"Where would I go?" I step forward to kiss her cheek.

She smells like Chloe roses, and her makeup is full beat.

"Darling, where do you ever go? I stopped trying to keep up."

She never tried to keep up. "Where are you headed?"

"Board meeting for next year's gala. Blake ordered supper if you feel like eating. You smell like a stable."

"Probably because I walked home."

"Good heavens, why on Earth would you do that? Roman would have brought the car down."

"I didn't want to be stuck in a car in traffic. I felt like walking."

She leans forward for air kisses then waves her hand. "Phew! Take a shower. You're all sweaty, and look at your hair."

"Love you, too!" I plaster on a saccharine smile.

"Don't wait up."

She's out the door, and I walk slowly towards the kitchen, wondering if Scar was really out there following me or if poor Dirk's cursing my name right now.

"How'd it go, babe?" Blake greets me as I enter our large, white and stainless kitchen.

None of us really cook, but it's a power-move to have an elaborate kitchen in a city short on real-estate. Mama is all about the shows of wealth.

"Mm, this smells good." Containers of beef and broccoli,

miso soup, and spicy noodles are arranged around the granite bar.

The cypress bars in Hutch's and Scar's homey kitchens are so much warmer than cold granite. An image of him working hard, muscles flexing, sweating and sanding, drifts through my mind, and I exhale a little growl. *Will I ever stop thinking about him?*

"Everything okay?" Blake frowns at me

"Sorry, yes! It was so great. Jill kept comparing me to these super famous photographers. I thought I'd pass out."

"I wish you'd let me go with you. You could've used the moral support."

"You're right." Picking up a fork, I stab a piece of dark-brown beef. "It's just… I'm tired of feeling like everyone is watching me or helping me. I need to stand on my own."

Her expression softens, and she walks over to where I stand. "You're right. You're not a baby, and you're fully capable of handling your business." Sliding a curl behind my ear, she tilts her head. "Still, even the strongest people like having backup in stressful situations."

Nodding, I think about Scar again. Another internal growl as I resist him.

"Thank you for setting this up for me." I wrap my arms around her waist for a hug. "You've always believed in me, and it means more than you know."

"You're my little sister." Her voice is warm.

"I know, but not all sisters are that way."

"We have the evening and the place to ourselves. Run shower. I'll make us some plates, and we can watch a Sandra Bullock movie."

More internal growling. "Not *Miss Congeniality*."

Her brow furrows. "You love that movie!"

CHAPTER 24

Scar

W E ARRIVED IN NEW YORK THIS MORNING AFTER TAKING THE redeye out of Charlotte. I didn't even unpack before heading to the Andover to stake out a good place to sit and wait for Hana to emerge.

Dirk offered to take the first shift, but I let him know I'd be taking all the shifts as far as she's concerned. She's pissed at me, but we're back at home base, ground zero for all the bad guys.

He can keep an eye on Blake for his brother, who at the last minute decided to stay home and deal with the Pepper situation, and while he's at it, he's also running his surveillance programs, hacking into street cameras and tracing cellphone pings to see who all's in the city and where.

I do my best to blend in with the masses of people crowding the streets. Hana took a cab from the apartment building to the Milo gallery, which made my job easy. Still,

I'm in all-gray from my hoodie to my gray jeans, doing my best to blend with the masses of people crowding the streets.

Once she went inside the gallery, Dirk connected to the security cameras in the building to monitor her movements. I found a comfortable spot at a park across the street to wait.

It's a mild spring day, but the wind blows in sharp gusts around the tall buildings and bits of trash and Bradford pear petals swirl in the air like urban snow.

Four hours later, when she still hasn't emerged, I get a little worried. Sliding out my phone, I send Dirk a quick text, *Still have eyes on her?*

It takes him a minute to reply which ratchets my anxiety higher. Is it possible she went out a different door? Finally he answers, *Still inside. Guess who else is in the city?*

Exhaling a growl, I roughly tap my reply. *I don't like guessing games.*

Dirk is nonplussed. *Trip Alexander. Home with Mommy Dearest.*

I'm not happy with that information. If Trip is staying with his mother, he's in the same building as Hana, which means they'll be in contact.

I only know of one thing to do. *Keep tabs on him.*

That guy knows at least as much as I do, and probably more. He knows where all the bodies are buried–and who has the shovels.

Another half hour passes, and I'm growing restless. Finally, like a drop of sunlight, Hana emerges from the small gallery on the first floor of the black, Manhattan highrise. Her blonde curls fly in wisps around her face, and she's wearing a long-sleeved, cream sweater and white pants.

I slowly rise, filtering into the pedestrian crowd across the street and down the block from where she stands looking up and down the wide sidewalk. It almost seems like she's looking for me. She knows Dirk and I are here, watching over her and her sister.

She hesitates a moment longer then seems to give up. I expect her to hail a cab, but she surprises me. She takes her phone from her pocket and begins walking north.

I hang back when she stops at the intersections, watching as she taps on her phone quickly. I wonder who she's texting. I wish I were at her side, holding her hand. Instead, I continue shadowing her, letting my eyes trace down the sway of her curls, the bounce of her little ass in those baggy pants.

It's like following my heart as it leaves my body, painfully dragging me behind. At least I can be close to her this way, keeping my eyes on her, ensuring her safety.

In Midtown, she almost sees me when she stops in front of the Empire State Building. She's making good time, and I'm moving at a rapid clip before I realize she's stopped. I quickly side-step around a corner, out of sight.

It's not necessarily a bad thing if she sees me. She knows one of us is here, after all. It's more other people seeing us together we want to avoid. She's more inclined to be angry if she sees me… and perhaps I want to see what she'll do now that she's back near all her old haunts with her old running buddies close at hand.

We never had that conversation before we left Hamiltown.

Her pretty eyes scan both sides of the street before crossing, and I give her a little more space before doing the same. We're at the southern border of Central Park, entering her Upper East Side neighborhood, and now that I know Trip is in town, I have to be doubly cautious not to be seen outside their building.

One last time she hesitates, looking around before entering. I exhale a sigh of relief, knowing she's indoors. It's not late, but my hope is she'll stay in for the night. I enter the hotel across the street and take the elevator to the small, empty room we reserved with windows facing the street entrance to their building.

Surveillance is the most grueling part of our job, but in this case, I'm highly motivated. It would be easier if she were speaking to me. I could ask her to text when she's coming and going. I could tell her I'm here, not to worry.

Hell, I could get one good night's sleep holding her in my arms instead of gradually wearing myself down, night after night, thinking about her. I miss the warmth of her small body curved into mine, the light-floral scent of her hair when her head rests on my shoulder. The space she filled is hollow and aching.

Closing my eyes, I see her gaze hooded and full of love, her soft, full lips curling with a smile as she leans forward to trace them along my brow as she straddles my lap.

My cock stirs, but I open my eyes again. No point going down that road to torture. I fix them on the front of the building as the pain of longing settles in my chest.

Our precious times were so short-lived, and I have no one to blame but me. Will I ever get her back?

The sun is setting, orange-purple over the park. Clouds create a low ceiling, and the twin spires of the San Remo rise over the trees behind her building. Dirk communicated with Blake, and they're staying in for the night. Still, I won't be able to sleep. I remember how Hana used to slip out after hours, when everyone was asleep, without her sister's knowledge.

I almost wish she hadn't told me all the things she did in her past. My one consolation is her determination to make Blake proud, to be better than how she was. She already is in so many ways.

I lean my back against the wall, sitting in the cushioned

window seat of the small apartment-style hotel room. My gaze is focused on the street below as the streetlights flicker on, creating arcs of yellow light on the pavement.

Dirk promised to set an alert if she leaves the building. He texts me to get some rest. We're going on twenty-four hours of no sleep, but it's difficult to relax without her beside me. I haven't slept well since the day we split apart.

Reaching in my pocket, I take out my wallet. Inside is the small print she made of the two of us in my bed. It was the first time we'd made love, the day she changed me for-ever. Her pretty eyes glow, and I look fucking awestruck. I promised to keep her safe always–even when she's angry, even when it's my fault.

Looking at the sidewalk far below, my heart is heavy, my eyes weary. It's possible I might slip into a tentative rest when my phone buzzes, and adrenaline spikes in my veins. I'm on my feet, ready to head out the door.

It's a text from Dirk. ***Check out what I just captured, fresh from the street cam outside Gibson's.***

Fuck, is it Hana? I'm on edge waiting for the grainy, night-vision picture to come into focus on my phone. An in-visible fist closes around my throat as I recognize the flat-brimmed hat and the baggy jeans. His puffer jacket is off the shoulders, wrapped like a cape.

Of course, anyone could dress this way. It's a popu-lar street style, not a positive identification. Still, going into Gibson's, dressed like a wannabe gangster…

Can you verify his ID?

Dirk's reply comes fast, ***Working on it. Checking the pings of the last cell number we found.***

My breath is shallow as I wait, as the seconds tick past, and I picture the bots combing through the tendrils of the dark web. The final rat emerged from hiding the same day Trip appeared at his mother's.

Hutch had hoped sending the girls to the city alone

might provoke movement in the organization. It's possible this is all a coincidence, but I'm feeling more certain my partner is right. These guys have been waiting almost a year, and most criminals are not patient. It's why they get caught.

Finally, Dirk's text appears. ***Positive ID. Ivan X.***

Our threat level switches to high, and I quickly text, ***Time to catch that rat.***

CHAPTER 25

Hana

M Y HEAD IS ON MY SISTER'S LAP, MY BELLY IS FULL OF BEEF AND broccoli, and we're giggling as Sandra Bullock slams naked into Ryan Reynolds then to the floor.

"I'm so glad you never had a dog like that." Blake groans, and I push to a sitting position.

"Excuse me, you were the one lobbying hard for a Yorkie all last year. I only wanted a kitten. Which I never got."

"Yorkies are not like that dog." She slips a bite of salted caramel ice cream into her mouth. "Anyway, Uncle Hugh has a million barn cats running around. Just claim one."

"Maybe I already have." I haven't, but she makes a good point.

"Not the solid orange one. He's mine. I named him Mr. Puffinstuff."

I pretend to be angry. "Mr. Puffinstuff is mine. I claimed him the first day we were back visiting the house!"

"That wasn't Mr. Puffinstuff. That was Lady Ginger. She has the little white boots on her front paws."

"Oh my God, you've named every freakin cat." I give her arm a shove. "Did you even leave one for me?"

"Trust me, there are plenty more to spare. Although I did tell Pepper she could take a couple. It's good to have cats in pairs. They keep each other company."

"That does it. I'm getting a white puffball dog."

"No!" she cries.

We finish watching the movie, cackling at Betty White wrapped in an Indian Blanket, dancing to "Get Low," squealing at the male striptease, and swooning at the final proposal scene.

I haven't felt this light since all that shit went down with Scar, and we bump hips every time we pass each other, carrying our ice cream bowls to the kitchen to clean up.

"I like seeing you smile again." Blake puts her arm around my shoulder as we head to bed.

Walking through the living room, I glance at the doors of our separate bedrooms. "What if we sleep together tonight? It's been a while since we shared a room."

My sister doesn't even hesitate, giving me a wink. "I think that's a great idea, since we're both used to having bed partners these days."

Sadness pinches my chest, but I force a smile. "I'll just change into my PJs real quick."

We're curled up in her king-sized bed a few minutes later with the lights of the park outside her floor-to-ceiling windows.

"I'll close the curtains in a minute," she says softly. "As much as I love being in Hamiltown with Hutch, I miss the lights of the city sometimes."

Snuggling closer to her side, I prop my head on her shoulder looking at the skyline of the Upper West Side.

"You seem so happy with Hutch. No regrets?" She inhales slowly, and my eyebrows rise. I lift my head to study her serious expression. "What?"

"I'm really worried about Pepper and all this Marie Kondo stuff. She just started all that after our engagement, and now she's quitting softball when she's so good at it? It's because she doesn't like me. It's because I'm marrying Hutch."

Pressing my lips together, I think about this. "I don't think it's you."

She rolls in the bed to face me, gray eyes round. "What is it, then? It can't be a coincidence."

"No..." I wrinkle my nose. "I really think it's puberty. She feels lost and things are changing. Oh, and she's having trouble in her English class."

"English?" Blake's voice is thoughtful. "I was always good at English."

"Maybe when we get back you can help her. I know she likes you."

"You think so?" I've never seen Blake so distressed, and I feel really protective of her all of a sudden.

Cuddling close, I give her a squeeze. "I know she likes you. She told me!"

"What about you?" She rubs my arm. "I want you to be happy, and this Scar thing..."

A knot twists in my throat, and I close my eyes. "He lied to me, Blake." My voice is so small. "About *that*. About *him*."

"Hutch said he's really broken over this. I don't think he had a choice in working for Victor, and when he knew... Hutch said he walked away."

"How can I trust him when he'd hide something like that?"

"Do you think maybe that's why he hid it?" Her voice is gentle. "I know I was on the fence for a while, but after seeing you together. I believe he really cares about you."

Her words hurt so much. I turn away, pulling my knees to my chest and holding them, assuming my usual position when I know I'm going to have to survive something unsurvivable.

"Hana..." She curls around my back, wrapping her arms over my waist. "I love you. I only want what's best for you."

"I know." My voice is a whisper, thick with unshed tears.

"Let's rest." Her cool hand smooths my curls off my

forehead. "I'm here for you, and you've got all the time in the world."

Placing my hands over hers, I close my eyes. I don't want to cry anymore, so I let my big sister comfort me like she's always wanted to do.

Standing in the darkroom as the massive, blown-up image of Scar slowly comes into focus, I think about Blake's words. His eyes, that intense gaze, looking back at me like I hold his heart in my hand hasn't changed.

The last time he stood in my bedroom, his eyes were so sad, so much like the pain tearing me apart. Still, I couldn't stop my automatic, internal response. It was the same as that morning in his bed, when his sexy words sent me into a tailspin.

I can't help that my body won't let me trust so easily, even with my heart bleeding out inside my chest. He withheld information he knew would crush me–does that make it okay? What happens next time?

Perhaps my sister is right. Perhaps there won't be a next time. Maybe this was the battle we had to face. Using the plastic tongs, I lift the massive print from the final bath and pin it to the line. I can't think about this right now. Now I have to think about the second big reason I'm here. Putting my past to rest.

When I left the apartment, I put the envelope holding the three checks in my bag. Glancing at the clock, I see it's after five. Too early for the party crowd, but hopefully not too early for the people who run this town.

Tapping quickly on my phone, I text Trip. **Picking you up in an hour. You're going with me to Gibson's.**

Mama scheduled Roman to pick me up at five, so I'm sure he's out there waiting to take me back to the apartment. I've got to figure out a way to lose either Dirk or Scar, whoever is tailing me today.

Shaking my head, I know it's Scar, and the last thing I need is him bursting into the room when I'm trying to do business, especially if he has ties to Victor's old crew. It would ruin all my plans.

I'm in the limo when Trip responds. *No thanks. Trying to curtail my day drinking.*

Exhaling a little growl, I text back. *Then have a soda. You're going with me. Also, plan an escape route. Don't want to be seen leaving the building.*

Gray dots bounce as I wait for his reply. *Back to your old ways, I see. Fine. Can't have you winding up dead, too. Who would I play with then?*

I don't respond. I have no intention of turning up dead or being reduced to one of his playthings. I'm not going back to my old ways. I'm burning those bridges tonight, hopefully for good.

CHAPTER 26

Scar

W E'VE HACKED INTO IVAN'S PHONE, AND DIRK IS FILTERING through his text messages trying to figure out his reason for being in the city. I'm in my position outside the Milo gallery waiting for Hana to emerge again.

She arrived later in the day today, but Dirk confirmed she did not leave the apartment last night. I've been on edge since Ivan showed up again. Blake was his primary target before Hana turned twenty-one and her trust fund matured.

Dirk was able to track down their conversations on the dark web to learn they were blackmailing Blake to get the money they claimed Hana owed in gambling debts and bar charges.

Now my only guess is they'll go after Hana directly, and guys like him don't mess around. They get their money or they take it out of your hide.

Anger prickles over my skin at the thought of that bastard touching my girl. He'd better pray I'm not around or nothing will be left of him.

It's after five before Hana emerges from the gallery, and she gets straight in her mother's waiting limo. While the exercise was nice yesterday, I'm glad she's not out on the street alone today–not that she's ever alone while I'm here.

I text Dirk she's on the move and hail a cab back to the hotel where my partner has set up a makeshift headquarters.

It takes almost as long to drive as it did to walk with traffic, or perhaps I'm impatient. Either way, by the time I'm entering the room where Dirk is busy typing, I'm anxious that she's been out of my sight for so long.

"Did she make it back?" I walk over to where he has three large monitors set up like a triptych with security camera footage covering all the screens. "She entered the building about ten minutes before you walked up."

"I'm taking a quick shower. Don't lose sight of her."

"And I thought Hutch was overprotective. You make him look like a slacker, bro."

"Blake was only in danger by association…" I don't finish that sentence.

I don't have to. Hana has made quite a bed we're trying to help her get out of, and Dirk knows as well as I do how dangerous the men searching for her can be.

I step into the bathroom to take the fastest shower ever. Being in the military taught me a lot, the most important skill is efficiency. I'm back in the room with Dirk, tying back my wet hair in less than five minutes.

Walking to the wall of monitors, I scan the six small squares on each screen, which include the street outside the gallery and their apartment building, the lobbies of both buildings, the street outside Gibson's and various street views I don't recognize.

Glancing at my partner, I notice his brow is lowered, and his lips are tight.

I'm immediately on alert. "What's wrong?"

His brow quirks, and he sniffs sharply, standing from the

chair. "I don't believe in coincidences, but it appears our man did not return to the city because Hana is here. He was summoned–they all were."

"Summoned?" I frown at the computer screen. "For what?"

"More like by whom. It appears someone big is in town, and he wants to meet with the capos at Gibson's."

"Sounds like our guy's been promoted. Last we heard he was a wannabe gangster."

"It's been hard getting information since our last visit, when Louis and the Brooklyn PD got involved. They must not have a mole there."

"Give 'em time." My tone is cynical, but I know these guys too well.

"If there was some way we could get a device in one of those rooms to record what they're doing…" Dirk taps on his keyboard, changing the street views on two of the cameras. "We could finally have concrete evidence to give Louis. He could secure warrants, and we could take down these assholes."

Sliding a hand over the back of my neck, I think about this. I don't want to be away from Hana for a moment, but I know that club better than Dirk does.

"Give me the recorder. I'll get over there and place it."

"You're the most conspicuous of the two of us. For starters, you're head and shoulders above everyone else, you look like a biker–"

"But I know my way around Gibson's, I know all the names, and during the day, when the club is empty, I can slip in and out without anyone noticing."

"I doubt they'll be that careless again, my friend."

"Has anyone said they saw me there last time?"

He presses his lips together, but he doesn't say yes. It appears, Rainey didn't tell anyone I was snooping around the office. Possibly because she wasn't supposed to be there either?

I sit on the bed to lace up my boots. "Just give me the device and tell me where to put it." Casting a glance out the window towards Hana's building, I start for the door. "Ping me if she goes anywhere, and keep your eyes on her. I'll be back in an hour."

Tying my hair back, I'm in a gray turtleneck and gloves as I step out of the cab in the Financial District. Getting all the way down here at rush hour took more than half an hour. I send Dirk a quick text that I've made it, and I'll likely be longer than an hour.

He ended up giving me two recording devices. We agreed one should go in the office where I found Rainey last time I was here. The other will go in the small back room where we believe the snuff film was shot.

I pass the glass double doors covered by heavy, velvet curtains, and jog down the steps to the alley entrance. The same, squat Italian is sitting on a chair seeming bored as he looks at his phone and smokes a cigar.

At the sound of my boots, he looks up, and his brow relaxes. It's been weeks since I was here, but clearly he remembers me.

"Thought you might be back around." He smiles like we're old friends. "I understand now why you were here before. Preparing for Petrovich?"

Fuck. Cold realization filters through my bloodstream. It makes sense now–the someone big in town is Simon. He never came to New York when Victor was alive, but now with his brother and his nephew gone, he must be coming to check on things personally.

My anxiety level is at an all-time high. I've got to get this done and communicate with Dirk ASAP–then I have to stick to Hana like glue. Hell, I might ask Blake if I can sleep in their guest room. The time for pretending they're alone is gone.

I hold my expression steady. "Did you get an ETA on his arrival?"

"That's above my pay grade, pal," he chuckles. "Figured if anybody'd have that information, it'd be you."

"Guess we're on the same pay grade." I'm doing my best to be chummy. "I'll give the place a quick sweep."

"I've already done it, but you guys are more paranoid than anyone I ever worked with."

"We have reason to be."

He puts the cigar between his thick lips and returns to his phone. "Knock yourself out."

I step carefully into the wine-red establishment and quickly scan for anyone who might recognize me. A few old guys are at the bar having happy hour. Otherwise, it's the usual set-up crew, busboys and waitresses in skimpy black dresses.

The recording device is burning a hole in my pocket, and I make a beeline for the small office. Not planning to make the same mistake twice, I crack the door just enough before entering.

Unlike last time, no one's here, and I go behind the desk, dropping to one knee to affix the bug under the drawer. Just as fast, I return to the door and look out. The coast is still clear, but I'm sweating like a pig. At any moment Simon and his men could walk down the stairs.

Going quickly to the short hall leading to the back room, I push through the leather-padded door. The entire room is black leather, with long bench seats along the walls. The door has a narrow window for observation.

I step up on one of the seats and affix the second bug in a corner. Hopping down, I hope I've got enough time to cross the open bar and get out before I'm detected.

My hand is on the door handle, when loud voices fill the space. "So I told him, suck on this, motherfucker."

"You're a cold-hearted man, Rick." A husky, smoker's voice chuckles. "You put your piece in his mouth?"

"And I pulled the trigger 'til it went click." He fakes an Italian accent, and I vaguely recognize the movie reference.

"You guys like all that new shit. Give me *Chinatown* any day," the older man growls. "That's some classic gangster shit."

"My sister, my daughter?"

"It's more than that."

A female voice joins the conversation. "I told Anthony the club is closed for a private party. He'll take his post up top. Let him know, security is in place."

"You know, I didn't believe you were up for this job." Rick's voice is cocky, overconfident. "I guess you proved me wrong."

"Which isn't very hard."

Their bantering fades as they continue to the bar, and I crack the door enough to see who's standing by the bar–Ivan X, whose real name is apparently Rick, a big guy I don't know, and Natasha.

She leaves them at the bar, heading in the direction of the office, and I lean back out of sight. I'm fucking trapped.

Sliding the lock on the door, I pull out my phone and send a quick text to Dirk. ***I'm stuck in the back room at Gibson's. Recorders in place. Simon is coming here. Guard the girls.***

Next, I take out my gun to be sure it's fully loaded. A bullet falls to the floor, and when I pick it up, my hand is shaking. *Fuck.* I'm nervous. I'm alone, I'm outnumbered, and if I don't handle this right, we could all get killed. *You're never prepared for hell....*

I don't know why Simon is in town, but my best guess is he's collecting debts. Which means he's here for Hana.

CHAPTER 27

B LAKE IS IN THE KITCHEN WITH MAMA, AND I CAN HEAR THEIR sharp voices muffled through my closed door. I don't know what they're arguing about–like it's anything new–but it buys me time.

Standing in front of my closet, I take down my cream sequined sheath dress and carefully fold it into a roll I can fit in my bag alongside my nude Louboutin pumps.

I texted Trip, and he said to meet him at the back stairs. He arranged for a car to take us to Gibson's. It'll be a while before anyone notices we're gone, and by then, I plan to be back with my past clean and ready for bed.

Hell, if it goes as smoothly as I hope, maybe Blake and I can watch another Sandra Bullock movie. It's been a while since I've seen *Two Week's Notice*.

God, I'm so ready to move into the next phase of my life–a phase where I'm clean, free from the past, all my debts repaid. I was such a fucking stupid kid. I thought I could do all these

things, and none of it mattered. Months of therapy taught me
to forgive myself and learn better coping skills.

The only problem is the people I owe don't care about
my reasons. They only care about their cash, and they want
it back–or else.

A shiver tickles over my skin, and I go to my door, opening
it as quietly as possible. Neither my mother nor Blake can see
what's happening in this hall, so it's easy to sneak out. When I
got home, I said I was tired, not to hold dinner for me. It's so
usual, they didn't question it.

I suppose I should be disappointed we're falling into our
old habits and roles, but I don't have time. Trip is waiting for
me in the alley, and I've got shit to do.

When I reach the back door, I hesitate, thinking about Scar
and wondering if he's out there somewhere, believing he's
protecting me. My heart aches at the thought of him watching over me, sadness filters through my chest, and I want to
see him again. I want to explain why I have to do what I'm
doing tonight.

Shaking my head, I know I can't, but when this night is
over, I'm going to force my insides to be quiet. I'll do meditation or breathing exercises or whatever it takes to calm the
triggers. My sister is right–he and I need to talk.

"First you hustle me like the building is on fire, then you
take forever to get down here." Trip sits in the leather backseat of his mother's Towncar, legs crossed, sipping whiskey.
"Where have you been?"

"Blake and Mama were quarreling in the kitchen. I had
to sneak out." I hop in the car and quickly whip off my thick
sweater and sweatpants and fish the sequined dress out of my
bag as we head south to the Financial District. "Anyway, I'm
here now, aren't I?"

"You've always had to sneak out. You're out of practice."
Trip looks out the window, bored as I change into my evening

attire. "So what's the plan, urchin? You're going to run in there like the fairy godmother tossing out checks like glitter?"

"No." I level my eyes on him. "The main person I need to see is there. The others you'll help me locate–perhaps they'll show up at some point. Seems like they were always together."

"This does not sound like a good plan at all."

"I've filled in the amounts I think I owe. If it's not enough, they can tell me the deficits, and you'll be there to witness everything."

"Again, a terrible plan." His hazel eyes slide to the side, sarcastic as always. "And what? They're going to fall to their knees and thank you, Saint Hana?"

"I don't expect anyone to fall on their knees. I expect them to acknowledge repayment, confirm we're good, and leave me alone." I take out my cosmetics bag and quickly get to work on my face.

"And if they don't?"

Trip's mother's luxury car floats over a bump in the highway as I apply mascara. My mind drifts to Debbie and her tragic end. She didn't deserve what happened to her. Was it my fault? Is that my fate?

Then I think about Scar's promise.

"If they won't, we'll have to find some sort of compromise." I slide tissue-thin, silk stockings up my legs. "I want to make peace. They'll have to come to the table."

"You have no idea the kind of people you're dealing with, Daisy cakes."

The car slows to a stop, and I glance out the window at the heavily curtained double doors covering the stairs leading down to Gibson's.

"I have an idea. It's time to end this."

Trip holds my hand as I step out onto the sidewalk. The sign says the club is closed for a private party, but that's nothing new. A short, stocky Italian man stands at the entrance. He's dressed in a dark gray, pinstripe suit and holds a thick cigar in his sausage fingers.

When he sees Trip, he doesn't hesitate. Stepping to the side, he opens the door for us, and we step into the lobby above the wide, maroon-carpeted stairs leading down to the smoke-filled main floor. Only it's early, so the scent of lost souls and dirty deals simply lingers in the heavy velvet.

My heart beats faster with every step we take, and I imagine us descending to the first ring of hell. I hesitate, and Trip puts his hand over mine.

"Having second thoughts?" For the first time in all the years I've known him, he actually sounds like he cares.

"Not if I want to end this." My smile wobbles, but I know how to fake confidence. I've been doing it for as long as I can remember. "I can't grow with this hanging over my head."

"I hope you're right."

Two men are sitting at the bar, and they look up when we enter. Both know Trip, and I vaguely recognize the one in the bucket hat and puffer jacket wrapped around his arms. *Wannabe gangster.* It's Rick Ivanov, and my throat goes dry.

The last time I saw him, he spent the whole night bragging about his aspiring film career and pushing himself on me. He wanted Debbie and me to be in a documentary he was planning about nuvo heroin-chic in the Manhattan club scene. I told him I didn't do heroin, but he insisted it would be a blockbuster. Looks like he's back from Hollywood.

"Yo, Trip, how's it hanging?"

"About mid-thigh these days."

The older dude I don't know barks a laugh, and Rick lifts his chin. Trip has no problem talking shit with these guys, and even when I was drunk or high, I was impressed by his ability to play it cool when nights got ugly.

The men return to their drinks and cigars, and Trip arches an eyebrow at me. "What are you waiting for?"

My brow furrows, and I look up at him. "What do you mean?"

"Hana?" We're interrupted by Natasha's annoying shriek. "*My beesh!* What are you doing here?"

She calls out like she's glad to see me, trotting over to give me a hug and air kisses at each cheek. Her minion Rainey hangs back near the wall.

"You look *amazing*." Natasha is such a faker, but I go along with it.

"Thanks, babe, so do you. So elegant." She's dressed in a dark green sheath, and her brunette hair is styled in a French twist.

"Pfft," she waves a hand. "I have to look the part now that I'm manager."

"Yeah, I heard you're running the club. That's crazy!"

"It's a job." *Such a lie*, but she carries on. "And I heard you have a big art show at the Milo next month. *That* is crazy! Tell me all about it."

Rainey doesn't join the conversation, which is new. It's been a year, but she's not smiling, not fanning around jumping at Natasha's heels. She's dressed in a tailored, wide-legged suit, and as we chat her eyes dart from Trip to me.

"Blake set it all up. Maybe you can come?"

"Nothing could keep me away!"

Our conversation starts to fade, and I inhale slowly. "So anyway, I just wanted to stop by and give you this." Taking one of the linen, business-sized envelopes from my bag, I hand it to her.

"What in the world?" Her brow furrows, and she flips it over, pulling the flap apart. "A check?"

"It's what I owe you… I think. I wanted to pay you back, say thank you for your patience, and I hope now we're even."

The fake friendship in her eyes frosts over, and she glances from me to Trip. "Five hundred? You owe me way more than five hundred grand, Hana van Hamilton. That's not even a drop in the bucket of what all I've done for you."

Rick perks up from his spot at the bar and looks over to where we're standing. "Hana van Hamilton? I thought I recognized you."

The back of my neck tightens as he saunters over to where we're standing. Rainey recedes further into the background, as if she's trying to disappear into the curtains, but Trip stands taller at my side.

"My buzz is fading. Can I get a whiskey, Nat?" He's trying to cut the sudden tension with his casual tone, but it only makes me more nervous.

Holding my smile steady, I address Natasha. "I wasn't sure the exact amount, but if you'll just tell me what I owe, I'm glad to–"

"You can't possibly repay me for what you did." She leans closer, lowering her voice to a hiss. "You took a man's life."

Blinking wider, my knees falter, and Trip's grip on my upper arm tightens. The female voice in my dream–I know it now. Rick is standing in the corner with a camera in his hand, and Natasha is behind me in the dark room. *You killed him…*

My head seems to lift off my body, and I can't find my breath. "I didn't."

Natasha's cruel voice continues, "There's only one way you pay for a life, Hana. Do you know what that is?"

I'm not going to faint. I won't faint. Still, I feel the cold waves drifting up from my toes, filtering through my bloodstream. "I didn't do it."

Scar said I didn't. Only, I didn't believe him. I saw the man at my feet.

"I was there," she hisses. "You were high as a kite."

I take a step back. I need to get out of here. "That isn't what happened."

Turning for the door, I take a step when Rick cuts me off

by sliding in front of me. "You're not trying to leave, are you? Don't you have a check for me?"

My eyes fly to Trip, and his brow is lowered. His casual demeanor is gone, and he's looking from Natasha to Rick to the man sitting at the bar. Rainey is nowhere to be seen, and my plan has turned into an ambush.

"I don't know what you're talking about." My voice grows louder as I force myself to be strong. "I didn't kill anyone. I couldn't."

"Yet you had the motive and the opportunity." Rick reaches out, but before his hand lands on me, a deep voice slices the air.

"Don't touch her." Scar enters the room, and my heart jumps in my chest.

"You." Natasha lashes.

My feet move before my brain can register. I run straight to Scar, wrapping my arms around his waist and tucking my head into his chest.

"You're here." My voice is lost in the violent beating of my heart.

A soft rumble vibrates his chest, and he wraps a strong arm around me, moving me to his side while keeping me close.

Strength filters through me as I hold onto my savior. He helps me stand taller, lifting my chin to face my enemies. I look from a scowling Natasha to a curious Rick to Trip, who inhales deeply and resumes his casual demeanor.

"I need a whiskey." He starts for the bar.

"You're taking her home." Scar's voice is level, and Trip makes a U-turn, sauntering back to where we stand.

"I want to stay with you." It's a quiet request, and he looks down, the warmth in his eyes removing all my fear.

"You need to go now. I've got business here, then I'll come to you."

His deep voice fills me with so much longing, I wrap my arms around him once more, and he kisses the top of my head, inhaling like he always does.

Closing my eyes, I hold him a beat longer, not wanting to let him go. He slides his hand up and down my back, and I do as he says.

"I'll see you in a little while." Then taking Trip's arm, I follow him up the stairs.

CHAPTER 28

Scar

MY GUN IS READY AT MY CHEST, AND I WAIT UNTIL I'M SURE MY beautiful girl is out of the pit before turning to face the snakes. "Why are you framing Hana for Victor's death?"

Natasha's eyes narrow, as she studies me. "What do you know about it?"

"More than you, apparently."

Rick steps closer. "You're familiar. Who do you work for?"

"Myself, now take me to Simon."

"No need." The voice I know so well, echoes from behind me. "As they say about those clowns, I'm already here."

Turning quickly, I face my old master.

"So the prodigal has returned." His dead blue eyes don't move as he chuckles. "I thought it would be more difficult, but what do they say about providing enough rope?"

"I'm not your son."

"A son would be more grateful. At least I hope. You on the

other hand are a recurring nuisance." He glances at Natasha. "Ask him again about Victor's death."

Natasha's black eyes turn to me, but I don't wait for her to follow his orders.

"When I found out what Victor did to Hana, I made a special trip to his loft in Manhattan. He was surprised to see me, so I brewed his favorite tea."

"You killed him?" Her upper lip curls like she smells something foul, and for a moment, I think she's going to charge me.

"I used the special Petrovich recipe." Anger radiates out of her like heat, but I'm not afraid of this girl. "Why are you framing Hana for something I did?"

Her lips part, but Simon cuts her off. "Speaking of Miss van Hamilton, where is my prized possession? I had hoped to take her off your hands tonight."

"She doesn't belong to you."

"Hana van Hamilton is payment for her father's debts. You should know I always collect what's mine."

"You're not taking her." My voice is a low growl, but Simon walks to the bar.

"Vodka, neat." The waitress takes down a short glass and pours two fingers of the clear liquor as he continues speaking. "You're delaying the inevitable. You can stop me now, but the date simply moves further down the road."

He lifts the tumbler and shoots the drink as I watch, the cold truth of his words sinking into my bloodstream. He'll never stop coming for her.

"One day you won't be there," he continues. "Maybe tomorrow, maybe in a year, maybe two. Maybe when she has a child."

He says the words slowly, as if to wait while my mind conjures the image of Hana and me together, happy. The two of us smiling, holding a beautiful baby with white, curly hair and large blue eyes, just like her mother's... just like mine.

A single gunshot to the head.

"I always collect." Simon's voice goes hard.

"Take me instead." The words fall from my lips on instinct.

The room falls silent. The five of us, the bartender, and the two bodyguards who came with Simon appear to stop breathing as I wait to see what happens next.

I say it again to be sure it's on the record. "I will take her place."

His brow arches, but he doesn't respond. Instead, he flicks his wrist at the bartender, and she pours him another drink, which he lifts and sips, slower this time. "You expect me to trust you?"

"I'll return to the fold in whatever capacity you see fit for as long as you say." As I say the words, pain twists harder in my chest. "My life for hers."

I know what this means, what I'm promising, the atrocities he could force me to commit. I know it means I'll have to say goodbye to Hana, possibly forever, a thing that will definitely kill me. Still, I promised to do anything to keep her safe from this monster. I won't break that promise.

"So you'll come back to me… However I see fit?" A line cracks the smooth plane of his forehead as he considers my proposal.

"In return, all their debts are forgiven. Their account with you is erased. The van Hamilton name is no longer part of your ledger."

Natasha makes a noise of disgust, but Simon takes a beat longer. He traces a finger along the lip of his glass, and his expression returns to neutral.

It's decided.

"I accept your offer." With a curt nod, he straightens, glancing around the empty room then nodding to his guards. "Let's go. We're returning to Minsk."

"Tonight?" My mind stutters to a halt. "I'm not prepared–"

"I will provide everything you need–clothes, weapons, money…"

"I can't leave without talking to Hutch. If I disappear, he'll come looking for me." It's the only thing I can think of to buy time. "I need to let him know I'm going with you willingly."

He glances to the guy sitting at the bar. "Marco will drive you. My pilot will have the plane ready for departure in two hours. I suggest you wrap up your business quickly. We leave at eleven. If you're not there, the deal is off."

With that he fastens the button on his blazer and starts for the door. The men in dark suits fall in behind him, and they quickly climb the stairs.

My chest is on fire, and my fists are clenched.

"Don't think this settles things with me." Natasha snaps, and my eyes flash at her.

"This settles everything. If you touch Hana, I'll make you wish you were dead."

Her gaze remains narrowed, but she backs down at my threat. I don't have time to deal with her bullshit. I'll have to trust my partners can handle this petty New York debutant.

Taking out my phone, the pressure of time weighs heavy on my shoulders. I have to move fast if I've only got two hours. I've got to talk to Hutch, and I need to be with Hana for the last time.

Dirk's voice is strained as he shouts into the phone. "What the actual fuck, Scar?"

My eyes strain through the window. Marco is driving, and the back glass is up as I speak quietly into my phone, wishing it didn't take thirty minutes to drive uptown.

"I need to talk to Hutch, and I need to see Hana."

"This is bullshit. You don't have to do this. We can totally get you out of this deal."

"The deal is made. I can't go back on my word." Scrubbing my fingers over my eyes, a block of concrete is in my stomach.

"If I don't do this, Hana will be a walking mark. At any time, he could decide to move on her, and we would never know when or where."

Silence falls on the line, and I know my friend is doing what he does best–sorting through all the possibilities, looking for a way out of what I've done. He's trying to find a solution to this problem.

Only there is no solution.

I've been around these guys long enough to know how they operate, and once you're in debt to them, there's no way out.

"I traded my life for hers. Now I need to talk to Hutch."

The reality of what's coming aches in me like a brand. Being with Hana has been the one thing that gave me a reason, now I have to leave her. If I know Simon, he'll make it so I never see her again. He'll twist the knife slowly, especially now that he knows I'm responsible for Victor's death.

He'll make my time in his service as painful as possible to make up for that hit.

"Indentured servitude is illegal…" Dirk is still going.

"*Illegal* doesn't exist in their world." My tone is resigned. "I'm going to hang up now, but I respect you, Dirk. You're a good man."

"Scar–" I hit the end button and immediately dial Hutch.

Thankfully, he answers on the first ring. "What's wrong?"

"Your girl is fine, Hana's fine. They're all good." He exhales a breath, but I don't have time to let up. "The situation has changed, and I'm going back to Minsk. Dirk will fill you in on the details."

"You can't go back to Minsk–" His voice is urgent.

"I don't have time to explain. I need you to do something for me." We're approaching the Andover building, and I speak faster. "Call Blake and tell her I need her help. I'm picking up Hana, but when I bring her back, I'll need her. Will you tell her that for me?"

"Of course, but I can't allow this–"

"You're one of the best men I know, Hutch. Thank you for your friendship. I was honored to serve with you."

"Scar–"

I end the call and hustle through the lobby of Hana's apartment building. Rusty gives me a wave, and I hop into the elevator.

"Mr. Alexander was just here with Miss Hana. He said you'd be right behind them."

My brow clenches. "I guess Trip knows me pretty well by now."

"He knows everything." The old man chuckles.

"Hold the elevator for me, will you? I'll be right back with Hana."

"You bet."

I dash down the hall, and the door opens before I knock. Blake greets me, her silver-blue eyes tense. "Is everything okay? Hutch just called. He said you needed me."

"When I get back."

Hana glides up behind her, and my chest swells at the sight of her. She changed out of the pretty sequined dress she was wearing, but she's still so beautiful in leggings and a thin, long-sleeved sweater.

"You're here." Her voice is so soft, so sweet.

Without hesitation, she walks straight into my arms, and I lift her off her feet. Her legs are around my waist, and her head is tucked into my neck. All the cracks in my heart and soul are filled, and I don't want to put her down. I want to memorize everything about her.

Blake studies my face, her smart gaze knowing something dark is coming.

"I'll have her back in an hour."

Blake nods, but Hana teases. "Only one hour?"

I lower my girl to her feet, spreading my hand over her pretty face. The hole in my heart paradoxically heals and rips larger as I gaze down at her. "I have to meet someone at eleven."

"Then we'd better hurry." She takes my hand, and we go to the waiting elevator.

We're across the street in the hotel room in record time. The lights of the city casting a pale blue glow throughout the small space.

Hana looks up at me the way she always has, like she believes in me, like she trusts me.

"Come here." I take both her hands and lead her to the bed. "Sit. I need to tell you some things."

Her blue eyes widen. "Okay."

"You asked me about my burns, and I told you how I got them. Now I need to tell you what happened after them."

Reaching out, she slides a cool hand over my wrist, where the ink stops at the seam of my injury. "I want to know everything about you."

Looking down, I thread her slim fingers with mine. "After this happened, my world went black. It had never been particularly light, but then Simon appeared and said I would work for him. He said my father gave me to him as a child, as payment for his debts. I never knew my father. I was disfigured and destitute, so I went with him."

Her brow furrows, and sadness is in her eyes. "What did you do for him?"

"Things I regret. Things I should have told you before we went so far."

She reaches up to touch my cheek. "I've done things I regret."

"I know, beautiful girl." Turning my face, I kiss her palm. A soft curl falls onto her cheek, and I slide it behind her ear, letting my touch linger. "The fire changed me. I didn't begin by accepting what had happened to me. I hadn't made peace with my scars."

"Peace can be one elusive bitch."

I know she's battled her own demons. I know she knows the story of searching for meaning.

"I found it with you." The words burn in my chest. My peace is right here in my hands, and it's slipping through my fingers.

My brow collapses, and she rises onto her knees, straddling my lap and pulling my face to hers. She kisses me softly, but with one touch, we're insatiable.

Lifting her shirt over her head, I lean down to kiss her shoulder, smell her skin as she unfastens her bra. I'm like a man losing his senses. I want to imprint these images on my subconscious.

With her bra gone, her small breasts fill my hands, and I kiss them, pulling the hardened nipples with my teeth, committing her small moans to memory as she pulls at my shirt. It's over my head, and her fingers slide down my back.

"You feel so good," she whispers before I cover her mouth with mine, tasting her sweet kisses as my chest simultaneously surges and shreds with every inhale, exhale.

Turning us, I lie her back on the bed and slide her leggings off. She's not wearing panties, and I carefully kiss her ankle, kiss her knee, the inside of her thigh.

"Is this okay?" I'm over her, sliding my hands under her ass. Her eyes are hooded, and she nods, dropping her legs apart.

It's all the invitation I need before burying my face in her pussy, tracing my tongue all over her clit, inhaling her sweet musky scent. Her back arches off the bed, and she moans, driving her fingers into my hair as I move faster, devouring her.

My dick is so hard, I'm afraid I'll come too fast. I want her with me, and my movements grow more insistent, pulling her soft pussy with my lips until her moans grow louder, orgasm trembling in her thighs.

Before she can finish, I move my mouth to the crease of her leg, higher, kissing her navel before I straighten to remove the rest of my clothes.

"God, I'm so close," she whispers, watching me, licking her full lips as I toss my pants to the side.

When I put my knee between her legs, she curls forward to take my hardened cock in her hand, guiding it to her mouth. Her hot tongue licks at my tip, almost sending me over the edge.

Catching her face, I lift her chin, leaning down to kiss her. "I want to be inside you."

Her arms rise to my shoulders, and I scoot her higher on the bed, settling between her thighs and sliding fast into her slick core.

"Oh, fuck," We both groan, and I hold for a beat, doing my best to hang on, to savor this time we have together.

"It's been so long," she sighs, and I lift my mouth to cover her jaw with kisses.

"Has it been a week?"

"It's been longer than a week." She catches my cheeks, kissing me roughly, pushing my lips apart, and sliding her tongue beside mine.

I like my aggressive sex kitten, and in spite of the pain, I smile, allowing her to push my shoulder, rolling me onto my back.

She's on top of me, rolling her hips and gripping my cock with her tight little cunt. "Fuck, Hana, I'm going to come."

"Me too," she gasps, rocking faster.

Her hands are above my head, and she rides my dick, panting and moaning as pink flushes her cheeks, her soft breasts. I catch a nipple in my mouth, giving it a pull.

"Yes," she gasps. "Slap my ass."

Her round little ass is right in my hands, and I give her a sharp slap.

"Oh," she moans as her body jumps, and a flash of orgasm shoots through my pelvis.

Fuck me, if she starts this, I'm going to lose control.

"Harder," she groans, and I squeeze her fleshy rear before spanking it again, harder.

"That's it." She gasps, her brow clenched as her mouth

forms an *O*. I smooth my palm over her hot skin, and my cock starts to jerk. I'm groaning as my orgasm slips through the gate.

I want to flip her over and nail her to the mattress, but she grips my shoulders, her voice trembling. "One more time…"

I don't hesitate, smacking her one last time as she breaks, jerking and moaning, her sweet pussy working my cock as she comes.

"Fuck," I groan, leaning back as I pulse again, deep inside her.

Hana's lips part, and she's breathing hard. My hands are on her legs, and I watch her in amazement as she comes down from that high. Her eyes blink open, and she starts to laugh, falling forward onto my chest.

"Oh my God, that was so hot," she groans, tucking her head under my chin. "I've always wanted to do that."

My large hands cover her sexy ass, and I gently stroke the places I spanked her. "Interesting request for a beginner."

She places her elbow on my shoulder, leaning her cheek on her hand and looking down at me. "I told you I'm a bad girl."

Lifting my head, I kiss her lips. "I think you're pretty damn good."

"You're pretty damn good yourself." She grins, covering my mouth with hers, and I roll us so she's on her back beneath me.

I'm still inside her, and I want to cover her with my body. I want to make her a part of me I can never lose. I want to go on her sexual journey; my heart breaks at the thought of her moving on with her life, without me.

Lowering my face to her hair, I kiss her, smell her, slide my hands across her soft skin. I'm running out of time, and every breath cuts more when I think of letting her go.

She squeezes her arms around my neck and exhales happily. "I love when you're on top of me."

Her legs wrap around my waist, and I bend my knees, lifting her off the bed and carrying her to the bathroom where we can clean up.

The feelings of dread are filtering back, and when we return, she curls into my side the way she always does when she sleeps in my bed.

I wrap a strand of her blonde hair around my finger in the quiet. "I killed Victor. The night I learned he hurt you, I couldn't rest until he paid for what he did."

She pushes up to a sitting position, blinking fast as she studies my face. "How?"

"A mixture of drugs that stopped his heart." My voice lowers. "I should've made it more painful."

"Why are you telling me this?"

"If anyone tries to say you did it. I want you to know the truth."

The room is still, the clock ticks, and her chin tucks as she slides her hand into mine. She lifts it to her lips and kisses my fingers, pressing them to her cheek. "Because you're mine."

It's the words my heart has said to her so many times. Now it's time to go. "Get dressed so I can take you back."

She doesn't argue, and we quietly pull on our clothes. My chest is a lead weight as I hold her hand, holding her close as we enter the elevator for the last time together.

Hana's cheek is against my arm, and I wrap it around her, holding her body close to mine, never wanting to forget this. With a glance at my face, Rusty can tell something is up.

"Hold it for me," I ask, and he nods gravely.

We slowly walk to her door. Her scent is in my hair, on my beard. I should have taken a piece of her clothing.

"I wish you didn't have to go." She pauses at the door, looking up at me with a smile. "Will you come back after your meeting?"

It's another twist of the knife. "No, angel, I won't be back."

Her brow furrows. "Why not?"

My chin drops, and I reach out to press the bell. "I'm going to make all your debts go away."

"How will you do that?"

"I made a deal with the owner of Gibson's, and he accepted it."

She breathes faster, noticing my dark expression. "What was the deal?"

I don't answer.

The door opens, and Blake's eyes are wide. Hana blinks to her sister then back to me. "Scar? What was the deal?"

I hold her eyes with mine. "You're safe now." Smoothing my hands over her cheeks, I kiss her forehead, her temple, inhaling her scent one last time. "For the rest of your life."

"What do you mean?" Her voice wavers, and her sister puts her arm around her waist.

"I want you to take care of yourself like I would. Eat. Remember you're so much more than your past."

"Scar…" Tears pool in her eyes, and she hesitates on the threshold. "You can't leave me."

Blake steps forward to hold her as I touch her one last time. "I'll always be yours."

"Scar…" Her voice breaks on a whisper. "Don't."

"I love you."

"No!" It's a broken wail.

Her knees go out, and Blake's arms wrap around her as they slide down.

Forcing my legs to move, I turn my back and walk to the waiting elevator. Rusty's gaze is downcast, and he gives me privacy as I collapse against the back wall. The noise of her sobs, crying my name, rips through my ears.

They don't stop until the doors close, but even then they echo in my mind. I inhale a shaky breath, pressing my fingers to my damp eyes. My girl, my angel, my broken daisy. I have to believe she'll be safe now, free to live a happy life, never having to look over her shoulder or pay for sins she didn't commit.

I stagger from the building, and Marco has the car waiting. With shoulders hunched, I slump against the door as we make the long drive east. The lights stripe the pavement, and I've lost the will to live. My only purpose now is standing in her place.

Simon doesn't look up from his phone when I board the plane. His security stops me at the door, removing my gun from its holster before giving me a complete pat-down. Knives gone, wallet gone, I know the drill.

Before he's done with me, the man holds out his hand. "Phone."

My new boss glances out the window as my fingers wrap around the device in my pocket. I knew this was coming, but I'm still not prepared to lose everything.

It leaves my possession, and my life here effectively ends.

Heaviness descends on me like a heavily weighted blanket. I walk to the back of the plane in silence, hoping I can spend the long flight in a back corner sleeping through the pain.

Alone in the darkness, I have one thing left, a small item I removed from my wallet before I left the car. With Hana's scent lingering in my hair, I lean my head against the plastic window and study our picture. My eyes burn with unshed tears. I close them and remind myself the reason I'm doing this.

Simon still hasn't spoken to me as we taxi into the airport in Minsk. He hasn't given me any instructions or told me where he wants me to serve.

Perhaps he wants to be sure of my loyalty? If he understands a fraction of my commitment to Hana, he'd make me his personal bodyguard. I plan to be a model employee as long as he lives up to his end of the deal.

Standing, he straightens his coat and walks off the plane as soon as the attendant opens the door. His men follow, and I glance at the staff collecting trash.

I have nothing, so I follow the way they went. It's a gray morning, and a cold wind blows across the open tarmac.

A small group of official-looking men stand in a clutch near a van parked at the bottom of the steps. I'm confused when I see Simon talking to them and pointing at me in a dismissive manner.

The moment my boots hit the concrete, I'm slapped in handcuffs, cold steel banging against the bones of my wrists.

In Russian, the man tells me I'm under arrest for the murder of Victor Petrovich, and I'm being taken to Lefortovo Prison.

Simon stands back, his face passive, and with crushing realization, I understand. "You never wanted Hana."

"What would I do with a broken doll?" His tone is calm. "You killed my brother. For that you must pay."

The man jerks my arm, and pain shoots through my wrist. I fight back before I'm forced into the waiting van. "What about our agreement?"

"We agreed you would serve me in whatever capacity I say for as long as I see fit." Simon steps closer, his eyes cold. "I want you to rot in a Russian prison for the rest of your sorry life."

My chin drops, and any hope I had dies.

"*Do svidaniya*, Oskar Lourde. I'll see you in hell."

CHAPTER 29

MY HERO IS A MONSTER.

My hero is a killer.

My hero would give his life to keep me safe.

I'm sitting on the concrete at the skatepark plucking petals off a daisy to my warped variation of *he loves me; he loves me not.*

I don't have to ask if Scar loves me.

He traded his life for mine, and I wish I was dead.

Blake said that was wrong. She said I have to live my life—it's the only way to honor his sacrifice. It's what she said the night he told me goodbye, the night I lay on the floor of our apartment crying until I couldn't breathe.

Mama was terrified, and forced Blake to give me a sedative. It changed nothing. I slept, and when I awoke the unbearable pain knotted me into a ball again. I stayed in my bed clutching my knees as the tears melted my eyes.

I didn't know love was like this. I didn't know it was cruel and dark. I didn't know it would destroy you. I didn't know it would take everything and leave you for dead.

Scar was my mate. He fought demons and nursed dark wounds. He had done things he was ashamed to talk about.

He belonged to me.

I belong to him.

I don't know where to go or how to live my life without him.

More sedatives. Blake brought me back to Hamiltown, hoping for the best, but I went to my bed in our family home and didn't leave. Norris would bring me food, and I tried to eat it. I tried for Scar. He told me to eat.

My stomach refused. My stomach can't let go of losing the love of my life, or knowing I'll never love anyone, ever again.

Hutch came to see me. He told me I'd been in bed for two weeks–*has it been that long?* He told me Pepper was worried about me. *I never want to hurt Pepper.* He told me Blake was frantic. She was considering calling off the wedding–*that doesn't make sense.*

Then he said the words that brought me back to life.

He put his large hand on my back, and said, "I'm going to find him, Hana. I'm going to bring him home. But we need you to be here when that happens."

Squeezing my eyes, I forced my lungs to expand. I forced my body to unfurl from the ball of pain paralyzing my muscles.

I forced myself to sit up and look at my future brother-in-law.

"I guess I look pretty rough," I said, but he forced a smile.

"You got this." Hutch took my hands and helped me to stand.

I managed to shower and go downstairs. I choked down real food and went outside to let the sun shine on me.

I want to be happy. I want Hutch's words to give me hope, but my old fears are back.

No matter how hard I try to believe in happily ever afters, I know they don't happen for people like me. I'm not pure and innocent. I don't deserve to ride into the sunset with a handsome prince.

My hero isn't a prince.

But oh, God, I want to believe in happy endings.

Looking down at the nub of my sad little daisy, all its petals plucked away, I think it looks like me. Stripped bare, nothing left to give.

I'm at the skatepark today because I agreed to introduce Teal to Pepper. I would've expected him to give up on my involvement, but he didn't.

Pepper's in the valley working on her stunts. Every few minutes, she'll skate over and give me a hug like she knows I need it. Like she recognizes the fragile bonds holding me together.

Looking up, I see Teal's car pulling into the lot, and I stand, dust off my butt and walk over to meet him.

When he sees me he smiles, stepping forward to give me a brief hug. "It's been a minute."

"Sorry I kind of fell off the planet on you." I shove a curl behind my ear.

"I got a lot done." He shoves his hands in his pockets as we walk towards the park. "I went back to Brooklyn and settled up my things. I sublet my apartment, and I'm looking into getting a place in town."

"That's a lot!" My eyebrows rise. "You're really serious about this."

"I am." I hear a tremor in his voice and I realize he's nervous. "I met a guy who hooked me up with the Little League organization in the area. I was thinking maybe I could get a job coaching at the school."

"You met Stinky?" I force my tone to be light, hoping to break the tension. "He's the man to know. Stinky's got his finger in hardware, snow cones, softball, this skate park."

Teal squints up at the sign. "Stinky's Skate Park. I'll be damned." We take another step, and he pulls up short, touching my arm. "Let's wait on the whole dad thing. Let's just meet first and see how it goes."

"Whatever you want. I'm here to help."

He inhales slowly, and we start walking again, going to the bench at the edge of the grass. The sound of roller skates fills the air, and Tommy and his crew are in the park as well, doing stunts and practicing.

"They're really good." Teal watches, leaning his forearms on his thighs. "Is that her?"

"She's the only girl out here today."

At that moment, Pepper looks up and sees us, and her slim brows furrow. She changes course and rolls over to where we're sitting, stopping on her toes at the edge of the concrete and marching over to stand beside me.

"Hey, what's going on?" She puts her hand on my shoulder, almost like she's protecting me, and a hint of comfort nudges my battered heart.

"Pepper, this is a friend of mine. He's new in town, so maybe we can make him feel welcome."

"Maybe." She squints at him. "You know, my friend here recently suffered a loss, so if you're thinking–"

"Oh, I wasn't…" Teal fumbles, and I jump in to help him.

"What I was saying," I stand, giving her an elbow. "This is Teal Masters. He's moving here from Brooklyn."

"Teal Masters?" Her tone changes to bright curiosity. "Shortstop for the Brooklyn Cyclones?"

"Yeah," Teal exhales a relieved breath, standing as well. "How did you know that?"

Pepper shrugs. "I used to keep up with stuff like that. What are you doing in Hamiltown?"

"Well, ah, since I retired, I was looking for something new." Teal clears his throat. "I was thinking about taking a job here coaching little league, or maybe something at the school."

"Kind of a strange choice. Do you know people here?"

He looks at me, and I redirect. "I told him you played short-stop for the Snow Cones. I thought you might introduce him to some of the kids."

"I could do that."

"Maybe you could throw the ball sometime, get to know each other." I glance at Teal.

"That would be great. I mean, if you don't mind." He smiles, and I feel sorry for him. He's clearly working so hard, and he's so awkward. "What if we head over to Shirley's bakery and have some donuts?"

Raising my eyebrows in approval, I give him a nod. "I would love a donut. Pepper?"

She squints towards Tommy and the boys then back at us. "Okay. I'll just put on my shoes."

We wait as she changes out of her skates, then we walk the two blocks to the specialty bakery.

Pepper's a little more chatty as we walk. "Shirly started with just cakes, then she added cupcakes, and now she's doing donuts."

"Very market savvy," Teal says, and I hang back, noting the similarities between them.

I don't have my camera with me, so I slip out my phone and adjust the settings. It's not as easy to manipulate, but I can get some good shots if the natural lighting cooperates. It's a partly cloudy day, which is perfect.

We walk up to the polished wood and glass case where an assortment of specialty donuts is on display, ranging from maple syrup and bacon to key lime.

"I don't do sprinkles." Pepper wrinkles her nose. "They're not tidy."

"They don't spark joy?" Teal jokes, but it breaks the ice.

"You know about Marie Kondo?" Pepper's defensiveness melts a little more.

"A little. I'm hoping to tidy up before I make my move."

"I can help if you want. I've tidied my uncle's house, Carmen's store… I even tidied Hana's room!"

"Would you? I'm not so great at folding, and I forget how she says to store things."

"Sure! I'm really good at folding."

They walk over to a table with their donuts, and I hang back, taking a few pictures of the two of them, amazed Pepper can't see how similar they are. She has his eyes, his hair color. She even walks the same as him.

"I guess you can't see the way you walk." Carmen sits on the couch, the television remote in hand, a bowl of popcorn in her lap.

I'm telling her all about the meeting today with Teal, and she's scrolling through the movies on the streaming service in Uncle Hugh's home movie theater.

I curl up beside her in a reclining chair, a bag of sunflower seeds in my pocket, and she pulls up the classic rom-com *Working Girl*.

"He was so nervous, it was almost painful, but Marie Kondo saved the day." I put a seed in my mouth and expertly extract the heart from the shell, which I spit in a little cup.

"Not that again," Carmen groans. "I'm going to suffocate Pepper with a perfectly folded shirt one of these days. This doesn't give me joy…"

"I think it's 'spark joy.'" I eat another seed.

"Whatever it is, I'm sick of it. She's constantly rearranging the store. I can't find anything. She says I'm not organizing the jewelry correctly."

"I'm hoping once Teal finally gets up the nerve to tell her he's her dad, she'll start playing ball again. She's so good at it!"

"I don't know. I kind of get where she's coming from." Carmen starts the movie. "She's hitting puberty, and she's interested in boys. She wants to be where the boys are, not on the ball field."

"I guess." I settle into the leather chair, doing my best to focus on the crazy hair and outfits, but sadness still twists in my chest.

I want to be where Scar is, and no amount of tidying or matchmaking is going to change it. Tears are in my eyes when Melanie Griffith leans into Harrison Ford and tells him she's *got a mind for business and a bod for sin.*

All I can think of is my last night with Scar and how things were just starting to get good between us. I dip my chin, trying to be sneaky and wipe my tears so Carmen doesn't see, but it's not a sad part. We've seen this movie so many times, she doesn't buy it.

Instead, she starts talking loudly. "I remember the first time I watched this with my mom, I thought Harrison Ford was so hot. I was younger than Pepper."

"He was hot." I clear the thickness from my throat, needing to sniff.

I'm still trying to hide my sadness. Carmen and Pepper have been working so hard to cheer me up. I feel ungrateful when all I want to do is hide in my bed and cry.

"He's a total skeez! He cheated on all of his wives, and I think he was a dick to Carrie Fisher."

I have no idea what Han Solo did with his personal life, but I know my friend is trying to distract me. "Didn't he marry somebody really young?"

"Yeah, I guess he's mended his ways." Carmen stuffs popcorn in her mouth. "She probably does butt stuff. Still, after a while it's just the same old butt you've been fucking for ten years."

A tear falls onto my cheek as I start to laugh at her disappointed tone. "It's true, but wasn't he like seventy when he married her?"

The movie continues with crazy Sigourney Weaver waving her crutches around. "What difference does that make?"

"Maybe he's less of a horndog now that he's old?"

"I don't think it makes a difference. Charlie Chaplin was having babies at ninety."

"How do you know that?"

"It was in *When Harry Met Sally…* We should watch that one."

Carmen shouts at the screen. "Hit him with your crutch, Siggy! I hate how they pit women against each other in old movies."

"Thanks for this." I lean my head on her shoulder. "You really are my bestie."

"I can't wait to be in the city for your show. It's going to be so great."

"Yeah." My voice is quiet, and I try not to be sad thinking how it won't be the same if Scar isn't there. "Can't wait."

Switching off the movie, she rests her head on my shoulder. "I know it's not the same. I wish there was something I could do."

"Maybe if I weren't such a fuck up, he'd be here now." It's a question I wrestle with nightly, as silent tears exhaust me to sleep.

"I think everything in our lives has to happen for us to get where we are." Carmen sees my confused expression and continues. "If you hadn't been mixed up in the stuff that was happening in New York, your uncle never would have sent the letter to Blake to get you here in which case you never would have–"

"Stumbled into Scar's arms?" She momentarily silences my inner guilt and presses her lips into a smug smile.

I concede. "Maybe you're right."

"I'm right." She scoots closer. "And I overheard Dirk talking about some guy they were bringing in to help. They have a plan."

Hope twists so hard in my chest, I almost can't breathe. "What is it?"

"Dirk found some guy in Chicago–I think he said he's a lawyer. That's as much as I know."

Chewing my thumb, I think about what she's saying. If Hutch has a lawyer could this mean he's found a way to bring Scar home? "But they're in Russia."

"That's something you haven't done in a while."

I look at my thumb and put my hands in my lap embarrassed. "One step forward, two steps back?"

She puts an arm around my shoulders. "One step forward,

two steps forward. You should stop by the office tomorrow and see what's new."

Nodding, I tuck my thumb in my fist. I plan to do just that.

"It's not the worst prison in Russia." Dirk has his back to the door when I arrive at Hutch's office the next day. "The most brutal prisoners are at Black Dolphin. Lefortovo is bad, but it's not that bad."

Cold filters through my bloodstream as I stand inside the entrance listening to his words. Hutch looks up from his desk to see me and immediately cuts off his brother.

"Interesting. Good research. Hey, Hana."

Dirk spins around to face me, and his expression is unmistakable. They've been keeping this from me.

"Scar's in prison?" It's a cracked whisper. "How long have you known this?"

Hutch crosses the room to where I stand at the door. "I asked our contact in Minsk to monitor his arrival, to help us know where they were going."

"So you've known from the beginning?" My heart drums pain through my chest into my back.

Dirk tries to recover. "I know it sounds bad, but from what we've learned, it's actually a good thing."

"How can Scar in a Russian prison possibly be good?" I'm actually shouting at him, something I never do.

"Hey," Hutch touches my arm. "It means we have a better chance of actually getting him back. If Simon dumped him in a prison, he's not using him to do anything illegal."

My eyes squeeze shut, and I want to scream. I'm so fucking helpless, and my Scar is in a fucking prison for me. Rage and misery and heartbreak and longing writhe in my chest.

I feel my insides spiraling, but Dirk throws me a lifeline. "It means we can get him home."

A sharp inhale hiccups in my chest, and I meet his eyes. "How?"

"Another PI I know, a Marine, was briefly imprisoned for killing a rapist." Hutch turns his phone to me, and it's a photo of a handsome man with light brown hair and hazel eyes in a designer suit. "This is the lawyer that got him out, Marcus Merritt. He had a unique argument that pitted the defendant's record against the victim's. I don't have all the details, but he got him off with time served and a small fine."

"You think he can do that in Russia?"

Hutch exhales heavily, and his face drops. "I doubt it. I don't even know who we could contact to try and make it happen, but I've been working on it nonstop." His green eyes meet mine, and the only thing as powerful as the pain in my body is the ferocity in them. "I won't let my friend die in a Russian prison for killing a child-molesting worm."

Blinking quickly, I hold back the tears. I don't want to appear weak in front of these strong men, especially after all Hutch has said about me in the past–all of which is true, sadly.

"How can I help?"

Dirk puts an arm around me, giving me a squeeze. "You can be strong a little while longer."

It doesn't feel like enough. "He killed Victor for me. I love him."

"I know."

Hutch's fierce expression softens. "He loves you. I'm going to get him out of there, and back home to you. I promise."

CHAPTER 30

Scar

'M BEHIND A LAYER OF BARS BLOCKING A SOLID, METAL DOOR INSIDE a four-foot-square cell.

A concrete slab serves as a bed, and beside it is a toilet containing rust-colored water. A small window high above my head lets me know if it's day or night. Otherwise, I'm completely alone.

As a child, I heard stories of men sent to this prison. They were accused of being political dissidents or spies. Often, they were shop owners who'd pissed off a customer who in turn reported them to the FSB, the new and improved KGB, for speaking out against the government or trying to stir up political protests–something no one was stupid enough to do unless they had a death wish or some foolhardy belief they could make a difference. No one makes a difference without violence, and no one has the stomach for violence.

Such is life in an autocracy, where neighbor spies on neighbor, and a petty grudge can turn into a life sentence.

When I got here, I was stripped and hosed down like I'd been exposed to radiation. The force of the water left visible bruises where my body is not covered in ink. I'm pretty sure I'm bruised all over, plus a few cracked ribs.

A painful body-cavity search, and I was given scrubs so stiff, they could stand on their own. The guards made me bend at the waist and walk to my cell with my handcuffed arms extended up behind my back–supposedly so I wouldn't see who I was passing or how I arrived at my cell.

I'm pretty sure it was for degradation as well.

One guard pressed my forehead to the wall and his gun to my temple as the other uncuffed my wrists to prevent me from attacking them. I had no intention of attacking them. I made this deal, and I'm here until I'm set free, which according to Simon will never happen.

Finally, I was alone in the silent darkness, in a room with no blankets or food. Only cold, brown water and a patch of fading daylight from a small rectangle near the ceiling.

My body aches, and I find no comfort anywhere. Still, nothing hurts as much as losing her picture. They took everything from me, and I can only hope one day, when I'm an old man, I might get it back. For now I'm alone in this cell with nothing but my memories–so many memories.

Closing my eyes, I see her soft blonde curls falling around her shoulders. I see the light in her eyes, shining when she would look up at me, and I even smile when I remember her sassy little self choking on a sunflower seed.

Rolling onto my side on the concrete slab, I brace my injured ribs as the pain of loss squeezes my heart. *I'll never see her again.* I'll never touch her soft cheek, hear her sweet laugh, place my lips at the base of her neck as I inhale the scent of her skin. It's a worse torture than anything they could do to me here.

When I made my deal with Simon, it was on impulse. I didn't imagine how I would manage being without her, but as the reality settled over me, I expected to distract my mind by working. Here, in this empty place, I have nothing. Here I've found an even worse torture than death.

Silence, space, time.

I've been thrown into an ocean alone. I've gone from constant contact to isolation and nothingness. How long will I live in this void?

Echoing in my ears is the pressing question that has always haunted me… *Why?*

With her, I found the answer. Now I have none.

A week has passed in this cell alone. The first night, I found a rock in the corner where the wall meets the floor, and I used it to scratch a line in the wall. I made one for every time the tiny window turned from dark to light. It gave me something to track.

I've never practiced meditation or any form of mental exercise, and I'm sorry for that. In its place, I've worked out a routine of exercise each day, counting the number of repetitions I would do, seeing if I can go one more round.

The pain of my injuries remind me I'm alive. Four times a day, a small pot of soup and a rock-hard piece of bread slides through my door.

When I dream, I hear her soft moans, a treasure lost to me now. When I wake with a hard-on, I handle it with my back to the door, standing close to the small, metal toilet. I'm sure they're watching me, a cold eye, tracking all my moves.

In the place of meditation, I have my own practice of spirituality. I don't believe I'm worthy of salvation, so it's nothing like that. I don't believe God would waste time on someone like me, so I take myself inward. I focus on breathing and observing the thoughts that pass through my mind. Some of them are tragic. Some are beautiful. I watch them like slides on a movie screen.

I remember being a small boy alone in the cold barn behind my foster parents' home. My bed was a cot, but I had a blanket. I loved the animals, especially the draft horse they used for farming. Kabarda was my first friend.

I remember leaving that house, saying goodbye to my friend, and moving to a large, childcare facility, where I slept in a bunk bed in a room with many other boys. I remember fighting because I was so skinny. Then after eating well and regularly, I grew tall. I started working out, and no one tried to fight me anymore. From there I moved to a hostel, then finally I joined the military.

I remember the first day I met Hutch, and how we became friends. He had an optimism I'd never seen before, a fierce belief in his view of the world. We were the same age, but he seemed younger in his aggressive optimism. Still, after the life I'd lived, I wanted to be a part of what he had.

Many times, I return to the day of the fire and how it changed my life forever. My military career was ending, Hutch was leaving, and I was afraid of going back to what I'd been before I met him, hopeless, pessimistic. Then the fire brought something out of me I didn't know I possessed—was it heroism as Hutch said or a pointless act as Simon characterized it?

It was an impulse I didn't find again until I saw the horrible things Victor did. I wasn't like him, and I wanted out of that world. I was a prisoner, and I escaped. I ran to the one person who I wanted to be, and in joining Hutch's world, I found my destiny.

I found Hana.

"Let's go." I startle at the sound of a voice.

After seven tick marks and nothing but the hum of machinery, silence, or the sound of myself, it's like an alien invasion. It's a welcome noise, even if it's an uncaring prison guard.

The double doors open, and I step into the empty hall, looking side to side, startled to see other men are standing outside similar confines. All this time, we've been so close to each other, human rats in cages.

A voice shouts, and we start to move, walking in a line down the corridor and out into an open yard with tall fencing topped by swirls of barbed wire. I squint against the bright sunlight, looking around at the hundred or so men doing the same.

I'm not the biggest thug in this gulag. I'm not even the most damaged.

Across the concrete courtyard from me is a man at least one inch taller who is missing an eye. Beside him is a bald man, same height as me, with the side of his face marred by some accident involving fire or acid.

I'm gazing at him in wonder when a voice barks at me from the left in Russian. "You're new here."

Glancing at the speaker, he's two inches wider than I am, but not as tall. I don't know how to answer his statement, so I don't. Returning my gaze to the yard, I continue inspecting my fellow inmates.

"Why are you here?" The man continues speaking in Russian.

Deciding I have no choice, I answer him. "Murder."

It's not the full story, but it'll do. I'm here because of Hana, but I'm in prison for killing Victor–if you believe Simon.

The man juts out his chin as if he's satisfied with that response. "Who did you kill?"

"A pedophile."

He sniffs. "Did he rape you?"

"No. He hurt the woman I love when she was a child, so I killed him."

He nods, and apparently this is acceptable. He holds out a hand to me. "I'm Ghost. Say you're with me, and they'll leave you alone."

I don't know who they are–the guards or other inmates– but I nod clasping his hand and thanking him. Then I go to the bleachers lining the yard and sit by myself. I don't need to communicate with these men. I only need to be around other humans.

Knowing they're here, we're all in this together is enough for me. I'm not alone.

"Lourde!" My name is shouted across the yard, and I look up to see a scowling guard standing at the fence.

I go to where he's waiting, and he pushes my shoulder with a black baton, speaking in Russian. "Shower."

Looking around, I see another guard standing at a door that leads into a room similar to a gym locker. Stepping inside, I see a wall of showers, and men standing under them quickly washing themselves with beige soap.

"Two minutes."

I glance at the man, and he turns his back to me. I guess the clock has started, so I quickly remove my scrubs and go to a vacant spot under a shower head. Beside me is a startlingly big guy with a bald head and prison tattoos on his face.

He slowly inspects my body, but I don't look at him. I quickly shower, thinking I can get this done in two minutes, even if this bar of soap doesn't lather. Rubbing it against my head, I quickly shove it under the spray, doing my best to get the week's worth of sweat and grime off me.

I'm startled when a hand touches my stomach, and I immediately slap it away. "I'm with Ghost."

The words come out fast, and the big guy turns, leaving me alone to finish. Every muscle in my body is tense, and I don't know what I've just said or what it means. I am certain if an assault were to happen here, the guards wouldn't care.

When I get back to my cell, I'm revived from the contact with other humans and the shower, but I'm shaken by my experience there.

A blank notebook and a pen are on my concrete slab-bed. I look at them for a long time, wondering what I might do with them. As the lights go down on my seventh day inside, I begin to write.

Our second trip to the yard comes exactly seven days later, and I strain my eyes for Ghost. He's there, same size, same abrupt line of questioning.

"What was her name?" He looks up at me.

"Hana." Saying it relaxes the pain in my chest, like soothing music.

In my notebook, I've written every thought I had from the first day I saw her in her uncle's pea-gravel driveway to the night I held her in my arms for the last time. I've documented the way she fills the cracks in my soul. I've drawn primitive doodles of her face, her long curly hair, her eyes. I would close my eyes and hear her cracked moans of ecstasy when I was deep inside her.

"Do you wish you could forget?" He's staring at the yard, like he's miles from here.

The lack of specificity in the question sends my mind down a rabbit hole that makes me worry I'm losing my grip. *Forget what?*

If I forget Hana, I would forget my pain. I'd never have to experience the agony of losing her, but I'd exist in this space of nothingness. Would I want to forget her? Would I do it if it meant I would lose the tiny daggers that never stop stabbing my insides.

"No." I answer flatly. "I want to remember everything."

I would suffer again and again, all the fiery levels of hell to remember the time I had with Hana. My memories of her are the jewels I have now replacing everything I've lost.

He lifts his chin and nods. "You're still sane."

This day in the shower, a different group of men are there. None of us look at each other. None of us speak. We're herded out of the facility, and again, our time is over.

Again, we're lined up and led back to our tiny cells for seven more days alone.

My throat tightens with each step closer to the metal door. I'm not sure I can do another seven days alone. Panic settles at the bottom of my gut, a desperation I don't recognize.

The years spread out before me, and I'm not sure if I can continue this way. I don't know if I can do this again and again, over and over for the rest of my life.

When I return to my cell, another book is waiting on my concrete slab. It's a book of poems by Alexander Pushkin.

May love yet show her smile of valediction… I toss the volume aside and pick up my notebook.

CHAPTER 31

Hana

"**O**H, I LOVE THIS ONE." BLAKE HESITATES, HOLDING A PIECE OF tissue paper over the black and white portrait of Pepper and Teal in Shirley's.

We're five days away from the show, and she's helping me pack the new pictures I want to include in it. I sent thumbnails to Jill, and we agreed on five additional images.

"I was thinking about memory, and it's the first memory they'll have together. I think it goes well in the series with the girls."

My sister's head tilts to the side. "I'm not sure if it's because I know the story, but it's like I can feel the tension."

Teal's smile is hesitant, and Pepper's eyes are curious. She has no idea she's sitting across from her father as they cautiously get to know each other.

"He's the only tense one. Pepper is clueless."

"He still hasn't told her?" She arches an eyebrow at me.

"It's only been a few weeks, and they're not together all the time."

"It's been long enough." She carefully places the tissue over the front of the sheet. "I'll have Hutch invite him to dinner when he gets back in town. It's time to get that ball rolling." She stops at another portrait, laying her hand on her heart. "I need a copy of this to frame."

It's a candid shot of Blake sitting on her fiancé's lap on his front porch swing. Her head is leaning against his, and his lips are pressed to the base of her neck.

Developing this image hurt so bad. Scar would always lean down and kiss my neck, smell my hair. Tears were in my eyes as I enlarged it, settling on a glowing sepia for the filter. Standing here now, my barely closed wounds tear open again.

Jill insisted it be in the show. The emotion is so strong.

"Your love is beautiful to see." I do my best to shake off my pain. "And to think, you always said you hated him."

"I was young–and I'd never seen him naked." Blake quips, wrapping an arm around my shoulders and leaning her head against mine. "You are so talented. I can't get over how you capture emotions."

"I have great subjects." Giving her a squeeze, I push back on my pain, sliding a tissue in place and stacking an image of Uncle Hugh on top of the print. "The Elder Statesman."

It's a shot of our uncle standing on his porch in his linen suit and gray Stetson, holding his cane, and it captures him in all his formal elegance looking out over his property.

"It's perfect." She slides a tissue over it and we roll the prints carefully before sliding them in the sturdy cardboard tube.

Setting it to the side, she takes both my hands in hers. "How are you feeling?"

Blinking up at her, I answer honestly. "I feel safe, and I feel miserable."

Pulling me in, we hug. "I wish there was something I could do. Hutch is determined, but I feel so helpless."

"When does he get back from Chicago?"

"He didn't tell you?" Her brows furrow, and she steps back. "He's on his way to Minsk."

My heart jumps, and I pull my hands out of hers. "I want to go with him. I need to be there. If he's able to see him, I want to see him."

"I guess that's why he didn't tell you. Scar's in solitary confinement in a maximum security prison. No one can see him."

Clenching my jaw, I try not to be angry at Hutch. I know he's doing all he can to help us. "It doesn't matter. He should have told me."

"I'm sure he didn't want to distract you from your show."

"Screw the show!" I throw up my hands. "Does he really think it's more important to me?"

She puts her arm around me again. "I know it's not. I'm sorry."

"If he can't see him, what will he do in Minsk?"

"He said he hopes to meet with senior officials or a diplomat–I'm not really sure how it works, but he's going to talk to them and try to work out an exchange."

"What does that mean? What kind of exchange?"

"Like if there's somebody in jail here, in the US, who they want, they can exchange them for Scar."

Crossing my arms, I consider this option. "He can do that?"

"Marcus Merritt said it's more complicated, since Scar confessed to the murder and the victim has family who claims to want justice."

"A family of criminals! It's freakin Russian mafia, for God's sake."

"Yes, and Scar is an American citizen. He helped the military in eastern Europe, and the man he killed was an established criminal."

"So he's going to ask if they want somebody to trade, then what?"

She exhales heavily. "Then they go to the President."

"Of the United States?" My eyebrows shoot up, and she nods.

Leaning heavily against my worktable, I don't know whether to laugh or cry. It feels like a monumental task, at the same time, we've met ambassadors and diplomats at my mother's gala events. We know senators…

"It's like something out of a spy novel." My voice is quiet, and I look to my sister to judge her response.

"Apparently it happens all the time."

"It does?"

"Well, not *all* the time, but it happens. Remember that news reporter who got her sister out of North Korea?" She lifts the cardboard tube and reaches for my hand. "We have to stay positive. Hope for the best."

"Hang on—we forgot one." The final addition to my show is a self-portrait I took last week.

I'm sitting in a window seat with a daisy in my hand, plucking the petals as I recite my twisted version of the game in my head.

I used a tripod and waited until the sunlight filtered through the window to create a halo around my blonde hair. With a little manipulation, I was able to appear glowing, remembering my love.

It's the perfect finale piece. The ultimate representation of *Memory*, the love I will never forget.

I hold a sheet of tissue as I explain. "In the original French version of the game, it's not about whether or not he loves you, but how much. *Un peu*, a little or *à la folie*, to madness."

Blake's voice is soft. "He loves you *a la mort*."

Lifting my chin, I give her a sad smile. "And I'll love him until I die."

"Holy cow!" Pepper yells from the passenger side of my golf cart. "We're only going to be gone three days!"

Carmen struggles to roll a suitcase as big as a steamer trunk down the short driveway from her mother's house to where we're waiting. "Shut up! I didn't know what to pack. It's my first time visiting New York."

"Looks like you need to—"

"Pepper Winston!" Carmen stops walking and points a finger. "If you say one word about tidying up or sparking joy, I swear to God!"

Pepper crosses her arms and falls back against the seat.

I hop out of the cart and jog around to help her lift her massive load. "As long as you didn't exceed the weight limit. Uncle Hugh said fifty pounds each."

Carmen's shoulders fall. "I think I exceeded the weight limit."

Hesitating, I glance from her to the cart. "We'll see what happens. I'm probably underweight, since I still have a lot of stuff at the apartment."

My bestie gives me a squeeze and a squeal. "I'm so excited! I can't believe I'm finally going to The Big Apple for a super prestigious art premiere for my bestie!"

"Just don't call it *The Big Apple*. Only tourists and journalists say that."

Pepper nods like she's an authority. "It's like calling San Francisco *Frisco*.'"

Carmen scrubs her finger in Pepper's hair. "Like you know anything."

"I know not to call it *The Big Apple* like some kind of dork."

"Is your dad flying with us or is he going to meet us there?" Carmen shifts around on the backseat bench then freezes when she realizes what she said.

My eyes are wide, and I'm pretty sure my heart stopped. "You mean my mom?" I say loudly, but my voice is too high and wobbly.

Pepper doesn't move, her lips are parted as she blinks several times. Slowly her face turns to mine, and her brow scrunches.

"Yes! Your mom!" Carmen cries. "I've been all mixed up all day trying to get Rashmi set up to run the store while I'm away and everything packed. What did I say?"

"You said my *dad*." Pepper's voice is eerily calm for the bomb we just dropped.

My bottom lip disappears beneath my teeth, and the only noise is the crunch of tires on gravel as we glide up to the front entrance of Uncle Hugh's mansion.

I bypass the waiting limo and park in his five-car garage, then I shift in my seat to face my little friend. "Say something, Pep."

She blinks twice. "Teal Masters is my dad?"

"I'm sorry!" Carmen puts both hands over her face. "This is why you should never tell me secrets. He wanted to tell you himself, and now I've ruined it."

Studying Pepper's expression, I can't tell what she's thinking. "He only found out a month or so ago, and he wanted to meet you."

"Why hasn't he told me yet?" Her brow scrunches harder. "Is he trying to decide if he likes me or something?"

"NO!" Carmen and I both shout at once, and Pepper jumps in her seat.

"I'm sorry." Scooting forward, I wrap my arms around her. "No—it's just the opposite. He's been so nervous you'd be mad at him for not being around or you wouldn't like him. I think he wanted to plan something special, but it's all been so crazy these last few weeks."

"That's why he's moving here." Carmen reaches across the seat to rub her arm. "He really wants to be a part of your life."

My voice is quiet, and I release her, looking into her big brown eyes. "If you want that."

"Your dad should be saying all of this." Carmen drops her chin. "I really screwed up everything. I'm sorry."

We wait, watching as Pepper's expression goes from stunned to settled. "We won't tell him."

Carmen's eyes flicker from Pepper to me. "I'm okay with that."

"If he's planning something special, I want to see what he does." Pepper nods, like the decision is made. "I can go on acting like I don't know, and it'll be our secret. Like a surprise birthday party or something."

"Okay…" I tilt my head to the side, trying to meet her eyes. "And you're okay with this?"

She shrugs. "I think so. I always wanted to know my dad. What does Uncle Hutch think?"

My chest squeezes, and I press my lips into a smile. "He's been a little worried about how you'll respond. We all have. We don't want you to feel ambushed."

"I don't." Hopping out of the golf cart, she hesitates before picking up her duffel. "If Uncle Hutch is okay with him, then I'll be okay with him."

She starts for the house, but I hurry to catch up with her, leaving Carmen grunting and struggling with her monster-bag.

"But do *you* like Teal?" She's walking fast in a way that makes me worry.

We reach the waiting limo, and Pepper puts her bag in the back before Uncle Hugh's driver can help her. My things are already inside, and Carmen is flapping like a goose, trying to roll her suitcase on the gravel.

"Don't worry about me," she yells sarcastically.

My uncle's chauffeur trots over to help her, and I take Pepper's hand, going around to climb in the backseat. Blake flew ahead of us to the city to be there when Hutch returned from his international flight, which has me even more anxious to get to New York.

"He's nice, but he's not like Uncle Hutch."

"What do you mean?" I sit across from her on the black leather seat.

"He's always asking what I think about things and worrying if I'm having fun. Uncle Hutch never does that."

Swallowing a laugh, I nod. "I think Teal was trying to find out what you like. The way you'd do with a new friend."

"Do you like him?"

"I do. He seems like a really nice man, and I think he'll work very hard to be a good dad."

"What'd I miss?" Carmen crawls in the limo. Her hair's a mess, and a sheen of sweat is on her forehead.

"Here." I pull out a body wipe. "We got it all sorted. You try not to spill any more beans."

"Are there any left? No," she groans, holding up her hands. "If there are, don't tell me!"

It's late when we finally arrive at the Andover. Rusty is delighted to meet the Hamiltown additions, in particular Pepper, who he immediately takes under his wing.

"I've never been in an elevator like this." She smiles up at him, watching as he holds the door open while Carmen struggles with her bag.

"I can call a bellhop if you need assistance, Miss," he says to her, but Carmen declines.

"I don't have any tip money!"

Rusty lifts his chin, then motions to the panel. "Your floor is twenty-seven. Right there."

Pepper presses the button and smiles up at him. "I bet you see a lot of stuff. Lots of hot gossip?"

"An elevator operator never tells." He looks to the top right corner, but a smile hints at his wrinkled lips.

Hutch is in the kitchen with Blake and Mama when we enter the apartment.

"My room is the last door on the left," I tell Pepper and Carmen before I go to where he's standing.

Pepper beats me to her uncle. She might be twelve, but she still jumps into a hug. It makes me wonder what she's really thinking about the Teal situation. I know Hutch is worried about her, but maybe she's worried about Hutch? I'd like to tell her it's all going to work out fine, but we're keeping that accidental revelation under wraps.

Also, I want to know what's happening with Scar.

"Of course, we have to invite Belinda and Cheryl." Mama is going down her guest list for the wedding. "The Hawthornes and the Bartholomews should also be invited."

"I hardly even know those people," Blake argues.

"They attend the gala every year, and they always make huge donations."

"We're trying to keep it an intimate affair."

My eyes are wide as I look from the two of them to Hutch, who is typing something on his phone. Reaching out, I touch his forearm, motioning for him to follow me into the living room.

Pepper is helping Carmen wrangle her suitcase to my bedroom, and I wring my fingers as I wait. "Any luck?"

He's been gone five days, first meeting Marcus in Chicago then going to Europe.

"They're going to let me know."

"That's it?" My shoulders drop, and mist heats my eyes. "You went all that way, and they're going to let you know?"

Hutch's deep voice is solemn. "It's not what I wanted to hear either, but it's a start. I made contact, and he's on their radar."

Rubbing my hand over my forehead, I swallow the knot

twisting my throat. "Were you able to find out how he's doing? Is he well?"

"He's being transferred to a labor camp about three hundred miles east of Moscow."

"A labor camp?" My heart sinks. "That sounds awful!"

Hutch nods, his expression dark. "He's been in solitary confinement since he got there, so it could be good. At least he'll be around people."

"Criminals!" I'm doing my best not to attract the attention of my mother, but I'm not sure how much longer I can hold back the tears.

Hutch puts a warm hand on my shoulder. "I know this is painful. I hate it, too, but we're making progress."

Nodding, I wipe my eyes. *Can I face another day without him?*

"I always thought he'd be with me at my show. It won't be the same."

I'm pulled into a warm hug, and a tear escapes, falling to my cheek. A moment later, I feel another pair of arms joining Hutch's around me.

"Hang in there, sis." Blake has my back, like always.

"Me too!" Pepper's voice rings out, and we all chuckle as she wiggles in at my waist, hugging me.

"Heck, I want some of that!" Carmen hugs Blake's back.

"I don't know what's happening right now, but I hope it's nothing serious," my mother calls from the kitchen.

It still hurts, but this time, I'm not cowering in the darkness alone. I've got a crowd of people surrounding me, holding me up, keeping me strong. It's not just serious, it's marvelous.

CHAPTER 32

Scar

Her eyes are like the deep ocean, inky blue, holding secret *treasures*… I write the words, and I sketch an oval shape the way I remember her face. I'm no artist, but I'm getting better at capturing her likeness.

Long, soft curls I can wrap around my fingers, full lips curling into the best smile. The sound of her voice is the only thing I can't capture on paper. I would call her for no reason just to hear her speak.

"Time to go." The sharp voice snaps my attention before the door slides open on my cell.

The order came yesterday. I'm being moved to a labor camp a half-day's drive from here, somewhere farther east, closer to the wastelands of Siberia, reinforcing my forgotten status. It's a nagging, dry ache in my chest.

I've lost weight living on a diet of soup four times a day, but my muscles are more pronounced from my daily exercise regime. Staying strong is as important in this environment as having friends. I wonder if I'll find another Ghost. I'm sorry I can't say goodbye.

Handcuffs are placed on my wrists, and this time I walk out standing straight. Passing the tiny cells, one after the other makes my stomach turn. No human should be housed this way for any period of time.

One of the guards puts a small bundle between my cuffed hands before I walk out the door. He doesn't make eye contact, and I do my best not to drop it as I'm shoved into the back of the van alone.

Sitting with my back to the cab, I realize it's the clothes I wore when I arrived. My wallet, shoes, and watch are all gone, but my chest squeezes as I quickly shove my fingers in the pockets of my shirt.

I can hardly breathe hoping, *Is it still there?* Fuck, it's got to be. I'm frantic, bouncing over rough roads, falling to the side, my fingers touch paper, and I exhale a yell. *It's here*.

Careful not to tear it, I slide the photograph from the pocket of my shirt. The minute I see her face, my chin drops, and I exhale a groan.

Swallowing the pain, I trace my finger over her pretty smile. I'm holding her in my arms, and I cast my mind back to that day, her soft body next to mine in the bed.

I can't smell her scent anymore, but I remember it. I remember the feel of her soft breasts in my hands, and the warmth of her laugh. Leaning against the wall in the back of that van, I hold the photograph to my heart and dream of a day when I'll hold her again.

"Get out." The sky is dark, and I'm confused when I open my eyes.

I must've fallen asleep, and we've driven much longer than

half a day. Shuffling forward, I stand up to see we're outside some kind of state building or a castle.

"Come this way." The guard speaks in Russian, and I follow him and another man up the concrete drive, past an elaborate fountain, around to a side entrance.

We step into a small room where deliveries are received. Boxes are stacked in a corner, and a dumb waiter is built into the wall. A narrow, black staircase is situated in the other corner, and I wait with my hands cuffed.

A second guard stands opposite me, but he doesn't make eye contact. He's indifferent to my plight, probably wishing he was off duty, somewhere miles from here. At least, it's how I'd feel if I were him.

The original guard steps through a dark wooden door, and motions to me. "This way."

It's all very cloak and dagger, and I'm confused as to what's going on. I'm supposed to be in a labor camp, but this is clearly someone's official residence.

I follow the guard into the main building, through rooms with enormous Oriental rugs covering polished wood floors. Chairs and sofas with opulent, satin upholstery are positioned beside tables holding stained-glass Tiffany lamps and crystal dishes.

In one room we pass, a grand piano is in the center with spindly wooden chairs arranged as if in preparation for a private concert.

Finally, we stop at a massive wooden door, and the guard taps lightly.

"Come." A male voice speaks sharply in Russian from inside, and the door opens.

I'm escorted into a large office with a heavy wooden desk in the center. A green lamp is on one corner and a brass statue of a cherub holding a harp and a cluster of grapes is on the other.

The walls are lined with bookshelves, and photographs of

a young woman and a little girl are arranged among the books. In each frame, the pair grow a few years older.

Behind the desk sits a man with thick white hair smoothed back from his prominent face. He's wearing a gray suit with no tie, and his white shirt is unbuttoned. He's casual, but clearly powerful.

"Leave us," the man orders, and the guard starts for the door. "Wait. Remove these handcuffs."

"Are you sure?" The guard is confused, but the old man cuts him a glare which elicits quick compliance.

Cuffs gone, I rub my wrists, waiting to see what's about to happen. I'm at a complete loss.

"May I offer you a drink?" The old man stands and goes to a small table beside a window.

He pours a short glass of vodka, but I decline. "It's been a while since I've had a drink."

And I have no intention of being drugged.

"You're probably wondering who I am and what you're doing here." He closes the space between us, leaning against the desk. "May I see your wrists?"

Adrenaline circulates in my veins. I don't know what kind of setup this might be, but I'm mentally preparing to punch this guy in the face and run.

"Please, if you don't mind."

"What do you want to see?" My voice is rough from lack of use.

"I heard you were severely burned over most of your body. I wanted to be sure I have the right person before I say what I'm about to say."

Placing my hands on the arms of the chair, I stand to my full height, five inches taller than this man. His eyes widen, and he straightens, moving around to the other side of the desk. It's reassuring to know I'm bigger than him—and he's afraid.

Without taking my eyes off his, I slide the prison-issue shirt over my head, exposing my full torso for inspection. "The ink covers my scars."

The old man's eyes widen, and he blinks down to the wooden desktop. His brow clutches as if he's reliving some secret pain, then he begins to speak.

"Eight years ago, I was in the Mediterranean, yachting back from Cannes to Istanbul. My daughter Ana was traveling with my granddaughter to meet me from her home in Varna." He pauses to inhale or to simply collect himself as if telling me this is difficult. "She made a detour… I don't remember why. I think it was to visit a farmer's market. She was very interested in handmade things at that time. Either way, they stopped at a place called Krasivoy Kafe for lunch."

His brown eyes lift to mine, and my shoulders tighten. I pull my shirt back on.

"The place no longer exists." His voice is solemn. "But perhaps you remember it?"

It's difficult to breathe, but I answer. "I remember."

"A tragic event occurred at that Kafe. A fire broke out and several people were killed. More were injured, and in the chaos, my daughter and granddaughter were separated. She was dragged out, leaving her daughter inside to die."

Swallowing the knot in my throat, I wish I'd accepted that drink. My mouth is completely dry.

He continues slowly. "They were in a very rural area, and the fire trucks took a long time to arrive. The ancient structure was burning fast, and my daughter was frantic."

He pauses, walking to his bookshelf where he lifts a framed photograph. "My wife died when Ana was a child. She and my granddaughter are the only family I have left in this world."

Pain grinds in my chest, and I wish he'd get to the point.

"Ana said two men appeared on the scene. One was an American, a Marine. The other appeared to be from our country. She said he was very tall, lean with long hair and wolfish blue eyes. She said he ran into the fire not once, but twice searching for my granddaughter. He found her. He saved her, but before he could escape, the roof collapsed. She feared the man had been killed."

He waits, and I look up at him, meeting his gaze.

He gives me a knowing smile. "As you know, that man was not killed. We tracked him down in America, but he disappeared before I could make contact. For seven years we searched, then a few days ago, my man notified me the Marine was in Minsk meeting with a state official, trying to work out a deal to save that man's life. You are that man, Oskar Lourde."

A surge of energy drives me to my feet. "Hutch was in Minsk?"

"He wants to make an exchange, some criminal in return for your life. Only, you are not a criminal." His flinty eyes lock on mine. "Are you?"

Hesitating, I'm not sure how to respond. If I say yes, will he send me to the labor camp? If I say no, will my deal to save Hana be canceled?

"I'll have that drink if you're still offering it."

He goes to the table and plucks a large square of ice, lowering it into a short crystal tumbler, then he pours clear vodka over it. Handing it to me, he waits as I drink it down.

Gazing at the empty glass, I speak the truth. "I killed a man in America."

His chin lifts, and he returns to sit behind his desk. "You killed a man in America, but you pay for it in a Russian prison? How does that happen?"

"The man I killed has connections in Moscow. I was briefly part of his network."

"I see." He leans back in his chair, sliding a hand along the edge of his desk. "Why would the Marine make a deal for your freedom?"

Shaking my head, I walk over to his bookshelf, lifting a framed photo of his daughter and the little girl. I recognize her now. She has a look about her, wise beyond her years. It reminds me of Hana.

"The man I killed was a very bad man, but his brother is even worse. He put me there."

"The Marine said the man you killed raped his little sister, the woman you love, when she was a child. Is that true?"

My jaw clenches, and my eyes squeeze shut. Returning the photo to the shelf, I drop my head as rage surges through my veins.

"Yes." It comes out as more of a growl. "I'd do it again. Slower."

The old man rises from his chair and walks to where I stand. "Do you know who I am, Mr. Lourde?" His voice is strong with authority.

Studying him, I answer honestly. "I don't."

I think he's going to tell me, but he changes his mind. "Perhaps that's how it should be. You saved my granddaughter with no knowledge of who she was, and for that I owe you a debt. Tonight I will put you on a plane for whatever destination you choose. You will not spend another night in prison in my country. My man will provide you with a number. If you are ever in trouble again, I hope you will allow me to help you."

CHAPTER 33

Hana

M

Y DRESS IS MAGENTA CRÊPE SATIN FROM THE SPRING VALENTINO collection. It's mid-thigh with cutouts at my ribs, creating the illusion of a halter top, and while it's not Versace, Debbie would approve.

Standing in front of my full-length mirror, I remember my friend. "Debbie would've been so proud of this night," I say softly.

Carmen gives my upper arms a squeeze, pressing her cheek to mine. "I wish I'd known her. She sounds like a lot of fun."

I lightly touch the tears from the corners of my eyes and force a smile. "She was wild, and she had bad taste in men. But her fashion sense was impeccable, and she was very loyal."

"Sounds like my kind of gal."

"You look amazing!" I step back admiring her shimmery purple sheath. "What's happening here?"

A solid red handkerchief is wrapped over her auburn hair,

and she squints her hazel eyes at me. "You hate it? I saw it online in the Versace runway show, but I'm not sold."

"I mean, it's a daring choice."

"That does it." She rips the kerchief off her head and throws it on the bed. "Help me cut bangs."

"We have to leave for the show. I'm not cutting bangs."

"Everyone in New York has bangs! Everywhere we went, all I saw was bangs bangs bangs!"

Grabbing her arms, I meet her eyes. "Aren't I supposed to be the one freaking out right now? I'll take you to get bangs tomorrow."

Closing her eyes, she nods quickly, sliding her hands down the front of her dress as she breathes. "You're right. I'm sorry." She inhales, exhales. "I was just thinking about all the rich and famous people who are going to be there tonight, and I look like a bumpkin with no fashion sense."

"You look really good, and I wouldn't just say that."

Pepper bursts through the door. "Hana, your mama said if you don't get down to the car right this minute she's going to drive straight to the airport and board a plane for Saint Moritz. I don't know what that means, but she is very dramatic."

My little friend's eyes are wide, and I grab her hand. "It means it's time to go."

Carmen waves her hands in front of her face, and somehow her freaking out actually helps me stay calm. Something along the lines of, one of us has to keep it together.

The three of us clasp hands, and we head for the door.

Jill clutches my arm as I sip my glass of champagne, trying hard not to be nervous. "This is the best opening we've had in years."

"How do you know?" I scan the neutral faces of the men

and women filtering through the gallery, sipping wine and pausing in front of each photograph to stare.

My heart sinks every time they do that.

"They don't smile," I turn to Jill's chest, putting my hand on my forehead. "They hate it."

"Honey." Jill hooks a finger under my chin. "Almost every print has sold. They're not smiling because they're awestruck. The reporter from the *Times* said he hadn't seen such a unique voice since Maier. As in Vivian Maier."

My eyes heat, and I think I might cry. "I'm not that good."

"That's exactly what makes you great." Wrapping her arm around my shoulder, she gives me a squeeze. "We'll have you back in the fall for another show, then next year we can do a retrospective."

"I haven't been around long enough for a retrospective."

She waves her hand, giving me a wink. "We'll see what happens. Just don't stop taking pictures. The new ones you sent are perfection." She does a chef's kiss. "The father-daughter portrait? *Tears*."

Oh, shit. I forgot it's hanging in the next wing. "Thank you so much, Jill!"

Moving as fast as possible through the crowd, I wind my way past Mama, who's going on about my grandmother's artistic eye and trips to Paris. I'm pretty sure she's making that shit up. Every time she gets drunk, she goes on and on about how far she's climbed from her West Virginia coal-mining roots.

Trip says something, but I don't stop. I've got to find Pepper, and I'm pretty sure I know where she is.

The gallery is dimly lit with spotlights illuminating the photographs to make them more prominent. The wings are arranged in a winding *S* pattern, following the timeline we created, guiding viewers through the stages of *Memory*. I round the fourth corner, and skid to a stop.

She's there, standing in front of the giant portrait of her and Teal sitting across from each other at Shirley's. In the picture, Pepper's hands are elevated as she tells some story, and at this size, the amazement in Teal's eyes at his daughter is vivid.

Chewing my lip, I walk slowly to where my little friend is standing, and as I get closer, I see her face is streaked with tears.

"Pepper?" I drop to my knees, putting my arms around her waist.

"I can't believe I didn't see it." Her voice is a whisper, and I hug her tighter. "It's so obvious. I really am stupid."

"You are not!" I lift my head and meet her eyes. "You are one of the smartest kids I've ever known in my whole life."

"I should have told you sooner." The male voice behind me causes us both to turn.

Teal takes a few steps closer, ducking his head. His hands are shoved in his pockets the way they always are when Pepper is around. "No denying the obvious here."

Rising to my feet, I hold out my hands. "Teal, I'm sorry. I didn't realize—"

"It's an amazing photo. I want a copy to frame and hang on my wall—after you sign it, of course."

"Of course."

Pepper looks up at him, and he drops to his knees, lifting his hands and hesitating before he touches her. "Can I hug you?"

She dives forward, wrapping her arms around his neck, and dammit, I'm crying.

"I need a tissue," I tell them before taking off to the ladies room.

It helps that I'm pretty familiar with this gallery from the days I've spent preparing for this show. Touching the scratchy paper towel to my eyes, I make sure I don't look like a raccoon before heading out into the fray once more. I'm going to be exhausted by the end of this.

Drifting into the movement of the viewers, I hang in the shadows to watch their reactions. My stomach tightens when I look up to see I'm in the most painful part of my collection.

I wish I'd kept that awful tissue on hand, because the oversized portraits of Scar bring all the pain flooding back into my chest.

It's a deep, soul-gutting pain. Somewhere out there, my love is in prison, possibly being tortured on my behalf.

Leaning my head forward, I inhale a sharp breath, knowing I can't do this right now. I have to hold on a little longer and break down when I'm alone.

Still, the pain is unbearable. As beautiful as this night is, it's only a phantom of good with him not here. If only I could send him letters. If only I could hear his voice.

Oh, God, if only I could touch him one more time…

"They looked good in the darkroom, but wow. I can't believe this is me." The deep voice beside me in the dark makes my knees wobble.

Am I hallucinating? Turning my head slowly, when I meet his eyes, I almost faint.

"Don't do that." Stepping closer, he scoops me up by the waist before, holding me close to his chest.

I'm surrounded by warm woods and clean man-scent. "Is this a dream?"

Blinking fast, I'm sure it is. I must have fallen asleep.

Leaning down, he traces his nose along my cheek before kissing my lips gently. "Jesus, you feel so good. I've dreamed of this for weeks."

"I don't understand…" Tears slide from my eyes, and I'm having trouble breathing properly.

His strong arms are around me. He's holding me tight against his chest, and the last time I felt this way, I was on mushrooms.

"Maybe we should start believing in God, because I think I got a miracle." He's smiling, and the love glowing in his eyes has my heart flapping higher and higher in my chest like it grew wings.

"I always believed in God. I just never believed he cared for me, because I'm such a fuckup."

"I guess you were wrong."

"How did this happen?" My hands are on his face, and I can't stop touching him. Leaning forward, I press my lips to his, and he kisses me back with a force that steals my breath again.

"I really want to fuck you right now." He's so happy. I'm so fucking happy.

"Okay!"

"But your big show."

"Are you kidding?" Grasping his hand, I drag him down the narrow hall, through the curtains, dividing the show from backstage areas, into the darkroom where I spent the last two weeks crying as I gazed at his oversized face.

Now, in this room, facing each other, I blink again, forcefully. It's real. He's standing in front of me in the same jeans and button-down shirt he was wearing when he left me outside my apartment.

He's leaner, but his eyes glow with the same white-hot hunger. His long hair is looped in that samurai bun, and his dark brow lowers. I'm about to be devoured, and my toes curl as heat races through my core.

"I can't breathe," I manage to speak.

Walking slowly to where I'm standing, he slides a curl behind my ear before leaning in closer. "You're the best thing I've seen in my whole life."

Our mouths collide, and he lifts me onto the table. The skirt of my dress rises above my ass, and I exhale a whimper as his large hands grip my hips, dragging my core flush against his prominent erection.

"Oh, fuck," I gasp. "Give it to me."

My fingers fumble at his waist while he quickly unbuttons the top buttons of his shirt and pulls it over his head. His torso is even more ripped, and I lean forward to press my mouth against his collarbone, licking his skin as salt fills my mouth.

"I love your body." Sliding my hands around his waist, I'm on fire.

Reaching for the button of his jeans, I manage to get it open, shoving them down as the pink tip of his cock emerges. Leaning forward, I lick my tongue over it, and his groan makes me wet.

"I don't want to tear your dress." His voice is thick with lust, and I'm ready to rip through the satin fabric myself.

I slide to the edge of the table, and he reaches under my skirt to my thong, ripping it off my body.

"Yes," I whimper, rolling onto my stomach. "Fuck me."

The skirt is over my bare ass, and he slides his cock up and down my dripping core. With a firm thrust, he's fully inside me, and we both groan.

"Oh, God…" I arch my back so I can take him further into me.

His large arm wraps over my chest, and he lifts my back to his chest, his lips pressing into my ear. "Fuck, I love you so much."

Everything in me melts, and my eyes squeeze shut as his large hand moves between my thighs, circling and sliding up and down my clit. It doesn't take much to have me rigid, vibrating with orgasm, and trembling in his arms.

He's thrusting harder, and my fingers cut into his forearm. "Yes," I gasp, feeling my orgasm rising again as his fat cock massages my deepest spots.

I don't know how this is happening, but I'm not questioning it. He's here in my arms, loving me raw and dirty. My dreams are all coming true, and I want to savor every moment of this reunion.

His fingers slap my clit, and I yelp, coming again, harder. He thrusts once more then holds, his cock pulsing deep, filling me as my body quivers, as emotions race through my chest, as I feel like I'm being swept up in a tidal wave of unparalleled ecstasy.

"Fuck, that's so good." He exhales a groan before pressing his mouth against my shoulder.

Clutching my fingers into his hair, I laugh at the joy radiating in my bones. "How is this happening?"

Strong arms encircle my torso, and his face is beside mine. We're wrapped in so much love and afterglow, it's like magic.

"I spent nine hours on a plane, planning out all the things I wanted to tell you." His voice is that gorgeous, deep vibration I've dreamt about so many times.

"I like this better." Turning in his arms, he slips out, and we frown.

I take his hand, leading him to the sink where soft towels are kept for cleanup.

"So they let you out?" Reaching up, I slide a piece of his hair behind his ear. He moves closer, pulling me into his arms.

"It was the little girl's grandfather." Closing his eyes, he shakes his head. "The one I saved from the fire. He put me on a plane, no questions asked."

Stretching higher, I cup his neck with my hand, and we kiss again, his tongue sliding firmly against mine, curling and claiming me as his. I'm levitating instead of standing, reveling in this waking dream. *He's here.*

I don't want to go back to the show. I want to go back to my bedroom–or a hotel room, and spend all night in his arms.

"I need to find Hutch." He smooths both hands down the sides of my head. "But I had to find you first."

Lifting my chin, I kiss him again. I can't stop kissing him. "You're right, but I hate it. I want you all to myself."

"We won't take long," he promises, spreading his hand over my cheek again and kissing me once more.

I have no panties, but my dress is still intact. Waiting, I lick my lips as he buttons his shirt and fastens his jeans. Threading our fingers together, I pull him towards the door.

"Here we go."

We're out the door and into the mix of spectators. My big, tall man is at my back, and I walk him through the show, stopping at my favorite shots and letting him tell me what he thinks. Every few steps, he leans down to kiss my ear, sending a shower of tingles down my shoulders and legs.

"See what you think of these." Dragging him to the last hall, we pass the image of Blake and Hutch.

"I'd like something like that of us."

"Me too." Lifting his hand to my lips, I kiss his knuckles.

The image of Pepper and her dad is next, and he exhales a little growl. "I don't like that guy."

"Stop!" I give his arm a tug. "He's nice, and he really loves Pepper."

"As long as he keeps his hands off you." I'm back in Scar's strong arms, and I'm giddy and light. I'm in heaven, sharing this with him, hearing his thoughts.

Finally, we reach the self-portrait at the end of the show. Stopping in front of it, I look at the image of me plucking the petals off the daisy. The sunset glows golden around my head, and what was once a painful moment of loss and longing is transformed into magic.

Now, it's beauty and love.

"I want this." He pulls me closer. "It's how I dreamed of you every day we were apart. You haunted my soul."

Turning in his arms, I look up into his beautiful eyes. "I don't love you a crazy amount." His brow quirks, but I continue. "I know how much I love you, and it's bigger than the universe."

Warmth radiates to me from his eyes, and leaning down, he presses his lips to mine. "You are mine, beautiful girl. Nothing will tear us apart again."

"So it worked?" Hutch's deep voice echoes in my mother's kitchen. "Fuck, I was so depressed coming home. I didn't think I'd accomplished anything."

I'm sitting on the bar behind Scar. He's leaning back

between my legs, and my arms are around his shoulders. He's retelling the story of his release to his partners, and I can't stop touching him. He never stops touching me.

Dirk claps his shoulder, giving it a shake. "You built up so many karma points saving that little girl, it had to come back to help you."

"I saw her picture. She's doing really well." Scar looks down at his hand on my thigh. "It's all good now."

"Were you happy with the show?" Blake taps my arm, pulling me out of my fixation of holding my man in my arms.

"What show?" I tease, wrinkling my nose. "Kidding! It was amazing. Thank you, sis."

Sliding off the bar, I give my sister a hug.

"You're a star." She leans back, holding my hands and smiling proudly.

Scar's massive arms surround me, and again, he kisses my neck. He hasn't stopped touching or kissing me since our reunion, and I am here for it.

"Hana's pictures are art. I could stare at them all day." Scar's compliments make me want to fly.

"Absolutely," Hutch and Dirk join in the compliments, and I exhale a laugh.

"Thanks, guys."

"Jill said she sold every print, and bidding wars broke out on several of them." Blake's expression is smug, and she nods. "She's already booked you for the fall."

"We talked about that." I slide my fingers into Scars, and he gazes down at me with love and pride and so much emotion. Blinking around, I realize everyone is watching us. "Where are Carmen and Teal and Pepper?"

"They went for cupcakes." Blake gives my shoulder a squeeze. "We can catch up tomorrow. It's late. Let's get some sleep."

"I booked you guys a room at The Plaza." Dirk calls as he heads for the door. "A car is waiting when you're ready."

Sliding my eyes from my sister, who's pulling Hutch down the passage towards her bedroom, to Dirk's sudden departure, I step closer to Scar's chest. "I'm ready."

He looks down at me like I'm his treasure, his eyes so full of pride and confidence and possession. "Let's get out of here."

A thrill races from my chest to my core, and I squeal when he sweeps me off my feet, carrying me to the door.

I'm sure our room at The Plaza is the ultimate in elegance, but I don't even notice. The only thing I see is him, my gorgeous hero, my savior who is a prince to me.

Our bodies entwine in ecstasy, sweaty and intense, biting, tasting, smelling, committing every sense to memory that will last through lifetimes.

Curling into his side, he folds his long body behind mine, my dark protector watching over me since that first day so long ago. My eyes close, and the voices are gone. His lips press to my head, and a wash of comfort flows through my skin.

We've fought demons and darkness, but we survived. Our scars remain, but they tell us we can heal.

We can walk through fire, and together, we'll make it through to the other side.

EPILOGUE

Scar

HANA IS CURLED ON MY LAP IN THE OVERSIZED RECLINER IN Hugh's entertainment room, and she's making me watch this movie about pageant girls.

She argues it's about more than pageant girls, but I'm watching Sandra Bullock have a makeover, a pajama party, a girls' night out where they get really drunk… She's playing music on crystal wine glasses holding water.

Finally we're at the part Hana said was the reason we're watching it, and I confess, I crack a smile. "You were not that good at SING."

"It's because your stomach is a wall of granite." She scoots around, studying my arm, tracing her finger over the new tattoo of a slim, mythical creature with long curls. "You added a mermaid to your sleeve. That's for me?"

Her chin tilts up, and she smiles so cute, I kiss her nose. The first time I saw her, she had me entranced. "It is."

"I love it."

"I love you."

She snuggles into my side again, resting her head on my chest, and I manage to get through the rest of this silly film. Okay, it's not the worst Sandra Bullock movie–it's not *Speed 2*. I had to turn that viewing into a makeout session, which gives me an idea.

"Why don't you sit on my lap?" I give her arm a little pull, and she slants her eyes up at me.

"Last time I did that, it turned into reverse cowgirl."

"Is that a problem?"

"No, but we're lucky nobody walked in on us. There's not a lock on that door."

"We should have movie night at my place."

"But we wouldn't have these luxury accommodations." Sliding up, she straddles my lap facing me. "And we wouldn't watch any movies."

She breaks one of her special sugar cookies in two, holding one to my lips as she eats the other. It's chewy and warm, and I arch an eyebrow.

"I love eating your cookies."

Leaning forward, she slides her lips along my cheek. "You do it so well."

I've got a boner in my pants, and I'm ready to slide it into her. Turning my head to kiss her. Her lips part, and when our tongues caress, she tastes like rich, sugary butter.

"You've seen this movie a lot." My lips are at her ear, and I pull the lobe with my teeth.

"How do you know that?" She rocks on my hard cock, and I groan.

"You quote all the lines."

"Then you watch while I play." Sliding to her knees, she blinks those blue eyes up at me as she slides my sweats down my hips.

My erection pops out over my belly, and she's on it,

pulling my tip between her lips, causing me to push back in the chair with a groan. Fuck, she's too good at this.

"Hana," I groan, sliding my hand in the side of her hair, but she's not stopping.

Her hot mouth pulls at my tip when her tongue slides out around the base, teasing as the orgasm tightens my ass. I am not watching the movie, and when her fingers tickle my sack, I lean forward and lift her off the ground, planting her on my lap.

"That does it," I groan.

She squeals as I reach under her skirt and pull her panties to the side, sliding fully into her slippery wet core. Damn, she feels like heaven.

Leaning forward, she pulls the ring in my lip with hers before making a pouty face. "I wanted you to see the movie."

Then she rocks her hips, pulling me deeper into her core. Fuck that movie. I catch the sides of her face and kiss her firmly. "I'd rather watch you ride my dick."

"Mm…" She sits up straighter, pulling her shirt over her head and giving me a show. "How's this?"

Cupping her breasts, she pulls her nipples as she rocks back and forth. "Gorgeous."

But when she licks her fingers and slides them between her thighs and starts rubbing her clit, I nearly blow. "Fuck, Hana. I like that."

"I do it all the time." She puts a hand on the chair beside my face and whispers in my ear. "When I think of you."

Fire floods my brain, and I grip her ass, rocking her harder as my orgasm builds. She gasps and whimpers, and I feel the back of her hand moving faster against my thigh. It's fucking hot as hell, and I'm not holding back.

Her back arches, and she exhales a loud moan as her pussy breaks into spasms. I lift my ass off the chair as the orgasm races through my cock, and we ride it out, my arm around her waist, straining and coming, holding each other as the tidal wave sweeps over us.

She's in my arms as her breath slows to normal. Her face is on my shoulder, and she lifts it to kiss my cheek. "We should do movie night at your place."

"We're doing pretty good right here."

Leaning to the side, she scoops her shirt off the floor and quickly pulls it over her head. "We really are taking chances, especially watching a rom-com. Anybody could walk in."

She curls into my side again, resting her cheek on my chest as I restore my pants over my hips. We should get cleaned up, but I'll give it a few more minutes.

Tracing her finger over my new tattoo again, she looks up at me. "I never have bad dreams anymore. Isn't that weird?"

"It's good. It means you feel safe."

"It's like the nightmares are over. All happy endings from now on."

Wrapping my arms around her, I close my eyes as I inhale her soft scent, flowers and sugar. Her nightmares are over, but we still have a few loose ends to tie up, or bury.

The claim ticket is burning a hole in my pocket. I have one thing on my mind today, but Hutch wanted me to stop by the office for a few minutes. He said he has news, but my eyes are on the antiques store and the plans I have for lunch.

Hana was curled up in my sheets when I left her this morning. She told me she's taking Pepper and some of her friends out with the horses for a photo shoot this afternoon, and I told her I'd be there.

What she doesn't know is the kids are helping me with something special.

"Hey, thanks for coming in on your day off." Hutch

clasps my hand when I enter, and Dirk's at the computer, as always, pulling up images.

"What's happening?"

"We just got this report from our man in Minsk." Dirk has the tone that means he's concentrating. "Just trying to verify it's legit."

We walk over to stand behind him, and Hutch explains what's happening. "A photo was circulated on the dark web last night. Simon Petrovich is dead."

Shock flashes in my chest, and I frown at my friend. "How?"

"That's the part I need to verify." Dirk's fingers fly over the keyboard, and I'm waiting for him to say heart attack. "Gunshot wound to the chest. The police report ruled it a suicide."

Stepping back, I slide my hand over my mouth. "No fucking way that's true."

"You were with him the last time any of us saw him. Any thoughts?"

"He had two bodyguards with him all the time." Leaning closer, I study the grainy image. "That's Simon, or someone made to look exactly like him."

"The coroner verified he had a very small star tattooed on the back of his knee."

My fists tighten. I know what it means, *I kneel for no man.* It's the old symbol no one talks about. "Did Simon have such a mark?"

"It's the only thing they have to go on, besides dental records," Dirk quips, rocking back in his chair and turning to face us.

"Someone killed Simon, and they didn't use the Petrovich method." Hutch's hands are on his hips, and he walks slowly to his desk. "Does that mean it's someone outside his network? Or is it someone on the inside trying to make it look like a hit?"

Exhaling heavily, I shake my head. "I can't say that I give a shit. With him dead, no one is left to bother the van Hamiltons anymore."

"What about you?" Hutch's green eyes level on mine.

"I can handle myself." My thoughts go to the phone hidden in my office. Who would answer if I used it now? I have no clue. "Honestly, I don't think anyone left remembers me."

Hutch nods, and Dirk stands, going to the wire basket on the filing cabinet. "This came for you in the mail."

I take the brown parcel and inspect it. The postmark is Muscovite, but I don't recognize the address. The three of us look at each other, and I rip it open at once. If somebody's coming for me, we all need to know.

What slides out squeezes my heart. "My notebook."

"What's that?" Dirk steps closer, inspecting the string-bound journal I was given in prison.

A short note accompanies it from the old man, and I summarize it for them. "He went to the prison to be sure all of my things were collected. He's sorry this was all they had left."

Flipping through the pages an ache twists in my throat. All the words I wrote, the things I didn't want to forget, the small doodles of Hana, it's all here. It's like a historical record of the things I hold most dear. I'll have to share it with her one day. Maybe on our wedding night…

"Damn, I really like that guy." Dirk grins, and I pat his shoulder.

"Me too, man." *Me, too.*

Closing the cover, I slip it in the backpack when I get to the truck. I make my quick stop in the small antique store in town to pay my bill and pick up the small package, then I head out to the pasture where Hana is working with the kids.

Pepper runs up to meet me as soon as I'm parked under a shade tree. "Everything's in place!" She's jumping all around, and her eyes are wide. "All you have to do is *it*! I'll get everybody back to the house."

Leaning into the bed, I take out the backpack and slide it over my shoulder while Pepper runs to where Hana has the group hanging upside down from the limb of a tree while she lies in the grass below them taking pictures.

My girl has the wildest ideas for portraits, but they always turn out incredible.

"Time to go! Sorry, Hana! We all have to get back to the house now." Pepper waves her hands, and her little boyfriend does a backflip off the branch.

That kid is always showing off. I guess it's what we do to impress our women. The other boy and girl climb down the old-fashioned way, and they all tell us goodbye as they hop on the waiting horses and gallop off towards the house.

"Wait!" Hana sits up frowning with her camera in her hands, but the kids are long gone. "I had a lot more planned for them to do! Why would they just run off like that?"

"Want to take a break with me?"

Her shoulders drop, and her cute face is scrunched. "I guess I don't have a choice."

"I'm not going to take that personally." Catching her hand, I give her a quick kiss after pulling her to her feet. "Let's walk down to the bluff."

She slides her hand in the crook of my arm, and her tone brightens. "As long as you're here, I can get some shots of you. Maybe with your shirt off?"

As we descend into the small valley near a stream at the beginning of the tree line, Hana's breath catches when she sees what we've done.

Pepper arranged a picnic blanket with pillows and a stone vase of bright pink daisies. If Pep were here, I'd give her a high five. It looks amazing and really romantic.

"What is this?" She walks forward, dropping to her knees and looking up at me.

I kneel on the blanket and place my backpack beside us. "Pepper helped me with it."

Unzipping the bag, I take out a bottle of champagne and two silicone flutes, and the most important item of all.

Hana's blue eyes widen as she watches me. "Scar…"

"Hana…" I clear my throat. "I wanted to do this the first day I met you, but it seemed crazy. Then as time passed, the only thing crazier was not doing it. Then everything blew up and I realized the true crazy would be to pull you into my world, making you a potential target for anyone wanting to hurt me."

"I'm not afraid." Her voice is quiet but firm, so different from before.

"Now we have no reason to fear. Our debts are paid, and I can come to you knowing my love won't put you in danger." Taking her hand, I study her slim, ivory hand in my large, olive one. "I'm not a prince, which is what you deserve, but I love you. I'll live my life for you. I'll take care of you and our babies…" She inhales sharply, and my eyes flicker to hers. She's blinking fast, but I see the shine of tears. Sliding my thumb over her cheek, I lean in to kiss her gently. "Will you be my wife?"

Her hands cup my cheeks, and she nods, pressing her lips to mine again. "I've always wanted to be your wife. I love you so much."

"Blake helped me find this through an antiques dealer." Taking out the vintage, maroon-velvet box, I open the lid to reveal a platinum and gold diamond ring with a large carat stone in the center and nine smaller diamonds arranged in a circle around it. Lifting it from the box, I slide it onto the third finger of her left hand. "What do you think?"

"It's a daisy!" She tilts her hand side to side then cradles it against her chest, looking up at me with bright eyes. "I love it so much!"

Pride swells in my chest as I look down at her, this

amazing woman who stole my heart the first day I saw her. She's going to be my wife.

"We got it." Shaking my head, I kind of can't believe it.

Blinking fast, she smiles, climbing onto my lap. "What do you mean? Got what?"

"A happy ending." Sliding my arms around her, I look up to the heavens, holding her tight against my chest. She always fills every crack in my heart. "I didn't think we would."

Leaning her head back, she cups my cheek before kissing my lips. "We're just getting started."

Thank you for reading FILTHY!

Up next is FOR YOUR EYES ONLY.

It's a forbidden, boss-employee romance that follows Trip to Miami, where he encounters a beautiful, mysterious dancer he can't keep his hands off. What happens might surprise you.

Keep clicking for a short sneak peek...

Get THREE FREE stories by me!

Sign up for my New Release newsletter and get a **FREE Tia Louise Story Bundle!**

And/Or get a text alert by texting "TiaLouise" to 855-902-6387.*
(Text available U.S. only.)

Can you love what you can't touch?

No touching.
It's the only rule in this business, and trust me, with my
money and power, "hands off" is not a problem.
I don't need the women I employ to satisfy my needs…
Until her.
She's different than the other girls, innocent,
intoxicating, impossibly seductive.
I can't take my eyes off her, and it's not long before
hot looks turn into hotter touches.
I'm the boss, after all, I call the shots.
And nothing's more fun than breaking the rules.
I came to this country to pursue my dream… but it was a lie,
a scam that quickly fell apart.
Desperate, I took the only job I could with no work visa.
They promised no one would know.
They promised no touching.
Until I saw him.
Dark scruff shading an arrogant grin, lean muscles
stretching expensive fabric, eyes like twilight sending
electricity from my stomach to my toes.
He's my boss, but the way he watches makes
me do dirty things.
For his eyes only, I'm uninhibited, experienced, a seductress.
Only, our game turns dangerous when a watcher threatens
everything, and my *hands-on hero* vows to save me.

**(FOR YOUR EYES ONLY is a STAND-ALONE, extra-spicy
romantic suspense with forbidden touches, organized
crime, and a virgin heroine. No cheating. No cliffhanger.)**

PROLOGUE

Giana

O BSESSION KILLED MY MOTHER, BUT IT'S NOT HOW I WILL DIE.
The detectives called it a *crime of passion*, but she would've hated that verdict. She adored passion and colors and beauty and music. She taught me to love these things. She taught me to sing and to sew and to dream…

"Your mother was a great beauty." Aunt Graziella jerks my head as she attempts to pull a comb through my thick, gnarled curls, forcing a yelp from my lips. "You are not like your mother."

I don't cry. It's true, I'm not beautiful like my mother was, but I try to be strong like her.

My mother would walk through the streets of our small, coastal village in southern Italy with her silky brunette hair shining in the sun. Her skin was smooth as the delicately carved ivory plaques of Mary and the baby Jesus in the cathedral, and when she passed, the men would lean back, closing their eyes like they smelled fresh bread straight from the oven.

They would follow her along the narrow streets, hoping

to pick up something she dropped or to help her carry a heavy load—all to see her smile and perhaps even say *grazie*.

My olive skin was tanned brown by the sun, and my aunt would rub lotion on me saying I'd never attract a man with the way I looked. It only got worse as I got older, and she said I looked like a peasant with round hips and a full bust.

But I wasn't looking for a man.

When I was ten years old, a man took away the life I loved, a life of happiness in which my mother and I lived in a pretty little apartment overlooking the sea. A man killed my beautiful mother, and then he killed himself. And I was sent to live with my aunt.

My father died in a fishing accident before I was old enough to remember him. He gave me my love of dancing and running around the streets barefoot, which made my heels as rough and calloused as a donkey's hooves, as my aunt would say.

I started dancing when I was thirteen, and to everyone's (mostly my aunt's) surprise, I was very good at it (for a girl my size, she would say).

I wasn't as slim as a reed, but I could dance well enough to draw the attention of the city company. I was talented enough to be paired with a boy as light on his feet as I was, a boy who asked me to marry him and then broke up with me—but that came later.

The memories I cherish are the ones I spent with my mother, sleeping with the windows open so we could breathe the salty sea air. I would close my eyes and dream of lifting my arms and riding higher on the warm currents, my stubborn curls flowing straight in the cool breeze, the stars illuminating my skin from the inside like a goddess.

My mother once told me butterflies work very hard to become the beautiful, flying creatures that kiss all the flowers. She said their metamorphosis happens when they're not even expecting it.

She said caterpillars root in the dirt and leaves, dreaming

of nothing, when all the time, deep inside they have the power to become magnificently gorgeous creatures that can fly.

I wrinkled my small nose and asked if she was calling me a worm.

She laughed and hugged me close. "What do you love, Gia?" She threaded her fingers in my wild curls until they were smooth coils around my cheeks. "Follow what calls to you, and that's how you find your passion. Then spread your wings and fly."

Then she was gone, and I was left with no one who believed I was special.

She made it sound so easy—believe, work hard, fly. I didn't know metamorphosis was dangerous and cruel. I didn't know how easily everything could go wrong.

I only thought it created a beautiful butterfly.

I didn't know it also brought death.

CHAPTER 1

Trip

Ten years later

"**Y**OU'RE OUT OF CONTROL, MOTHER." I EXHALE, straightening the lapel on my dark brown, Brioni suit. Agitation itches beneath my virgin wool collar, but I don't let it show. I never let my irritation show. I study the Manhattan skyline through the oversized windows of our Upper East Side apartment and collect my thoughts.

At twenty-five, I'm well-connected and highly invested in the obscenely wealthy shadows of the city's real-estate, gaming, and nightclub scenes. I operate on the razor's edge of what's legal and what's, shall we say, *morally gray*.

Players from around the globe operate in my world, and high-priced lawyers use many words to construct the shady legality of our deals. The margins are thin. At any moment, someone's number could come up, in which they discover they owe more than they can repay.

Such things don't happen to me.

Remaining off the record, in the deep background, protects

me. I never stick my neck out for anyone. It's a world of poker players, and I've got the straightest face in the group—or should I say, the most detached smile.

"Don't speak to me that way." My mother acts offended, but she's not.

Turning from the window to the mini-bar, I pour a tumbler of vodka casually. "Forgive me. I wasn't trying to be rude. Would you like a drink?"

"Of course." She touches her hair lightly with her fingertips, preening like a goldfinch in her bright yellow Balenciaga caftan. "The very idea of you sleeping with my best friend, a woman twice your age. What would your father say?"

"He'd make some crack about my manhood." I glance at the bronze urn on the mantle holding his ashes. "He'd wonder aloud why I couldn't land a girl my own age or something like that."

William Robert Alexander II took great pride in tearing his only son and namesake to shreds. He'd focus his green eyes on me like a hawk, ready to rip through any exposed weakness or vulnerability. I hated him, but he taught me to be strong.

He sent me to the finest boarding schools his inherited wealth could buy. He made sure I got into Columbia, then when I realized I didn't need him, I quit wasting everyone's time and dropped out.

Naturally, he had many unkind things to say about that decision, and what he dubbed my failure to finish anything, as if he had any idea the deals I was closing. But I had stopped listening to that old bully a long time ago.

"Your father was *difficult*, but he took care of us financially. We can be thankful for that."

Did he? For starters, it wasn't his fortune to leave, not that it matters to me, and secondly, his finances always came with strings—or barbed hooks.

"I find other things to be thankful for." I hand her the drink.

She can live off the spoils of an unhappy marriage,

pretending to be unaffected by years of emotional abuse, but I'm doing everything in my power to divorce myself from that man's legacy. I'm so close to being completely, utterly, independently wealthy. I just have to stay focused, then I'm cashing out, leaving the game.

"Still," she continues, "I don't know why you'd want to validate his low opinion of you by sleeping with that woman."

Taking a sip of my drink, I decide it's time to prick the air out of her precious gossip bubble. "I didn't sleep with Belinda Desayda-Rice."

Her eyes narrow, and I can tell she's trying to decide if I'm being honest. *Give me a break.* Of course, I didn't sleep with Belinda. I could murder Grish for putting me in this position. He's the one who can't keep his dick in his pants.

Greg Peters is one of my most trusted business partners—because we're the same age and equally hungry. He's from Moscow, so while *Grisha* is the Russian diminutive for Greg, I shorten it further to *Grish*.

Shaking her head, she sighs. "I confess, I wasn't sold on the story. Belinda isn't your style, and you've been friends with Debbie since you were a child. It would be too bizarre." My mother lifts the olive from her drink, chewing as she speaks. "But why would anyone spread such a lie? It must be a terrible strain for you, Trip dear."

I can think of several reasons Belinda would allow people to think I was her lover. For starters, it feeds her ego. It makes her look desirable if an ambitious twenty-something wants to fuck her, but more importantly, it distracts everyone from the fact she's actually sleeping with her daughter's boyfriend.

Fucking Grish. My clever Russian pal thinks he's scored a pair of queens, but he's got a seven and a two—a notoriously bad hand in poker.

"It'll blow over in a few days." I pause at the mirror to straighten my yellow silk tie.

My thick brown hair curls around my ears, and dark

stubble is on my cheeks. I need a trim and a shave, and I want to be anywhere but this goddamned city. I'm not in the mood for bullshit.

In that moment, I decide. "I'm going out of town for a few weeks. I'll check on our properties in West Palm…" *And my own business investments* while this drama dies out.

In south Florida my work is more colorful and a lot more relaxing.

"Sounds lovely." Mother walks over to give me air kisses. "I'm leaving for Saint Moritz on Monday, so before you go, would you be a dear?"

She smiles sweetly, which means she wants me to transfer money into her account. My father couldn't stop her from pursuing other interests (a.k.a., *other men*) after he died, so in his will, he put me in charge of her purse strings. Barbed hooks.

As long as she remains single, she's entitled to as much of the family estate as I am, but if she ever remarries, she's out. Our eyes meet, and I catch a flicker of apprehension in hers.

It fucking pisses me off.

My father put me in this position of power because he hoped it would turn me into him. It gnawed at him when I would watch him be a racist, elitist bastard and not laugh at his jokes. It infuriated him when I drank vodka instead of scotch. He called me names and said I thought I was better than him.

I didn't think it. I *knew* I was better than him, and the idea that he'd put me in a position to make my mother cower stirs an anger so deep in me it almost breaks my façade. Does she truly think she has to beg for what she deserves?

I suppose all those years of having to account for every penny created a mindset she can't break. My father was a nouveau-riche dipshit who didn't realize the truly wealthy never think about money.

My mother might drive me crazy with her frivolous

behavior, but I've become protective of her as I've gotten older. I've learned how prolonged exposure to cruelty can change a person, and I only want her to be happy now.

"You can always have as much as you want." I slide my phone from the inside pocket of my blazer. Tapping the face, I quickly move ten thousand from the family endowment to her personal account. "Text me if that isn't enough."

BOOKS BY TIA LOUISE

STAND-ALONE ROMANCES

THE BRADFORD BOYS
The Way We Touch, 2024*
The Way We Play, Oct. 2024*
The Way We Score, Jan. 2025*
The Way We Run, 2025*
The Way We Win, 2025*
(*Available on Audiobook.)

THE BE STILL SERIES
A Little Taste, 2023*
A Little Twist, 2023*
A Little Luck, 2023*
A Little Naughty, 2024*
(*Available on Audiobook.)

THE HAMILTOWN HEAT SERIES
Fearless, 2022*
Filthy, 2022*
For Your Eyes Only, 2022
Forbidden, 2023*
(*Available on Audiobook.)

THE TAKING CHANCES SERIES
*This Much is True**
*Twist of Fate**
*Trouble**
(*Available on Audiobook.)

FIGHT FOR LOVE SERIES
*Wait for Me**
*Boss of Me**
*Here with Me**
*Reckless Kiss**
(*Available on Audiobook.)

BELIEVE IN LOVE SERIES
Make You Mine
*Make Me Yours**
*Stay**
(*Available on Audiobook.)

SOUTHERN HEAT SERIES
When We Touch
When We Kiss

THE ONE TO HOLD SERIES
*One to Hold (#1—Derek & Melissa)**
*One to Keep (#2—Patrick & Elaine)**
*One to Protect (#3—Derek & Melissa)**
One to Love (#4—Kenny & Slayde)
One to Leave (#5—Stuart & Mariska)
*One to Save (#6—Derek & Melissa)**
*One to Chase (#7—Marcus & Amy)**
One to Take (#8—Stuart & Mariska)
(*Available on Audiobook.)

ACKNOWLEDGMENTS

I'm incredibly blessed to have an amazing, supportive group cheering me on and anxiously awaiting each new adventure. I don't know how I'd make it without you—seriously. (That includes _you_, dear reader!)

Every day, I'm more grateful for my husband "Mr. TL" for his encouragement when I'm struggling, and for still always wanting to read my books.

Thanks to my beautiful daughters who have left the nest but still believe in me, make me laugh, and support me from afar. I love you ladies!

Thanks so much to my alpha readers Renee McCleary, Maria Black, and Ilona Townsel for your encouragement and feedback in the early stages. You guys are my rocks.

Huge thanks to my awesome betas, Jennifer Christy, Amy Reierson, Courtney Anderson, and Amanda Shepard for your enthusiasm and fantastic notes!

Thanks to Jaime Ryter for your eagle-eye notes (_made you cry!_), to Lori Jackson for the gorgeous cover design, to Wander Aguiar for the perfect Scar, and to Stacy Blake for the beautiful paperbacks!

Thanks to my dear Starfish, to my Mermaids, and to my Veeps for keeping me sane and motivated while I'm in the cave.

I can't begin to put into words how much I appreciate the love and support of all the book-bloggers/tokers/gramers, of my author-buds, and of my readers and friends. I love you guys!

I hope you all devour this new story and come back begging for MORE! I confess, I'm a little obsessed with this world.

Stay sexy,
<3 Tia

ABOUT THE AUTHOR

Tia Louise is the *USA Today* best-selling, award-winning author of super-hot and sexy romances. She'll steal your heart, make you laugh, melt your kindle... *and have you begging for more!*

Signed Copies of all books online at:
http://smarturl.it/SignedPBs

Connect with Tia:
Website
Instagram (@AuthorTLouise)
TikTok (@TheTiaLouise)
Pinterest
Bookbub Author Page
Amazon Author Page
Goodreads
Snapchat

** **On Facebook?** **

Be a Mermaid! Join Tia's Reader Group at
"Tia's Books, Babes & Mermaids"!

www.AuthorTiaLouise.com
allnightreads@gmail.com